THE GHOST

AND THE NEW NEIGHBOR

HAUNTING DANIELLE

THE GHOST

AND THE NEW NEIGHBOR

USA TODAY BESTSELLING AUTHOR

BOBBI HOLMES

The Ghost and the New Neighbor
(Haunting Danielle, Book 31)
A Novel
By Bobbi Holmes
Cover Design: Elizabeth Mackey

Copyright © 2022 Bobbi Holmes
Robeth Publishing, LLC
All Rights Reserved.
robeth.net

ISBN: 978-1-949977-72-1

I

Dedicated to Sadie the Lab who loaned her name to Sadie the Golden Retriever. Sadie, like the Hunny who inspired our fictional Hunny, has traveled the Rainbow Bridge.

ONE

Heather Donovan thought her living room looked bare without the Christmas tree. Three days prior, on New Year's Day, Brian had helped her take it down. She would have left it up longer, but the dry pine needles piling up under the tree, along with the drooping noble fir branches weighed down with ornaments, had reminded her of an exhausted and disgruntled worker—one that might set fire to her house.

With a sigh, she turned from where the tree once stood and admitted she felt some satisfaction knowing she had put away all her Christmas ornaments and cleaned her house, so when she got home after work, she had the entire weekend to relax and do something fun.

In less than two hours she would discover any plans for fun weren't happening this weekend.

Heather glanced around and looked for her calico cat, Bella. She normally took Bella to work with her, but today Bella would stay home. Yesterday Heather had taken her car to the shop, so instead of her morning jog, she planned to walk to Pier Café, pick up breakfast for her and Chris, and walk down to Chris's house. After the two ate breakfast, she would ride to work with him.

After Heather spied Bella napping in the corner, she walked to the coat rack and grabbed her raincoat and slipped it on. She removed her purse from the coat rack. Before draping its strap over one shoulder, she picked up her cellphone from a hall table and dropped it into her purse.

Once outside, Heather closed and locked the door behind her. Turning to the street, she looked up. Judging by the clouds in the sky, she didn't foresee morning rain. A few moments later, she reached her front gate and was about to step out onto the sidewalk when she heard the gate over at Pearl's house open and slam shut. Pausing, she glanced next door and watched as two women walked out from Pearl's front gate onto the sidewalk.

It was no longer Pearl's house, Heather reminded herself. Someone had murdered her cranky neighbor several months earlier. But Heather imagined she would always think of it as Pearl's house despite the fact someone had bought the property. Had Adam or Pearl's trustee sent someone over to check out the house?

Heather was about to call out to the women, whose backs were to her, when the tallest of the two turned and looked Heather's way. Their eyes met, and the woman quickly looked away. Heather's cellphone rang.

Instead of calling out to the women, Heather shoved her hand into her purse and pulled out her cellphone. She glanced at the caller's identification. As she answered the cellphone, she watched the two women hurry up the street, in the opposite direction of the pier.

"Morning, Chris," Heather said into the phone.

"Have you left yet?" Chris Johnson, aka Chris Glandon, asked.

"I'm just leaving my house now." Heather stepped onto the sidewalk. "What's up?"

"I'd like to change my order…" Chris began.

AFTER HEATHER REACHED PIER CAFÉ, she took a seat at the counter, gave Carla a to-go order, and then watched as the server filled her cup with hot coffee. While Heather preferred tea, she didn't care for the brand of tea Pier Café served. Heather glanced around the diner, noting all the empty booths.

"I heard about Danielle," Carla whispered after she finished pouring the coffee. She set the pot on the counter and then leaned forward, resting her hands on the edge of the countertop. Since before Christmas, Carla's spiky hair had grown out, and was now blond, with streaks of pink framing her face.

"Who told you?" Heather picked up her cup and took a sip.

"No one actually told me," Carla said. "But I overheard Melony and Adam talking about it last night when they came in. Is it true?"

Heather set the mug back on the counter and gave a shrug. "I guess it depends on what you heard."

In response, Carla made a hand gesture.

Heather gave another shrug. "It's not really my place to say."

"If true, it's going to be a big change for those two. I can't even imagine." Carla shivered and then changed the subject. "Adam told me your new neighbor is moving in this weekend."

"Yeah. I wish it were Adam and Mel." Heather set her mug on the counter.

"Frankly, I never understood why Melony wanted to live there. Sure, Beach Drive is a great location. But seriously, who would want to live in that creepy place? If ever there was a candidate for a haunted house, that would be it. Its backyard was practically a graveyard, not to mention Pearl was murdered there."

Heather chuckled.

"I know you didn't like Pearl."

"While Pearl wasn't my favorite person when she was alive, she kind of grew on me after she died."

Carla, who knew nothing of Heather's paranormal abilities, nor the fact Heather had gotten to know Pearl's spirit before she moved on, stared dumbly at Heather. Noticing Carla's peculiar expression, Heather flashed the server a sheepish grin and asked if Carla would check on her order.

HEATHER HEADED up the street to Chris's house, to-go sacks in hand. Instead of walking on the beach, she stayed on the sidewalk. Dressed for work, she wore a long black skirt and sweater under her rain jacket. Instead of wearing her black hair down, she had braided it that morning and fastened the braids around her head, making her look like a Goth milkmaid with straight bangs barely covering her eyebrows.

When she passed Ian and Lily's house, she glanced their way, noting all the window coverings drawn. She then looked across the street to Marlow House. Their window blinds were also closed.

"Looks like everyone is sleeping in," Heather muttered aloud. "If they had real jobs, I bet they wouldn't still be sleeping."

When she reached Chris's house, she entered by the front door without knocking. Chris's enthusiastic pit bull, Hunny, greeted her. Hunny wanted to jump on Heather, but resisted the temptation, while her wiggling butt and tail moved behind her.

"Hey, Hunny Bunny," Heather cooed at the dog, offering her a pat with her free hand after closing the door behind her. Hunny continued to prance around Heather, her nose sniffing at the sacks of food. Chris walked into the entry hall from his bedroom and relieved her of the food so she could properly greet Hunny.

"CARLA KNOWS ABOUT DANIELLE," Heather told Chris as the two sat at his kitchen table eating the food from Pier Café.

"Can't keep anything from Carla. Did Danielle tell her?" While drinking his coffee, Chris looked over at Heather, waiting for her reply.

"No. She overheard Mel and Adam talking about it. I didn't confirm it."

Chris chuckled. "Wait until Carla hears about Lily."

About to take a bite of food, Heather paused and looked over at Chris. "Someone was over at Pearl's this morning. They left out the front gate. But I didn't see a car."

"They were inside the house?"

4

Heather shrugged. "I just saw them coming out the front gate. Two women. And then they headed down this way."

"If you didn't see a car, probably someone taking a walk, saw the for-sale sign, and got nosey. I'm surprised Adam didn't take the sign down right after escrow closed."

"You know Adam, doesn't miss a chance for free advertising."

Chris chuckled. "True."

"At first, I wondered if Brandon sent someone to check on the house one last time before the new owners move in. But when they took off up the street, and I didn't see any car..." Heather shrugged.

Fifteen minutes later, after Heather and Chris finished eating and cleaning up, they headed out the front door, with Hunny by their side. Chris hadn't bothered putting Hunny on a leash. The well-behaved dog normally stayed by Chris's side, following any command he might give her. Yet the moment Chris shut the front door, Hunny raced off, heading toward the street.

"Hunny!" The dog ignored Chris and ran down the sidewalk. Chris called out again. When Hunny continued to ignore him, Chris let out a curse and sprinted after the dog, with Heather trailing behind them.

Hunny stopped a few doors up from Chris's house, her nose shoved between two large evergreen bushes. Chris and Heather, now on the sidewalk and a short distance from Hunny, slowed to a walk.

"What does she have now?" Chris grumbled. Annoyed, he marched toward his dog. "Hunny, get out of there! What are you getting into?"

So focused on his dog, Chris failed to notice what Heather had. It wasn't until Heather grabbed Chris by the back of his shirt, pulled him to a stop, and then pointed—not at Hunny—but at something protruding from the side of the bush closest to them. It hadn't been visible from where they stood moments earlier.

"Feet?" Chris squeaked. They weren't bare feet, but feet wearing a pair of sneakers. By the exposed ankles, neither Chris nor Heather assumed they were simply seeing a pair of abandoned shoes.

"Damn, don't tell me there's a body attached to those," Heather groaned.

Chris let out a sigh and muttered, "To be honest, I would rather find an entire body than severed feet."

"True," Heather agreed.

Chris gave the dog another command to come, and this time, she listened. Hunny rushed to Chris's side and sat down, yet continually looked back at what she had been sniffing. Hesitantly, Chris and Heather approached the bushes while Heather pulled her cellphone from her purse, preparing to call the police station. Normally, she would have called Brian directly, but at the moment, he was at the dentist getting a root canal.

Once in front of the bushes, Chris hesitantly pulled the branches to one side while he and Heather looked down to the body attached to the feet.

Sprawled under the bushes lay a lifeless woman with her head turned to one side, her face not visible because of the foliage covering it. A bloody wound stained the back of the woman's clothing.

Heather gasped. "That's one of the women I saw leaving Pearl's house!"

Now kneeling by the body, Chris felt for a pulse. There was none. "How can you tell? You can't see her face." Not wanting to disturb the evidence, Chris did not move the body. He stood up, letting the branches fall back into place.

"I didn't see her face when she left Pearl's, either. But she's wearing the same thing one woman was wearing. Same hair coloring. It's her." Heather looked around. "I wonder where the other woman went."

"Call the police, and I'll look around," Chris told Heather. "Maybe her spirit is still lingering, and she can tell us what happened."

TWO

Joe Morelli responded to Heather's call on Friday morning. Moments after his arrival, more responders showed up, including some from the coroner's office. When they removed the body from under the bushes and placed it on the gurney, Heather blurted, "She worked at the library!"

Joe walked from the other responders to Chris and Heather, who stood about ten feet away, watching. Hunny stood between the two. Chris had leashed her not long after Heather's call to the police. With tail wagging at Joe's approach, the dog leaned forward, desperately wanting to greet the officer.

Once Joe reached Chris and Heather, he absently scratched under Hunny's right ear and said, "Yes. It's Betty Kelty. She's a local librarian. She lived across the street from Eden and Shannon Langdon."

"I can't believe someone killed her. On our street!" Heather said.

Joe cocked a brow at Heather. "This sort of thing isn't all that uncommon for Beach Drive."

"I guess you're relieved Pearl's trustee didn't accept your offer on Pearl's House," Chris snarked.

Joe shrugged. "I was never thrilled with the idea. Kelly wanted to live close to her brother. But a lot happens on this street. Doesn't it ever bother you?"

Heather frowned. "Well, yeah. Of course. Finding a dead body is never the high point of my day."

"What does the coroner say so far?" Chris asked.

Joe glanced to the van where they had just loaded the body. He looked back at Chris. "It looks like she was standing on the sidewalk when someone stabbed her. When she fell, it appears her killer shoved her body back and down between two bushes, out of sight, giving the killer a chance to escape. If we're lucky, they left some DNA on her body."

"Find the woman she was with, and I imagine you'll find her killer," Heather said.

"Did you find the murder weapon?" Chris asked.

Joe shook his head. "No, not yet."

"Perhaps the killer took it with her," Heather suggested.

Someone called out to Joe. He paused, looked back, and then turned to Chris and Heather and said, "I was hoping you would go to the station and give your statements. We have more questions, but there are things I need to wrap up here."

THIRTY MINUTES LATER, Chris and Heather walked into the interrogation room with Brian Henderson. Also with them was Hunny, who, after greeting Brian, curled up under the table to take a nap.

"How's your tooth?" Heather asked Brian after giving him a quick kiss and taking a seat at the table.

Chris rolled his eyes but did not comment on the affectionate gesture. Silently, he sat next to Heather.

"It wasn't bad." Brian reached up and rubbed his jaw before taking a seat across from the pair. He let out a sigh, looked at Heather and said, "So, you tripped over another dead body?"

"Technically, this one is Chris's. He found her first."

"Not really. You noticed her feet before I did," Chris reminded.

"I'm assuming you didn't run into her... umm... her ghost?" Brian asked.

Before answering, Heather glanced at the one-way mirror. She looked back to Brian and said, "You'd better hope Joe didn't get back and is in there watching us... and listening."

Brian grinned. "No. I just talked to him. He was at Pearl's, checking out her house. It's all locked up. Doesn't look like anyone broke in. They called Adam, and according to him, they didn't let anyone into the house. Now, about my questions..."

Heather shook her head. "No. We didn't see her ghost. And the entire thing is so bizarre. I saw her about an hour before we found her body. And about twenty minutes after I initially saw her, I was walking down Beach Drive, in her direction. I didn't see her anywhere. Certainly not standing on the sidewalk a few houses from Chris's place."

"Are you sure she was alive when she left Pearl's yard? Perhaps it was her ghost," Brian suggested.

"No. That first time, she didn't have a bloody hole in her body."

"Tell me more about the woman with her," Brian asked.

Heather let out a sigh, slumped back in the chair and said, "The first thing that comes to mind, Cruella de Vil."

Brian frowned. "Cruella de Vil?"

"Yeah, like from *One Hundred and One Dalmatians*," Heather told him.

"You're telling me a cartoon character was with our murder victim?" Brian asked.

"No, of course not. But she made me think of her. About a third of her hair was white, and the rest jet black. Like Cruella de Vil. It was shoulder length and kind of curly. She was tall, my guess around five nine, at least. Thin. Umm, I'd say she was in her late forties or fifties. Or who knows, maybe a well-preserved sixty. She wore this interesting quilt jacket. More Etsy than Amazon."

"What does that even mean?" Brian asked.

Chris laughed and then said, "I think she means it looks like a handcrafted jacket, like something you'd more likely find at Etsy."

Brian shook his head and muttered, "I don't even know what Etsy is."

"Also, she has dark brown eyes. She looked right at me, and I got a good look at her face." Heather paused a moment and added, "Oh crap. She knows I saw her with Betty before she killed her, and she knows where I live."

"With that timeline, I'd be surprised if Cruella wasn't the killer," Chris said. "And if you saw them together coming out from Pearl's front yard, they obviously were acquaintances. I'd say friends, but what kind of friend stabs you?"

"Why were they at Pearl's?" Heather asked.

Brian leaned back in his chair and crossed his arms across his chest. "Good question. Like I told you, Joe already checked out Pearl's place, and nothing seems to have been disturbed. All the doors were locked, and according to Adam, no one was supposed to be over there."

"So we have two women taking a walk. They decide to poke around a house that has a for-sale sign out front. They then continue walking, this time up the street. And within the next twenty minutes, they get into some argument. One stabs the other, shoves her into the bushes, and then runs off. Is that about right?" Chris asked.

Still leaning back in his chair, his arms crossed over his chest, Brian shrugged in response.

WITH JOE and Brian busy in the field, investigating the murder, the chief sat in his office, waiting for Josephine Barker, the head librarian and Betty's supervisor, to arrive. She had called him. After hearing about Betty's death through the Frederickport rumor mill, she had called the chief to find out if it was true, and to tell him Betty had been at her house early that morning. She offered to come right over from the library.

Before Josephine arrived, Brian called to tell him they found Betty's car parked in her own driveway. It was unlocked, and they found what they believed was Betty's cellphone between the driver's seat and console, as if it had slipped down out of sight. Either Betty hadn't realized where it had fallen, or she chose to retrieve it later. While the car was not locked, her house was.

Ten minutes later, he greeted Josephine in his office and motioned for her to take a seat in a chair facing the desk. As she made her way to the chair, he noted she clutched a tissue in one hand and a purse in the other. Perched on the tip of her nose, she wore gold-rim glasses, secured to a beaded eyeglass strap.

He took a seat behind his desk, and when he looked over the desktop at her, it reminded him how much she looked like Blanche Devereaux from *The Golden Girls*. She wore her hair the same style and hair color, without a touch of gray. He hadn't been the first one to notice the resemblance. It had been his son Eddy, who, when watching a *Golden Girls* rerun at his aunt Sissy's house for the first time, pointed at the television and blurted, "That's the librarian!"

Later, when the chief had picked his sons up at his sister's house, she had told him what Eddy had said. They both laughed and, after considering the observation, wondered how they hadn't noticed the resemblance before. Now he could no longer unsee the doppelgänger comparison.

Setting the silly observation aside, the chief focused on the more serious matter at hand. "Thank you for coming in."

"I couldn't believe it and had to call you. I thought, it can't be true." She sniffled and dabbed her nose with the tissue.

"You say she was with you this morning?"

Josephine nodded. "Yes. She came over to my house."

"Why don't you tell me everything you remember about this morning?"

Josephine gave a nod, let out a sigh, and sat back in the chair. "I don't have a car, but I have a garage. When the library committee initially discussed the need to look for a storage facility to rent, I suggested my garage. I rented the space much lower than a storage unit. As I'm sure you've heard, I'm retiring in a few weeks, and while I'm going to continue renting them the space, I thought it best if the new head librarian inventoried what's in storage. Betty came over this morning early to start the inventory."

"That's right, Betty was going to be the new head librarian," the chief muttered.

Josephine nodded. "Yes. She was so excited."

"Tell me everything that happened this morning."

"Well, Betty arrived early. Before six. After she arrived, we had coffee together. And then I remembered there was a box I meant to bring over from my office in the library. It needed to go into storage, and I wanted it included in the inventory. Since Betty was busy, I offered to get it. She let me use her car. In fact, you can ask Darren Newsome about it."

"Who?"

"He's the current janitor, replaced Kenny. He's only been with us for a couple of weeks. But he's in Bend, visiting family. He's supposed to be back Thursday. Anyway, he had left something at the library and was picking it up when I borrowed Betty's car to pick up the box for storage. I think it was about six. But you might want to check with Darren on the time. Anyway, when I got back from the library, Betty told me she got a call. It was an emergency, and she needed to leave."

"Did she say what kind of emergency? Or who called?"

"She just told me she would be back this afternoon if that was alright with me. I said of course." Josephine sniffled and blew her nose.

"About an hour before they found her body, she was seen with a woman. They described the woman as white, tall, thin, with hair that was black on one side and white on the other. Do you have any idea who that might be?"

Josephine frowned. "No. I don't. But that sounds a little like our new librarian. The one replacing Betty. But of course, I've never seen her in person, just during our video chats for the interview. And she's never met Betty, and she's not arriving until Monday. She lives in California."

"Do you have any idea why Betty might have been over on Beach Drive?"

"Her best friend lives on Beach Drive. Becca Hammond. She works at the grocery store, and her husband, Dave, works for the city. Have you contacted Betty's family yet?"

"I was hoping to get her family's contact information from you. If you have it. I don't want them to learn about this from someone on the street, and after your call to me today, it's obvious the news is already out there."

"Her family lives in Astoria, so I doubt they're aware anything happened. But I have her contact information back at the library."

"Are you aware of anything that might have been bothering Betty?"

"No. Not really. She seemed very excited about her promotion."

"Did anyone have a problem with her?"

"Certainly not. Betty was a sweet girl. She got along with everyone. No one would want to hurt her. This has to be some random incident. I don't understand what's happening to the world. On the news, we're always hearing about a stranger shooting up a bunch of innocent people. What is the world coming to?"

THREE

After waking up Friday morning, Danielle hadn't bothered braiding her hair. She wore it freely flowing around her shoulders, its curl from yesterday's braid still evident. She also hadn't bothered changing out of her plaid pajama bottoms and oversized T-shirt. Unlike her denims, she could still pull up her pajama bottoms around her growing baby bump—barely. She just needed to loosen the belt looped within the pants' waistband. Yet it wouldn't be long until they no longer fit. Danielle stood at her bedroom window and stared down at the street below, noticing the last police car had driven away.

Walt walked into the bedroom. "Looks like things are quieting down."

Danielle glanced from the window to her husband and smiled. Unlike her, he had dressed that morning and now wore gray slacks and a crisply pressed cotton dress shirt, its button unfastened at the neckline. *Walt is far more put together than me*, she thought.

Their housekeeper, Joanne, ironed all Walt's clothes. If they didn't have a housekeeper, Walt would iron his own shirts. Danielle never pretended to be a 1950s housewife, and she was annoyed with him, anyway. Yet if she was honest with herself, it wasn't annoyance she felt—more fear.

Walt walked to Danielle, wrapped his arms around her, and pulled her to him. Her back pressed against him as she again looked out the window. She let out a sigh and said, "I have to admit, it's nice having you here while a killer is on the loose."

"Does this mean you're no longer mad at me?" he whispered before kissing her ear.

"This is all your fault."

Walt chuckled and held her tighter.

"Your mother could have at least warned us," Danielle grumbled. It wasn't the first time she had made that comment.

"If you will remember, I said it could happen."

"You're happy about this, aren't you?" Danielle asked, already knowing the answer.

"Ecstatic." He kissed her ear again.

"You are a monster," Danielle said with faux drama.

"Probably. But you're happy too, admit it."

"And afraid," she confessed, no longer teasing.

"Don't be. I'll be by your side every step of the way." Walt turned Danielle around in his arms so that she faced him. She looked up into his blue eyes and wrapped her arms around his neck. "Have I told you today how much I love you?" he whispered.

Unsmiling, she stared into his gaze. Finally, the corners of her mouth twitched upward, and she said, "It's a good thing I love you so much."

Thirty minutes later, they sat together at the kitchen table, eating lunch, when a knock came at the kitchen door followed by, "Hey, I see you guys in there; it's Heather!"

Arching her brows, Danielle looked to Walt. "You locked the door?"

"Like you said, we have a killer on the loose." Walt looked at the door leading to the side yard, focusing his energy on its deadbolt. His telekinetic powers turned the lock mechanism and then slowly opened the door, all the while he remained sitting in his chair.

Heather stood just outside on the kitchen porch, watching as the door opened. She peeked inside the house and grinned. A moment later, she stepped inside, looked at Danielle, and said, "Hi, little mama."

"No hello for me?" Walt teased as Heather shut the door behind her. "After all, I opened the door for you."

"Yeah, and you didn't even bother getting up." When Heather walked to the table, Danielle noticed the manilla envelope in Heather's hand.

"Afternoon, Heather. I understand you had a crazy morning," Danielle greeted her.

Heather tossed the envelope on the table and sat down. "Who told you? I imagine you noticed the police cars."

Danielle glanced briefly at the envelope and then looked up at Heather. "We didn't until Lily told me. And then we looked outside and saw them down the street near Chris's house."

Heather frowned. "Lily?"

"Joe told Kelly. Kelly told Ian. And Ian told Lily," Danielle explained.

"Ahh." Heather gave a nod.

"Did you lock the door?" Walt asked. Heather glanced at the door and cringed. She started to stand up when Walt told her to stay put. The next minute, he used his powers to turn the deadbolt.

Heather turned back to face Walt and Danielle. She removed a photograph from the envelope and tossed it on the table. "Brian asked me to give this to you guys. If you run into her, she's dead."

Danielle picked up the photograph and studied it. "Lily said she worked at the library. I recognize her. Tragic." She handed the photograph to Walt.

"I was afraid it was Betty." Walt let out a sigh.

"You knew her?" Heather asked.

"Yes. She was always helpful. I spent a lot of time over there when researching my first book. I hope we see her before she moves on, and she can tell us what happened." Walt set the photograph on the table.

"Have they found the woman who was with her this morning?" Danielle asked.

"No. Not yet. Is it okay if I hang out over here until Brian gets off work? Until they find the mystery woman, I don't feel comfortable staying home alone."

"No problem," Danielle said.

Walt picked up the photo and handed it to Heather. "And you can meet our new neighbor."

Heather frowned. "What do you mean?"

"Adam called. The buyer arrived a little early. Adam's in Portland, and Leslie had to go home early. She didn't feel good. So she locked up the office. Anyway, a while back, Adam gave us a set of keys to Pearl's house, in case there was an emergency," Danielle explained. "He told the buyer to pick up the house keys from us."

"What do you know about the buyer?" Heather asked.

"She's a woman," Danielle said.

"A single woman? Does she have a family? I've heard nothing about her. Other than our new neighbor outbid Joe and Kelly, and Adam and Melony," Heather said.

"Yeah, a cash offer, over asking price," Danielle said, although Heather already knew that bit of information.

"I just find it bizarre she bought the house without looking at it. Aside from the listing photos," Danielle said.

"You moved here sight unseen," Heather reminded her.

Danielle chuckled. "Hardly the same thing."

"I suspect Adam was relieved. I don't think he found the idea of living in Pearl's old house after his experience with the Marymoor spirits comforting," Walt said.

Danielle nodded. "Especially now, since there has been another murder on our street."

"I guess Adam already knows what happened," Heather said.

"Yeah. He told me someone from the police station called him to find out if anyone was supposed to be over at Pearl's house this morning," Danielle said. "He was out of town when they got ahold of him, but they told him what happened. And now his buyer is showing up today."

"Not the best welcome to your new home. A murder on your street," Heather said dryly.

"No kidding," Danielle agreed.

"Guess who else is relieved they didn't get Pearl's house? Joe," Heather said. "At least that's pretty much what he said this morning."

"What exactly happened this morning? The version I got from Lily, who got it from Ian…"

"Who got it from Kelly, who got it from Joe," Heather finished for Danielle. She then told them all that had happened that morning.

"Yeah, that's pretty much what Lily told me," Danielle said when Heather finished her telling.

"Oh, and when I was at Pier Café this morning, umm, Carla knows." Heather glanced toward Danielle's belly.

"She knows what exactly?" Walt asked.

Heather made the same hand gesture Carla had made that morning. She held up two fingers.

"Who told her?" Danielle asked.

"She overheard Mel and Adam discussing it. So I guess you don't really have to tell anyone else. Carla will spread the word for you." Heather chuckled.

Danielle looked down at her belly and gave it a pat. "Well, I'm sorta getting used to the idea."

Heather flashed Walt a grin. "She's not mad at you anymore?"

"She called me a monster a little while ago," Walt said with a faux pout.

Heather shrugged. "Well, you are responsible for all this. When you can't control your swim team, this is what can happen."

Danielle giggled. "Yes, competitive little guys, each seeing who could make it to the finish line first, and when they saw they each had a chance, they took advantage of the situation."

"I always said you can't trust those sneaky tadpoles."

"I can't believe this conversation," Walt grumbled, no longer teasing.

Both women laughed. Finally, Danielle said, "I guess people didn't talk so freely about this stuff during your last life."

"Not exactly," Walt said.

"Well, I'm excited about it," Heather said.

"You who vows to never have kids of her own," Danielle teased.

Heather shrugged. "That mommy thing is just not for me. But I love being the doting auntie."

"It's probably a good thing Lily said nothing to Mel or Adam about their news," Danielle noted.

Heather nodded. "No kidding. Can you imagine Kelly or her parents going to the diner and having the waitress tell them about Lily?"

"Just remember, if Kelly ever asks if you or Chris heard before she did, lie and say you didn't," Danielle reminded her.

"Yeah, yeah, Chris and I understand. But this is Lily's fault. Before she spilled the beans to you, she should have asked if Marie or Eva were with you."

Walt glanced at the clock. "The buyer should be here any minute."

"You didn't tell me. What's the scoop on her? Does she have a roommate, boyfriend, girlfriend?" Heather asked.

"I haven't heard. To be honest, I don't think Adam knows much about her. He wasn't her agent."

"Yeah, Ray Collins brought the buyer." Heather chuckled. "For some reason, that agent really bugs Adam."

"It's too bad Adam didn't get both sides of the deal, would have been twice the commission," Danielle said.

"And Adam likes his commission!" Heather grinned.

"He doesn't know much about the buyer aside from the fact she bought the property in her name only and paid cash," Danielle said. The doorbell rang.

DANIELLE AND HEATHER stood by Walt's side as he opened the front door. When he did, he found a woman standing on the front porch. She appeared startled, finding herself looking not at one person, but three people staring in her direction.

"Hello, I'm Olivia Davis," the woman introduced herself.

"Adam Nichols from Frederickport Vacation Properties said I could pick up my keys here. I bought the house next door."

Danielle grinned and handed the keys to the woman. "It's so nice to meet you. Welcome to the neighborhood. My name is Danielle Marlow, and this is my husband, Walt."

Walt offered his hand to her, which she accepted, while he said, "Nice to meet you. As Danielle said, welcome to the neighborhood."

"And this is our friend and neighbor, Heather Donovan. She's your neighbor on the other side," Danielle said.

Silently, Heather and Olivia stared at each other. Instead of offering her hand, as Walt had done, Heather took a step back, awkwardly shielding herself behind Walt.

Olivia continued to stare at Heather. The faint smile she'd worn a moment earlier vanished. Tersely she said, "Thank you for the keys." Without another word, she turned and bolted down the walkway toward the street.

Confused, Danielle looked from their new neighbor to Heather and then closed the door. "What was that all about? I was just about to ask her if she wanted to come in and have a cup of coffee."

"It was her!" Heather screeched.

"Her who?" Walt asked.

"The woman I saw with Betty Kelty this morning. Before someone murdered her!"

FOUR

D anielle peeked out the narrow window next to the front door and watched as their new neighbor disappeared down the front walk. She turned to Heather. "Are you sure?"

"Yes, I'm sure! And by the way she looked at me, she recognized me."

"Explains why she was at Pearl's house," Walt said. "She probably arrived in town and was eager to see it."

"But it doesn't explain why she killed Betty!"

"Heather, we don't know if she killed anyone, just that they were together an hour before the murder. You don't know what happened in that hour," Danielle reminded her. "All we can do is call the chief and let him know you've identified the person you saw with Betty this morning."

Heather considered Danielle's words for a moment and then let out a deep sigh. "Yeah, you're right. I hate when people jump to conclusions about me. Maybe she had nothing to do with the murder, but she could have seen something."

"And if she is innocent and knows nothing about the murder, she could be in danger. Perhaps she saw something after she left

Betty, something she doesn't even realize is significant," Walt suggested.

Together, the three returned to the kitchen while Danielle called the chief to tell him they knew the identity of the person of interest.

"She could have parked in the alley," Danielle said after she ended her call with the chief. She now sat at the kitchen table with Heather and Walt. "Just because you didn't see her car on the street doesn't mean she didn't drive over here."

"I suppose you're right. She obviously knew Betty. Maybe she came over to show her the house. Since they didn't have a key to get in, they decided to walk down to the beach. I know one of the first things I did when I got here was take a walk on the beach. It's possible Betty was meeting someone, and Olivia returned to get her car and left without Betty," Heather suggested.

THE MOVING van would arrive Monday with Olivia's furniture and most of her belongings. But there was a blow-up bed in her car, along with suitcases filled with clothes and basic essentials, so she could stay at her new house through the weekend, until the movers arrived. She had brought nothing into the house aside from her purse and laptop computer. Everything else was still in her car. She wanted to check out the house before bringing everything inside. After inspecting the first floor, she went upstairs to see the bedrooms. Just as she started back downstairs to unpack her car, her doorbell rang.

When she opened the front door, it surprised her to find a police officer standing on her front step.

"Olivia Davis?" the officer asked.

She frowned at him. "Umm, yeah. How can I help you?"

"I'm Sergeant Joe Morelli. I understand you're the new owner?" Joe said.

"Yes. What is this about?"

"This morning, a woman was murdered down the street from your house."

Olivia's eyes widened. "Murdered? Have they arrested the killer? What happened?"

"No, we have not apprehended the killer," Joe began. "I was hoping you could come down to the station. There are some questions we need to ask you."

Olivia frowned. "I don't know why you'd want me to go down to the station to answer questions. I just arrived in town thirty minutes ago, and I don't know anyone here."

"The woman who was murdered was seen on your property an hour before her death. We would like to ask you some questions to help fill in the blanks so we can get a clearer picture of what might have happened."

Olivia said nothing for several moments and just stared at Joe. Finally, she said, "Okay."

———

BRIAN and the chief stood together in the office next to the interrogation room, watching through the one-way mirror. They had brought Olivia to the room and told her the officer would be there shortly. She now sat alone at the table, her back straight, and her hands folded before her on the tabletop. Glancing around, she took in her surroundings. After a few minutes, Joe arrived, carrying a large manila envelope.

After greeting Olivia and thanking her for coming down to the station, he sat down across from her at the table.

"So why did you choose Frederickport as your new home?" Joe asked congenially.

"I've always wanted to live at the beach. And property along the Oregon coast is more affordable than in California. And I got a job here."

"Really? Can I ask you where?"

Olivia shrugged. "It's no secret. And if you're a reader, you'll probably run into me again."

Joe frowned in response. Olivia smiled at his confusion and said,

"I got a job at the Frederickport Library. I'm a librarian. I start a week from today."

Joe's eyes visibly widened. He stared at her a moment, his demeanor shifting to a more aloof tone.

"You mentioned you just arrived today…" Joe pulled a photograph out of the envelope yet didn't show it to her.

"Yes. I flew into Portland this morning."

"And you rented a car and drove to Frederickport?"

Olivia smiled. "No. I mean, yeah, I drove here from Portland. But it's not a rental. It's my car."

Joe placed the photograph on the table and slid it across to Olivia. "Please tell me what you know about her." He watched as Olivia turned the photograph around so it was no longer upside down from her angle. He noted how her eyes widened, and what he deemed an expression of recognition crossed her face.

After a moment, she cleared her throat and asked, "Who is she?"

Joe frowned. "You don't know her?"

Olivia shrugged. "Why would I? Is this the woman who was murdered today?"

"Are you saying you don't know her?"

"I told you, I just moved here today. Is she the one who was murdered?"

"Yes. She was. Are you sure you don't know her?"

"Why do you keep asking me that?" Olivia asked impatiently. "I already told you I don't know her."

"And you have never seen her before?"

Olivia looked down at the photograph again, studying it before answering. Finally, she looked up at Joe. "No. I don't think so."

Joe arched his brows. "You don't think so? You don't know for sure?"

"I don't know. I see people all the time when working at the library, but it doesn't mean I'll remember their faces if someone shows me a picture of them."

"Her name was Betty Kelty. She worked at the Frederickport Library, where you'll be working."

Olivia picked up the photograph and stared at it. Lost for a few moments in private thought, she muttered, "So that's who she is."

"Where were you this morning between six and seven?"

Olivia looked up into Joe's eyes as they intently studied her every reaction. Slowly, she set the photo back on the table and said, "I imagine about thirty-five thousand feet in the air."

Joe frowned. "Excuse me?"

"I told you I flew into Portland this morning. Our plane didn't land until around 7:30."

"And you can prove this?"

"Why do I have to? I just arrived in town this afternoon. I didn't know this person. And I certainly don't know why she was on my property this morning."

"Someone saw Betty Kelty leaving through the front gate of the Beach Drive property you just purchased. This was about an hour before they found her body. That was around 6:30. But she wasn't alone. She was with a woman who fits your description."

Olivia shrugged. "Obviously it was someone who looks like me, because it wasn't me." She pushed the photograph across the table toward Joe.

"Same hair color, same jacket?" Joe returned.

"Coincidences happen." She picked up her purse, opened it, and fished out some papers. The next moment, she tossed them across the table.

Frowning, Joe picked up the papers.

"That's the information on my flight this morning. One nice thing about flying these days, they check your identification before you get on a plane. And there are cameras everywhere. So I suggest you do your research so you can check me off your suspect list. And if it's okay, I'm leaving now." She stood.

DANIELLE SAT on the living room sofa with her stockinged feet pulled up on the cushion, watching Heather, who sat on the chair across from her, talking on her cellphone.

When Heather finished her call, she looked at Danielle. "That was Brian."

"Yeah, that's what I kinda figured."

"He said the chief wants to talk to me. He wanted to know where I was, and he's coming over here."

"What did he say about our new neighbor?"

Heather shrugged. "When I asked Brian, he said he couldn't say anything right then. I think he didn't want to discuss it in front of whoever was nearby. I wonder why the chief wants to talk to me. Do you think they arrested her? Maybe she got out on bail, and he's warning me?"

WHEN WALT LET the chief into the living room fifteen minutes later, they found Danielle still sitting, curled up on the sofa, and Heather on the chair across from her.

Heather greeted the chief with, "Did you arrest her?"

"It wasn't the woman you saw," the chief told her as he walked all the way into the room while Walt trailed behind him. Before taking a chair next to Heather, the chief walked by Danielle and gave her a pat on the shoulder.

"What do you mean she wasn't the same woman I saw this morning? Yes, she was!" Heather insisted.

The chief, now sitting next to Heather, shook his head. "No, it wasn't. She was on a flight when you claimed to have seen her. It's obvious you saw someone else."

"The woman had the same freaking hair. Same hairstyle. Same dark brown eyes. Heck, she even had the same quilt jacket. I bet anything that's a handcrafted jacket. No way there are two women who look identical, each wearing the same handcrafted item. Unless she has a twin, and they have matching quilt jackets."

The chief frowned at Heather. "Are you sure?"

"Yes, I'm sure," Heather said emphatically.

Walt looked at the chief. "Edward, is there a chance someone else took that flight for her? To give her an alibi?"

The chief considered Walt's question and let out a sigh. "I'll have to request footage from the airline and airport. But that will take a few days. By the way, it seems your neighbor is starting her new job next Friday. At the library."

Danielle sat up straighter on the sofa. "That's where Betty worked."

The chief nodded. "Yes. She was going to be your neighbor's new boss. But according to the current head librarian, who is planning on retiring, that job may go to your neighbor now."

Danielle arched her brow. "So she starts a new job and immediately gets a promotion?"

"I called the library after your neighbor left the station. I spoke to the head librarian. Apparently, Ms. Davis initially applied for the head librarian job. But then Betty applied for the position before they made their final decision, and they promoted from within. They ended up offering Ms. Davis Betty's old job," the chief explained.

"I wonder how Ms. Davis felt about that," Heather mused. "Especially if she applied for the head librarian job first."

"She now has the job she wanted," the chief said.

FIVE

After Olivia returned to her house from the police station, she brought what luggage she had in her car inside, along with two folding chairs, a box with the blow-up bed, and a sleeping bag. Instead of setting the bed up in the master bedroom upstairs, she left it in the living room. She didn't want to haul it up the staircase. Olivia had planned to pick up some groceries, but the trip to the police station had eaten up her time, and now she was simply too drained and exhausted to go shopping. This meant she would have to run out later and pick up something to eat.

Olivia dragged the blow-up bed from its case, unfolded it where she intended to sleep, and then plugged its cord into an electrical outlet. Just as the bed finished filling with air, her doorbell rang. When she got to her front door a few minutes later, she looked through the peephole and saw a familiar face. It was Josephine Barker. While she had never met the woman in person, she recognized her from the video conference calls during her job interview.

After unlocking her door, Olivia opened it. "Josephine Barker?"

Josephine smiled and then held up the basket in her hands, which Olivia hadn't noticed when looking through the peephole.

"You recognized me! I bought you a little welcome-to-Frederick-port gift from the library."

Olivia smiled and opened the door wider, motioning for Josephine to enter. "I'm surprised you knew I arrived. I told you I would arrive on Monday."

"But then here you are." Josephine handed Olivia the basket after Olivia closed the front door. "You'll find living in a small town like Frederickport, news gets around fairly quickly."

Now holding the basket, Olivia silently inventoried its contents: gourmet coffee beans, muffins, chocolate chip cookies, crackers, and an assortment of Tillamook cheese. "This was very thoughtful of you. Please come in. But let me set this in the kitchen. I'm afraid my furniture hasn't arrived yet."

A few minutes later, Olivia returned to the living room after setting the basket on the kitchen counter. She sat in one of the folding chairs, with Josephine sitting in the other one.

Hesitantly, Olivia asked, "Do you know what happened down the street from here this morning?"

"I assume you mean what happened to poor Betty Kelty?"

Olivia nodded.

"I still can't believe it. She wasn't just a coworker. She was my friend. Were you here this morning when all the commotion was going on?" Josephine asked.

Olivia shook her head. "No. I was in flight. From what the police told me, my plane hadn't even landed when it happened."

"You talked to the police?"

Olivia nodded. "Apparently, someone saw your friend shortly before they found her body. She was leaving my yard through the front gate onto the sidewalk, and she was with a woman, who, by the description given, the police thought might be me."

"But it wasn't?"

Olivia let out a snort. "Not unless I could pop down from my flight while it's thousands of feet in the air, and then pop up again."

"I wonder who it was," Josephine mused.

Olivia shrugged. "I have no idea. It just wasn't me."

"I understand you'll be busy next week getting moved in after your furniture arrives. But I was hoping you could come down to the library sometime next week—at your convenience—to discuss your job."

Olivia arched her brow. "I thought I was supposed to start Friday, anyway. Is there a problem? Do you need me to come before that?"

"We just need to make some changes now that dear Betty is gone. We would like you to consider taking the job of head librarian. I'll stick around until we can find a replacement for Betty and help you get settled into your new position. I suppose we can just discuss it more on Friday. But I would like you to consider taking the job."

EXHAUSTED, Carla sat at Pier Café's lunch counter; it had been a long day. Business had picked up after they found Betty Kelty's body up the street. After rubbernecking the crime scene, locals stopped into the diner to get something to eat and to pump Carla for any details she might have. But that had since settled down, and now just the regulars drifted into the diner.

Instead of going home after her shift, Carla took a seat at the counter and ordered herself a burger. She had no desire to go home and cook dinner. She was just about to take a bite of her burger when a woman she had never seen before walked into the diner. The woman glanced around. Less than half of the tables and booths were occupied, with Carla the only customer at the counter. The woman looked toward the counter and started that way.

A moment later, the woman took a seat at the counter. One stool separated her from Carla. Carla looked her way and said, "Hi. You're not from around here, are you? We don't get a lot of tourists at this time of year."

The woman smiled at Carla and said, "Actually, I just moved here. I bought a house on Beach Drive."

"Really? Pearl Huckabee's old house, I bet."

"Oh, you know the property?"

"Yeah. If you're here alone and would like some company and the scoop on your new neighborhood, you're welcome to sit with me. My name's Carla. I work here, but I just got off."

The woman looked to Carla, silently studying her for a moment, and then took Carla's offer and changed stools. "Thank you, Carla. Yes, I'm the new owner. My name is Olivia Davis."

Carla reached down the counter in the opposite direction from where Olivia sat and grabbed a menu. She handed it to Olivia and said, "Welcome to Frederickport. By the way, the food is actually pretty good here."

"Thank you." Olivia accepted the menu, opened it, and began reading the entrée options.

"Did you hear about the murder?" Carla asked.

Olivia glanced up from the menu to Carla. "Yes, I'm afraid I did. Not a terrific first day in my new home." She turned her attention back to the menu.

Carla shrugged. "Beach Drive seems to have more than its share of that sort of thing. Sometimes I wonder if we have some weird cosmic energy hovering over this neighborhood that attracts that type of negative energy." Carla took a bite of her burger.

Olivia set the menu on the counter and frowned at Carla. "What do you mean?"

When Carla finished swallowing her bite of food, she picked up a napkin, wiped her mouth, and looked at Olivia. "Well, you know, Pearl was murdered in the house you bought. Pushed down the staircase."

"I didn't know."

Again, Carla shrugged. "If it makes you feel any better, they locked up her killer. Not in prison, I heard they put her in some looney bin. According to Police Chief MacDonald, she's not fit to stand trial. And then, of course, there were those bodies found in Pearl's backyard." Carla paused a moment and looked at Olivia. "Of course, it's your backyard now. But those bodies aren't there anymore, and I don't think you need to worry about finding any more. I think the police really checked out the place. Plus, their killer's behind bars, too."

"Lovely," Olivia said dryly. The next moment, a server came and took Olivia's order and brought her iced water.

"Aside from that, you have some great neighbors on this street," Carla said when the server left to put in Olivia's order.

"I do?"

"Yeah. There's Walt and Danielle Marlow, who own Marlow House. They run a B and B, but I don't think they'll have it open much longer. She's having twins."

Olivia arched her brows. "Twins?"

"I can't even imagine one, much less two." Carla shivered. "Marlow House is like one of the oldest houses in town, built by the founder of Frederickport, Frederick Marlow. Walt Marlow is some distant cousin of his. But the funny thing, Danielle inherited the house from some aunt—no relation to Marlow—and it was after she was living there when she met Walt Marlow. He was a guest at the B and B. Came with his fiancée. But she died. Long story."

"Umm… I guess."

"And then there's Lily and Ian Bartley. They live across the street from Marlow House. Lily moved here after Danielle did. They're best friends. Have you ever heard of Jon Altar?"

"Sure. He's a writer. I've always loved his work. I know he lives in Frederickport."

"Jon Altar is Ian Bartley's pen name."

"Really?"

"Yep. I have no clue why he doesn't write under his own name. I think that would be awful confusing to go by two names."

"I can't believe he practically lives across the street from me."

"Walt Marlow is also an author."

"He's *that* Walt Marlow?"

Carla nodded. "Yeah. I can't remember the name of his book, but they were going to make a movie of it, but, well, that's a long story too. Let's just say the movie didn't get made."

"Interesting neighbors," Olivia mused.

"Ian and Lily have a little boy. She used to be a teacher, but now she's a stay-at-home mom. They're both really nice." Carla took a drink of her soda and then said, "And your neighbor on the other side, that's Heather Donovan."

"I met the Marlows and Heather Donovan earlier today. I had to pick up my keys from Marlow House. The Marlows seemed friendly, but that Heather Donovan, she didn't say a word. Seemed very odd."

"Well, don't be too hard on Heather. She and Chris are the ones who found the body this morning. And this is not the first time for Heather. She kind of has this reputation in town for finding dead bodies. She does it all the time."

Olivia's eyes widened. "What do you mean all the time?"

Carla shrugged. "Just that if a body washes up on shore, nine times out of ten, it will be Heather who finds it."

"Umm… that is a little weird."

"Welcome to Frederickport." Carla laughed. "And then there is Chris Johnson. Who is totally worth the trip to Beach Drive."

"What do you mean?"

"Chris lives up from Lily and Ian, on their side of the street. He is, like, the hottest guy you will ever see, seriously. And he's nice. And single."

"Is he gay?"

Carla chuckled. "I seriously doubt it. He had a thing for Danielle before Walt came along. And according to Heather, he dates a lot, but typically not in Frederickport. He and Heather work together at the Glandon Foundation."

"I've heard of that. It's the philanthropic foundation set up by Chris Glandon, right?"

Carla smiled knowingly at Olivia. "Yes. It is. You know who Chris Glandon is?"

"Sure, I've read about him. He's some reclusive billionaire who inherited his fortune from his parents. Likes to give away money and travels the world."

"That's him. Both Chris and Heather work for the foundation. Basically, Chris manages it, and Heather is his assistant."

"Does Chris Glandon ever come to Frederickport?"

"He has a couple of times, but if he comes, no one ever sees him. He likes his privacy."

"Have you ever seen him in Frederickport?"

Carla didn't answer immediately. She chewed her lower lip a moment while considering her answer. Finally, she said, "Well, I met him once when he came to town."

"What does he look like? The only pictures I've seen of him he's got this overly bushy, scruffy beard, long hair, and sunglasses."

Carla looped a lock of pink hair around a fingertip and twirled it a moment before saying, "Chris Glandon? Well, umm... he's kinda average looking. Forgettable. Not sure how I would describe him."

SIX

Lily buckled Connor into his car seat as Ian tossed the diaper bag in the back of the car. She glanced back at him, the hatch open, and asked, "Does this mean we have Sunday to ourselves?"

"Looks that way." Since Ian's parents had moved to Frederickport, Ian, Lily, and Connor, along with Ian's sister, Kelly, and her boyfriend, Joe, had been having Sunday dinners with Ian's parents. But earlier that week, Ian's mother, June, had asked them if they could come for dinner on Friday instead of Sunday, as she and her husband, John, had other plans for Sunday.

Ian slammed the rear hatch closed while Lily shut the back car door and then opened the door to the passenger side of the vehicle. Wearing denims and a green pullover sweater, Lily sat on the passenger seat, closed the car door, and began buckling her seatbelt. She had her red hair pulled back in a high ponytail, and the only eye makeup she wore was a hint of green eye shadow, thin brown eyeliner, and mascara.

"I think we should go to Pearl Cove Sunday," Lily told Ian as he got into the driver's seat a few moments later.

"Hey, we're going out to dinner tonight. Two times in a weekend?" Ian teased while shutting the door behind him.

"The weekend doesn't officially start until midnight."

Ian chuckled and buckled his seatbelt.

WHEN THEY ARRIVED at Ian's parents' house, Kelly and Joe were already there, sitting in the living room with June while John prepared cocktails.

"I bought olives," June told Lily after snatching up her grandson and showing him the new toys she had purchased for him. Placing Connor on the floor with the toys, June told John, "Make Lily a martini."

"Thanks, June, that's sweet. But I really don't feel like a martini tonight." Lily took a seat on the loveseat with Ian.

"Do you have a headache?" June asked.

"No, I feel great." The moment Lily said the words, she regretted it.

"John, fix Lily a martini; she'll change her mind," June insisted.

Lily and Ian exchanged glances but said nothing.

A few minutes later, John brought Lily a martini. As he handed it to her, he looked at Ian and asked, "What can I get you to drink?"

"I don't really want anything right now. Let me think about it," Ian told him.

John gave a nod and walked across the living room and took a seat next to his wife. By his feet, his grandson played with the toys.

Lily glanced at the martini glass and then looked at Ian. He smiled, reached over, snatched the glass from her, took a sip and looked over to his parents, who were currently in a discussion with Joe about the murder on Beach Drive. They didn't look his way. He took another drink of the martini and removed the toothpick with the olives. Ian popped them into his mouth.

Lily frowned at Ian. The next moment, he removed the toothpick from his mouth. The olives were still intact. He grinned and handed them to her. "I removed the vodka for you," he whispered.

Lily giggled and accepted the offering. She ate the olives while

Ian set the now empty glass on the table. "I'm going to have to drive home," she whispered.

"Ian, you really need to sell your house and move," June said, now turning her attention to Lily and Ian. "Beach Drive is not a safe neighborhood."

"We are not moving," Ian said with a sigh.

June glanced from Ian to the table, spying the now empty martini glass.

"Lily, see, you changed your mind. My, you drank that fast. You might want to slow down," June chided.

Lily flashed June a weak grin.

Returning to the conversation about the murder, John said, "I can't believe they haven't located the woman who was with her this morning."

"Didn't Heather find the body?" June asked.

"Her and Chris," Kelly said.

"Heather was certain the buyer of Pearl Huckabee's house was the same woman with Betty Kelty an hour before they found the body. The description matched, even down to what she was wearing. But it couldn't have been her. The woman was on a flight at the time of the murder. She gave us copies of her flight information. And it looks like she was telling the truth," Joe explained.

"Perhaps it wasn't her flight information. Another possibility, they were forged," June suggested. "If Heather described the woman's clothing and said she looked like the same woman, it's possible those papers she showed you are fake."

"They aren't fake. But the chief is requesting video footage of the flight, to verify she was on it. That will take some time, but from what the chief told me before I left work, I don't think we'll need it," Joe said.

"Why is that?" John asked.

"After the flight arrived, there was a car waiting for her at the airport. Apparently, she purchased a new car and had it delivered. The dealer wanted to take a photograph of her for their website— to promote their customer service, and she agreed. The chief spoke to the dealer this afternoon, and he emailed copies of the photos they took this morning. Unless the dealer is in this with her, I don't think she's the same woman Heather claimed to have seen. It's a bizarre coincidence that both women wore the same jacket and look so much alike."

"And there are no leads on that poor woman's murder?" John asked.

Joe shook his head. "Unfortunately, no."

"Well, I'm glad they didn't accept your offer for that house. At least one of my children is safe!" June said.

June stood up and excused herself to go check on the dinner. When she returned a few minutes later, she said, "Dinner will be ready in about ten minutes. Does anyone want another cocktail?"

"You want a drink now?" John asked Ian.

Ian shook his head. "No, thanks, Dad, I'm good."

"Well, I'm not going to ask Lily if she wants another drink," June chided. "Not considering how she guzzled that last one."

Lily flashed her husband a frown.

"But Lily always says martinis are like—" John began.

"Yes, yes, you don't need to say that with Connor here," June scolded.

Ian laughed. "Mom, Connor knows what a woman's breast is. He was breast fed, remember?"

June rolled her eyes, and Ian laughed again. On Lily and Ian's first date, Lily had told Ian a martini was like a woman's breast. One was not enough, but three was too many. Thinking it funny, Ian had shared the joke with his parents. His mother did not find it amusing.

"Did you want another martini?" John asked Lily.

Lily looked to Ian. "We should tell them. We were going to tell them on Sunday anyway, and since we aren't coming on Sunday."

"Tell us what?" June asked.

"Yeah, what's going on?" Kelly asked.

Ian reached over and took one of Lily's hands in his. "We have an announcement." He looked at Lily and said, "You want to tell them?"

Lily smiled and said, "Connor is going to be a big brother."

The room went silent. After a moment, June gasped. "You shouldn't be drinking martinis!"

"Mom, you forced it on her," Ian teased.

"But she shouldn't have taken it!" June shrieked. She looked at Lily. "What were you thinking? Don't you know how harmful alcohol is to the unborn child?"

"Mom, settle down. Lily didn't drink the martini," Ian said, no longer teasing.

June pointed to the empty glass on the coffee table. "What do you mean she didn't drink it? The glass is empty!"

"I think what Ian is saying, he drank the martini," Kelly said.

June stared dumbly at Kelly. She turned to Ian and frowned. "You drank it?"

Ian nodded. "Yes."

"Ian never mentioned you were trying to get pregnant," Kelly told Lily.

"We weren't trying. But birth control is not a hundred percent," Lily said, not sounding upset. "And while we wanted our kids to be three years apart, I guess it might be nice if they're less than two years apart. And it's kinda cool that my best friend is pregnant at the same time."

"Oh, another grandbaby!" June exclaimed, as if the full announcement finally registered.

"When is this baby due?" Kelly asked dully.

"End of July," Lily said.

"July?" Kelly squeaked.

"Oh my. The wedding's in July," June muttered.

"I understand this complicates things, but we'll work something out," Lily promised.

Kelly didn't respond, but sat quietly. The others continued to discuss the upcoming pregnancy. After ten minutes, June announced they should take the discussion into the dining room.

Kelly stood up. "Excuse me, but I think that wine didn't sit right with me." She looked at Joe. "Can you please take me home?"

KELLY BEGAN to cry the moment she got into the car. It wasn't until Joe got into the driver's seat that he noticed her tears.

"Are you sick?" he asked, sounding concerned.

"No, I'm not sick!" Kelly snapped. "I want to get out of here! Hurry before one of them comes out here."

"I doubt anyone is coming outside; they were all sitting down for dinner." Joe shoved his key into the ignition and turned on the engine. "If you're not sick, why are we leaving and missing dinner?"

"Lily ruins everything!" Kelly sobbed. "I wish my brother had never come to Frederickport!"

With a frown, Joe pulled the car out into the street and headed home, silently driving while Kelly cried. They were about halfway home when Joe said quietly, "If your brother hadn't moved to Frederickport, we wouldn't have met."

Kelly made a hiccup sound, pulled a tissue out of the glove compartment, and blew her nose. No longer crying, she said, "It's just that Lily ruins everything. She's taken my brother away from me."

"You see Ian all the time."

"And they promised we could have our wedding at their house."

"Lily said they would work something out."

"Think about it, Joe. This isn't going to happen. Lily is going to be nine months pregnant in July. Ready to pop at any minute."

"She said she wasn't due until the end of July. The wedding's mid-July."

"It's a good thing we haven't ordered the wedding invitations yet."

"Why?" Joe asked.

"We can't have a wedding in July at their house. How do we have a wedding where the hostess is waddling around, about to have a baby at any minute? And what if she goes into labor early, in the middle of the wedding?"

"It would make for a memorable wedding," Joe teased.

"This isn't funny."

Joe let out a sigh and reached over and grabbed one of Kelly's hands, giving it a quick squeeze before returning his hand to the steering wheel. "I get this messes up our plans. But we have time to figure something out, and aren't you a little excited about having a new niece or nephew? You are crazy about Connor."

Kelly slumped back in the seat and looked out the window into the dark night.

After a few moments of silence, she said, "I am a horrible person."

"You are not a horrible person."

"Yes, I am. I learned something about myself tonight. I didn't even realize it."

Joe glanced to Kelly. "What's that?"

"I didn't realize how jealous I am of Lily. Not really. But when she said she was due in July, it was like this flood of emotion came rushing out. I had to leave, or I would say something really horrible to Lily, and Ian would hate me."

"Ian would never hate you."

"Yes, he would," Kelly said in a dull voice, still staring into the darkness. "If I had said what I was thinking, he would hate me. And I would hate me too."

SEVEN

"I wish you could go to breakfast with us," Heather told Brian as she watched him get dressed on Saturday morning. Already wearing green leggings and a long sweater, she sat on the bed, leaning against the headboard, her stockinged feet crossed at the ankles.

Brian slipped on his shirt and smiled over at Heather. "I'd like to. But I'm going back over to Eden's. She was the only one of Betty's nearby neighbors not home when we were there yesterday, but one of the other neighbors claimed Eden was at her house yesterday morning. I'm hoping she saw something."

"Thanks for staying with me last night." With the recent murder on the street, Heather didn't feel comfortable staying at home alone.

"My pleasure." Brian paused from buttoning his shirt and looked over to Heather, flashing her a mischievous grin.

Leaning back against the headboard, Heather let out a deep sigh.

Brian resumed his buttoning and asked, "Why the weary sigh?"

"I just wish Marie would get back."

"You're hoping she might know something?"

"No. I doubt she knows anything. After all, she and Eva have been at that theater thing since Thursday. But I hate missing my morning run."

Brian frowned. "I don't get it."

"If I don't want to stay here alone at night, I certainly don't want to go running on the beach alone. Not when Betty Kelty got stabbed twenty feet from where I usually run."

"You want Marie to go jogging with you?"

"She could keep me company. And if anyone messes with me, she'd be my guard dog."

"If you want a guard dog, ask Chris to let you take Hunny jogging. I bet Hunny would love it."

"Hunny? A guard dog?" Heather let out a snort.

"She is a pit bull. Looks damn scary. And while she's more of a lover than a fighter, I'm sure she would rise to the occasion if someone threatened you."

"Yeah, I'll consider that."

Brian left Heather's house fifteen minutes later, going out the back door. He made his way to his car, which he had parked in the driveway off the alley. Heather fed Bella, grabbed her purse, and headed out the front door to start for Pier Café. She knew Walt and Danielle would leave their house any minute, so she wouldn't be alone for long.

The moment she locked the door behind her, she heard her front gate open and shut. Turning to the sound, she let out a gasp when she saw her new neighbor, Olivia Davis, standing in her court-yard, staring in her direction.

"Oh, did I scare you?" Olivia asked in a quiet voice, her facial expression blank.

Heather's eyes widened. "Umm, you just startled me."

Olivia smiled and took a step toward Heather. "I was hoping we could talk."

"I… I was just leaving. I'm meeting someone, can't be late. We can talk later."

"This will just take a minute." Olivia walked toward Heather and stopped when she was about five feet away. "When we met yesterday, you were very quiet."

"Umm…"

"I understand you were the one who found the body yesterday."

Heather nodded.

"That must have been awful. Did you know her?"

"Umm, no. Not really. I've talked to her a few times at the library. But I can't really say I knew her."

"It's rather frightening learning there was a murder just a few doors down from where you live. Especially when the killer is still out there."

"Umm, yes. I guess it wasn't the best welcome to your new house."

"No. No, it wasn't. Tell me, you didn't happen to see Betty yesterday. Before she was killed?"

Heather stared at Olivia a few moments before answering. "If I did, I didn't know it was her."

"Did you see anyone else?" Olivia asked.

"If I did, I would have already told the police."

To Heather's relief, she spied Walt and Danielle walking down the street. Without hesitation, Heather called out to them and waved. She looked at Olivia and said, "It really was nice talking to you, but Walt and Danielle are waiting for me." The next moment, Heather darted to the sidewalk, leaving Olivia alone in her courtyard.

HEATHER SAT at a large table at Pier Café with Walt, Danielle, Lily, Ian, and Connor, with Connor sitting in his highchair between Heather and Lily. Heather had just finished talking about her morning encounter with Olivia Davis.

"That's so weird. And you're sure it was her you saw yesterday with Betty?" Lily asked.

"If it's not her, it's her identical twin or some wild doppelgänger wearing the same jacket. But according to the airline, she was on that flight. They're still waiting for the videos taken on the security cameras to verify that. But no way was it her on that flight. It was so weird her asking me questions while we both knew she was with Betty, yet neither of us would say it out loud."

"Joe said some guy she bought a car from also verified she was at the airport around the time of the murder," Ian said.

"I know. But he's wrong. I know it was her I saw," Heather insisted. "Heck, I described her and the jacket before she came to Marlow House to pick up her keys. How could I have done that if I hadn't seen her?"

"Perhaps she does have a twin," Danielle suggested. "And maybe they're in this together. That's the only logical conclusion, providing she really was on that flight."

"That should be easy enough to find out," Ian said.

"Now that you mention twins." Lily looked down at Danielle's belly.

"Don't tell me you're having twins, too?" Danielle teased.

"Oh, gawd no!" Lily cringed. "It's going to be bad enough having two in diapers at the same time, but three? But when you mentioned twins, I thought of your twins. Which made me think of my baby. Basically, what I was getting around to saying, we told Ian's family about the baby last night."

"Ahh, so how did they take it?" Heather asked. "I bet June was thrilled."

"Yes. After she realized Ian had been the one to drink the martini."

Heather frowned. "What martini?"

"And I don't think Kelly took the news well," Lily added.

"That's not true," Ian said. "She just left because she wasn't feeling well."

"What martini?" Heather repeated.

Lily looked at her husband and rolled her eyes. "Ian, didn't you see her face when we said the baby was due in July?"

"That doesn't surprise me," Danielle said. "I kinda wondered how she would take it when she realized her wedding was so close to your due date."

"Oh, and whatever you do, Heather, you can't let anyone know you knew about me being pregnant," Lily reminded her.

"Okay, but first you have to tell me about the martini," Heather said.

"I would like to know about that, too," Walt chimed in.

It took Lily a moment to register what they were asking. When she did, she told them about the martini June had pushed on her. After the telling, Heather asked, "Does this mean I can tell Brian now?"

"You really haven't told him yet?" Walt asked.

Heather shook her head. "No. The only reason Chris and I knew is because blabby Marie was so excited when she heard Lily telling Danielle that she couldn't contain herself and immediately came over to the office and told Chris and me, because she just had to tell someone."

"To Marie's credit, she felt terrible about it afterwards," Danielle said.

Lily turned to Heather. "You can tell Brian. It's not a secret anymore. I called my mom last night."

"You hadn't told her yet?" Heather asked.

"No. I really couldn't. Mom wouldn't be able to keep it from Laura. She's worse than Marie."

"And Laura would tell Kelly," Heather said.

Danielle lifted her glass of orange juice in a toast and said, "Well, now all of our secrets are out."

WHILE HEATHER HAD breakfast with her friends at Pier Café, Brian sat with Eden Langdon at her kitchen table, drinking a cup of coffee and discussing Betty Kelty.

"Yes, I saw Betty yesterday morning. It was pretty early. Before six. I was just leaving myself. She was pulling out of her driveway when I was getting into my car. We didn't talk, but we waved."

"And you didn't see her return?"

Eden shook her head. "No, like I said, I was leaving myself. I drove into Portland and spent the night. I got back about twenty minutes before you showed up." Eden took a sip of her coffee and then shook her head. "I can't believe someone killed Betty. Why would anyone want to hurt her? She was such a sweet girl."

"Did you know any of her friends?"

"Not really. Just Becca Hammond. But I don't think they're friends anymore."

"Becca Hammond, who lives over on Beach Drive?"

Eden shrugged. "I'm not really sure where Becca lives. Wasn't Betty murdered on Beach Drive?"

"Yes. About five houses down from where Becca Hammond lives."

Eden arched her brows. "I assume you've already spoken to Becca?"

"Not yet. Like you, she wasn't home. But can you tell me why they aren't friends anymore?"

"Whatever falling-out they had, I really don't see Becca killing her old friend over it."

"Please, just tell me what you know about this falling-out."

Eden let out a deep sigh, set her coffee mug on the table, and leaned back in the chair. "I know Becca from the historical society. I joined after I moved to Frederickport, attended some of their meetings to meet people. But frankly, everyone was old enough to be my grandmother, so I dropped out. Everyone except for Becca. She seemed nice enough, but we never really hung out. Anyway, I used to see her over at Betty's. They were friends. Well, they were until about a month ago when I saw them standing out in front of Betty's house, and Becca was going off on Betty. She was pissed about something. Betty sorta just stood there, saying nothing, and then Becca got in her car and raced off. And I mean raced. She left skid marks on the street."

"Any idea what it was about?"

"I was sorta curious, so I went over to Betty's later that afternoon, asked her if everything was okay. She knew I'd seen Becca yelling at her. Betty didn't tell me what had happened, just said something about how she probably lost a friend. She seemed pretty bummed about it. I felt sorry for her, but I have no idea what it was all about. After that, I never noticed Becca's car over there."

"Aside from Becca, you never saw Betty hang out with anyone?"

"No. Not really. I know she has family in Astoria. She used to go there a lot on her days off." Eden paused a moment and then said, "Oh gosh, have you told them?"

"Yes. The chief called them yesterday."

Eden shook her head and let out another sigh. "Betty was so nice to me after Shannon died."

"What are you going to do now? Last we talked, you were planning on moving."

"That was sort of put on hold while I get the estate settled." Eden studied Brian for a moment and then asked, "So what's the deal with you and Heather Donovan? You two still dating?"

Brian smiled and gave a nod. "Yes, we are."

Eden grinned. "Well, she is a better woman than me. You drove me nuts when we dated."

Brian laughed.

Eden studied Brian. "You know, you seem different."

"Different how?"

Eden shrugged. "I don't know. You had this enormous chip on your shoulder. I'll confess, when I found you were dating Heather Donovan, I didn't believe it at first. I mean, you and Heather?"

"I didn't realize you knew Heather."

"Oh, I don't. I've just seen her around town. She's kinda hard to miss. Not someone I would have thought was your type."

Brian shrugged.

"I hope you're happy, Brian."

"I am. You?"

Eden considered the question for a moment. "I'm more in limbo than happy."

"Why in limbo? Because you're waiting for the estate to get settled so you can move from Frederickport?"

"I suppose. While I never wanted anything to happen to my cousin, I will confess I feel a sense of liberation. I don't want to call that being happy. I don't want to be happy Shannon died. But I do feel free. Free to find happiness."

EIGHT

Carla had just brought the check to their table and walked away when Heather's cellphone rang. Heather picked up the phone and then frowned when she saw who was calling. A moment later, when she answered the call by saying, "Morning, Chief, this is a surprise," everyone else at the table stopped talking and looked her way.

When she got off the phone a few minutes later, Danielle asked, "Is everything okay?"

"I imagine you would have gotten that call instead of me if you weren't pregnant," Heather told her.

"Is this about the murder?" Danielle asked.

Heather nodded. "Yes, the chief is going to pick me up in a few minutes to take me to the morgue."

"Ghost hunting?" Walt asked.

"Yeah, he hopes Betty is hanging out with her body," Heather said.

Walt shrugged. "If her spirit wasn't with her body when you found it, chances are she already moved on."

"Or went somewhere else. If she didn't realize she was dead, she could have gone home," Danielle suggested.

"If it were me, I'd be following my killer and trying to harness energy," Lily said.

"You won't follow him if you don't understand you're dead," Walt reminded her. "If anything, you'd run away from your killer."

"That's what Pearl did," Heather said.

"Why isn't Brian taking you?" Danielle asked.

"Brian's busy in the field. I suspect they would've asked me to do it yesterday, but Joe was working, and I don't think the chief wants to deal with having to explain to Joe why I am at the morgue in case he happened to see me there. Joe's off today, so that shouldn't be a problem."

Danielle glanced at her watch and looked back at Heather. "Tell the chief hi for us. But Walt and I need to get home. We're going to that baby shop in town to look through some of their catalogues. I'm hoping we find the cribs we want and get them ordered. Then we want to stop at the hardware store and check out paint samples so Marie can paint the room."

"I thought you were going to wait and fix up the nursery later so you can use the room for the B and B," Heather asked.

Walt and Danielle exchanged brief glances, and then Danielle said, "Walt and I talked about it, and we decided to put the B and B on the back burner. Oh, if something comes up, like Kelly needs a place for wedding guests to stay, we'd be okay with that. But we have a lot on our plate right now. And once the babies get here—well, things are going to change for us. We don't want to tie ourselves down right now, and it's not like we need the money it generates."

"That's probably wise," Ian said. "While I love being a dad, once you become a parent, your life changes in ways that will never be the same. Enjoy this time with just the two of you."

"Not to mention the fact twins sometimes come early, so best to be prepared," Lily added.

***

PERCHED on the windowsill in one of the south-facing bedrooms of Marlow house, Danielle's cat, Max, looked out at the backyard, watching and waiting for Walt and Danielle's return. He had a hankering for some of that catnip Chris had given him and Bella for Christmas. Walt claimed the gift was from Hunny, but Max seriously doubted the goofy canine had anything to do with it.

Motion caught Max's attention. At first, he thought it was Danielle, but when he pressed his nose to the window, focusing on the person below, he realized it was not Danielle in the side yard, but a woman he had never seen before. With his black tail twitching back and forth, he continued to watch the woman. She made her way to the side door off the kitchen. The porch's overhang obscured his view. Unable to see where she had gone, he turned and leapt to the floor. Like a miniature black panther on the prowl, Max quickly moved from the bedroom to the hall and then the staircase.

When Max reached the bottom of the staircase, he paused. There, coming down the hall from the kitchen, was the woman he had seen walking across the side yard to the kitchen door. Max sat on the bottom step, his tail swishing back and forth. He silently watched the intruder.

She moved down the entry hall, looking into each room. First the dining room, then the living room, and the parlor. As she walked into the parlor, Max heard sounds coming from the kitchen. He leapt from the step and made his way to the kitchen. Halfway there, he heard Walt's and Danielle's voices. They were home.

Before continuing to the kitchen, Max turned and went back toward the parlor to see where the woman was so he could warn Walt. But when he got to the parlor, she was no longer there. He jumped up on the windowsill and looked outside. There was the woman who had been in the parlor minutes earlier, now going down the front walk, heading to the street.

Max jumped from the windowsill to the floor and hastily made his way toward the kitchen. He encountered Walt and Danielle just as the pair stepped from the kitchen into the hallway.

Max meowed loudly.

"Hi, Max," Danielle greeted the cat before leaning down and scooping him up in her arms. Max looked to Walt and let out another meow, this one louder and higher pitched.

Curious, Walt looked at the cat while Danielle calmly petted and cooed over the feline. Curiosity shifted to concern, and Walt blurted, "Are you sure she's gone?"

Max meowed again.

Danielle looked up from the cat in her arms and frowned. "Who's gone?"

Instead of answering Danielle, Walt stared at the cat, who met his gaze, never looking away. Danielle patiently waited for the pair to conclude their silent conversation.

Finally, Walt looked at Danielle. "Why don't you wait in the living room? I'm going to check the doors, and I'll be right back."

Five minutes later, Walt found Danielle sitting on the living room sofa, Max on her lap.

"What is going on?" Danielle asked.

Walt took a seat on the sofa. "We must have left the back door unlocked. Someone came into the house. From how Max described the person, I assume it was a woman. She came in through the kitchen and then walked down the hallway, into the parlor. And then she must have left out the front door."

Danielle glanced around nervously. "Are you sure she's not still in the house?"

"Max didn't see her leaving out the door, but he saw her out the window, walking toward the street. I suspect she heard us coming in the kitchen like Max had, so she left out the front door. I suppose we should be grateful she locked it when she left."

"Who was she?"

Walt shrugged. "Max had never seen her before. But the doors are all locked now."

"Walt, I know I locked the kitchen door when we left. I double-checked."

"He didn't see how she got in, only that he saw her walking across the side yard toward the kitchen door. It's possible she came through the pet door. I know an average-size adult would have a problem getting in that way, but Max is not great at giving descriptions, and that includes size."

"Or perhaps she's not a living person," Danielle suggested.

Walt stared at Danielle for a moment. "You think it might have been Betty Kelty?"

"It very well could be. If her spirit ran off after the attack and she doesn't realize she's dead, she could be wandering around trying to figure out what's going on."

"Then if that's true, Heather's trip to the morgue will be a complete waste of time."

Fifteen minutes later, Max enjoyed catnip in the kitchen while Danielle was upstairs getting ready to go into town to shop for the nursery. When she came back downstairs, she found Walt in the living room, sitting on the sofa, surfing on his phone.

"You know, for a man born in a previous century, you certainly adapted quickly to the digital world."

Still sitting on the sofa, cellphone in hand, Walt smiled up at Danielle. "You ready to go?"

"In a minute. I have to find my shoes." Danielle glanced around the room. "I think I left them in here."

"Under the desk," Walt said, turning his attention back to his phone's screen.

Danielle retrieved her shoes from under the desk, sat down on the sofa next to Walt, and put her shoes on. The doorbell rang.

Walt stood. "I'll answer it." Minutes later, he returned to the living room, their new neighbor by his side. Danielle had just finished putting on her shoes.

"I'm sorry to bother you," Olivia said.

"No bother. How are you settling in?" Danielle asked.

"My furniture doesn't arrive until Monday, as I was just explaining to your husband. They were supposed to hook up my cable and internet on Friday, but they tell me they won't be out until Monday afternoon. I was hoping I might use your Wi-Fi this week-end. I'll be more than happy to pay for it. But if you don't feel comfortable, I understand. There's Wi-Fi on my cellphone. I just thought I would give it a shot and ask."

Danielle smiled. "No problem. We give our B and B guests a password to use our Wi-Fi. I'll be happy to give it to you too. But you don't need to pay us."

Olivia glanced to the open door leading to the hallway and back to Danielle. "Oh, do you have B and B guests now?"

"No. None at the moment." Danielle's gaze moved to Olivia's unusual quilt jacket. "That is a lovely jacket. I've never seen one quite like it."

Olivia absently touched the hem of her jacket's left sleeve and then smiled up at Danielle. "Thank you. I made it."

"Really? You're talented." Danielle then turned her attention to Walt and asked, "Can you hand me one of the cards and a pen from the desk so I can write down the Wi-Fi password?"

Walt walked over to the desk and opened the drawer. As he retrieved the card and pen for Danielle, Olivia said, "Oh, thank you so much. I'll be able to use my laptop now!"

As Walt brought Danielle the pen and card, Max returned to the living room from the kitchen, his panther stroll weaving back and forth from the effects of the catnip. When he saw the woman Walt had brought into the living room, he stopped and sat down while studying the human. After a moment, he let out a loud meow.

All heads turned to the black cat.

"Oh, you have a kitty," Olivia cooed.

Max ran over to Walt and leapt into his arms.

"Do you like cats?" Danielle asked as she handed Olivia the card with the password.

"Yes, I am definitely a cat person. I like dogs, but I confess, I prefer cats. What's his name?"

"Max."

While Danielle and Olivia chatted a moment about cats versus dogs, Walt and Max had their own private conversation. After a moment, Walt, still holding Max, asked, "So tell me, Olivia, what have you been doing your first morning in Frederickport? Have you seen much of the neighborhood?"

Olivia looked at Walt and cringed. "To be honest, since hearing about the murder on this street, I've spent the morning locked up in my house. Do you know if they have any leads on the case?"

"Not that I'm aware of. So you've just been in your house all morning?" Walt asked.

"Yes. And there's not much to do. My furniture and the rest of my things don't arrive until Monday. I do plan to run to the grocery store. I don't have any food in the house. Last night I ate at Pier Café. Brought leftovers home, which I had for breakfast. But my pantry and fridge are empty, so I need to go."

They chatted for a few more minutes before Olivia thanked Danielle again for the use of the Wi-Fi and then said her goodbyes.

"What was with all the questions about her morning activities?" Danielle asked Walt after Olivia left. "I got the distinct feeling that there was something else you were really asking her, but I couldn't figure out what it was."

"That's because you know me so well," Walt said after he took a seat on the sofa next to Danielle.

"And?"

"Max finally identified our intruder."

"Who was she?" Danielle asked.

"Our new neighbor. Olivia Davis. That's who Max saw walking through our house before we got home."

NINE

"Thanks, Chief," Danielle said before ending her phone call. A moment later, Danielle set her cellphone on the coffee table and looked at Walt.

"What did he say?"

"He was glad I called him, but like we thought, nothing he can really do about it. The only one who saw her in our house was Max, and the chief is reluctant to use the testimony of a cat." Danielle added an eye roll to the last sentence.

"No surprise. Anything new on the murder?"

"No. But I'm not sure I want to go shopping today. Maybe we can go Monday? Or perhaps later this afternoon?"

Walt reached over and patted Danielle's knee. "Whenever you want."

"Thanks. I'd like to do a little research on our new neighbor. The chief is going to send me everything he has on her."

Walt frowned. "What kind of research?"

"The chief said she's from California. Not sure if she was born there, but if she was, I should be able to find her birth certificate on one of my genealogy websites. I want to see if she has a twin out there. That would explain how she was seen in Portland at the same time Heather saw her next door." Danielle let out a sigh and then added, "I wish Marie and Eva would get back. It would be nice if one of them could hang out with Olivia for a while and see what she's up to."

"Have Edward and Heather gone to the morgue yet?" Walt asked.

"They were just leaving when I called him. Betty's spirit wasn't there."

"Is he bringing Heather home?"

Danielle shook her head. "No. He's taking her over to Betty's house in case she's there."

"If they don't find her spirit at her house, she's probably already moved on," Walt suggested.

"That's what I'm thinking. Where is Eva when we need her?" Danielle grumbled before standing up to go to the desk where she had left her laptop earlier.

Danielle spent the next thirty minutes on her computer. Finally, she looked at Walt and said, "I can't find her birth certificate. I can't find much of anything, actually. While she obviously uses the internet—or she wouldn't have borrowed our password—I don't think she's on social media."

"I thought everyone was on social media."

Danielle grinned at Walt. "I guess not everyone."

Walt returned her grin.

"I was thinking we should probably tell Lily and Ian about our new neighbor's penchant for walking into houses uninvited. You want to go over there with me?"

DANIELLE JOINED Lily on the sofa while Ian sat across from them on the recliner. Nearby, Walt absently played trucks with Connor on the floor while he and Danielle explained what had happened that morning with Olivia Davis. Sadie, Ian's golden retriever, curled up by Walt's side, her head resting on his knee.

"She just walked into your house without knocking?" Lily asked after Danielle finished telling them about Max witnessing Olivia in Marlow House before they returned from breakfast.

Walt shrugged. "Maybe she heard Marlow House has an open-door policy for its neighbors. It's not like anyone else knocks before they come in."

Danielle rolled her eyes at Walt and said, "Well, they rarely come in through the pet door."

"She came in through the pet door?" Lily asked.

"She must have. I locked the kitchen door before we met you for breakfast this morning. Max saw her in the side yard, walking toward the kitchen. He didn't actually see her enter the house. But that's where he saw her go when he was upstairs, and then when he came downstairs, she was already in the house," Danielle explained.

"You really need to figure out what to do with that pet door. Especially now, with a killer out there. We all need to keep our doors locked, but it doesn't help if people can get in through the pet door," Lily said.

"I know." Danielle let out a sigh.

"I think it's time to invest in one of those locking pet doors," Ian said.

Lily glanced at Ian. "Oh, the ones where you have a remote gadget on the collar that automatically opens the door when the pet gets near it?"

Ian nodded, and Danielle said, "I've always been hesitant to put a collar on Max. Not safe for a cat if he's climbing on a tree."

"You can buy break-away collars," Ian reminded her.

"Then he couldn't get back into the house," Danielle countered.

Their discussion ended when Sadie's ears perked up, and then she leapt up and ran to the front door, barking.

Instead of yelling at Sadie to be quiet, Ian got out of his chair and followed her to the front door. After a few minutes, he returned to the living room with Kelly and Joe by his side. The moment Kelly spied Walt and Danielle, she abruptly stopped walking and said, "Oh, you're here."

"Hi, Walt and Danielle. How are you feeling, Danielle?" Joe asked, ignoring Kelly's less than friendly greeting.

"Since morning sickness became a thing of the past, pretty good, thanks." Danielle flashed them both a grin.

Kelly looked at Joe and said, "Maybe we should come back later?"

"Hey, you aren't interrupting anything," Ian assured his sister.

Kelly looked at Ian. "It's just that we need to talk to you about something. Alone."

Danielle and Walt exchanged quick glances before Danielle stood and announced, "Actually, Walt and I were just getting ready to leave, anyway. We're going to town and order our cribs."

"Cribs, as in more than one?" Joe grinned. "While I understand twins are more work, I forgot you have to buy two of things like cribs, highchairs, and car seats."

Kelly looked at Lily and said, "I guess you're going to have to buy those things, too."

"Yep. Connor will be about old enough to move out of a crib when the baby comes." Lily glanced briefly at Connor and then looked back at Kelly. "But we decided to buy a new crib. We don't want Connor to feel like the new baby took his bed. We'd like him to adjust to this change without giving him unnecessary reasons to feel jealous. It would be different if he had been out of the crib a while before the baby's arrival."

"Yeah. Jealousy can be a bad thing with siblings," Kelly muttered.

After Danielle and Walt left, Lily took a seat on the floor with Connor while Kelly and Joe sat on the sofa where Lily and Danielle had been ten minutes earlier.

"So what's going on?" Ian asked.

"Joe and I had a long talk last night," Kelly began. "And we're moving the wedding up to March."

"March?" Lily asked. "An outdoor wedding in March?"

Kelly looked at Lily. "We decided we're not having a beach wedding."

"But we appreciate your offer to have it here," Joe added.

"Is this because I'm expecting?" Lily asked.

Kelly didn't answer immediately. Finally, she said, "In a way.

There is no way we can expect you to host a wedding here during your last month of pregnancy. And once Joe and I started discussing it, we realized we really didn't want to wait until summer to get married. We only pushed it out that far so we could get married on the beach. But we'd like to get married sooner."

"Where are you going to get married?" Ian asked. "March is only two months away. What does Mom say?"

Kelly smiled sheepishly. "I haven't said anything to her yet. And I would appreciate it if you wouldn't tell her until I have a chance to break it to her. It's not like we're planning a huge wedding. It's just close family and a few friends."

"I have an idea," Lily said. Everyone looked at Lily. "How about having it at Pearl Cove? They do private events mid-week, and it has a magnificent ocean view. You would get your beach wedding while being indoors, out of the rain. Not a beach wedding exactly, but you will be able to see it while you're exchanging your vows."

Kelly chuckled. "Yeah. I wish. But Mom and Dad are on a fixed income, plus they're building a house, and even though Joe and I are paying for half the wedding, that would still be over our budget, especially if Joe and I want to buy a house."

"I was thinking Ian and I could pay for it. It would be our wedding gift to you."

Speechless, Kelly stared at Lily. Finally, she asked, "Why would you do that?"

Lily shrugged. "Well, you are Ian's baby sister, and he adores you."

Kelly looked at Ian, who sat quietly, smiling at his wife.

"That would be too expensive," Joe said. "We couldn't accept that."

"Sure you could," Ian said. "I think it's a great idea."

"Come on. It will be a beautiful place for a wedding. We can stay dry from the rain while still having a magnificent ocean view. And I've heard the food on their catering menu is amazing. I've always wanted to go to a wedding at Pearl Cove. But before we do this, there is only one condition," Lily insisted.

Curious, Ian looked at his wife, wondering about her condition.

Kelly frowned. "Umm, I'm not saying we're accepting the offer, but I am curious about the condition."

"Me too," Ian muttered.

"I want to approve your menu. And the reason for that, I don't want you cutting corners by picking the less expensive menu options. Since I've moved to Frederickport, I've heard about the amazing appetizers on Pearl Cove's catering menu. Items they don't offer on the restaurant's regular menu. I've always wanted to try things like their caviar canapes, or the prosciutto-wrapped persimmons with goat cheese, the lobster dumplings, oh, and that seafood and vegetable platter I've heard about! Of course, that's just the appetizers. You'll have to decide what to have for the main entrée, with beef, seafood, and vegetarian options for the guests."

Ian chuckled. "It's the baby."

Joe looked at Ian. "What do you mean?"

"When Lily was pregnant with Connor, she went through a ravenous stage," Ian told him. He then looked at Kelly and said, "You need to accept Lily's offer. After all, she is pregnant. Do you want to deprive her of all that gourmet food?"

OLIVIA DAVIS STOOD at the master bedroom window, looking down at Beach Drive. She had watched a car pull up to the house across the street from Marlow House, and then minutes later watched as Walt and Danielle Marlow had come out of that house and then crossed the street to return home.

When talking to Walt Marlow earlier that morning, she had the strangest feeling he knew she had been in Marlow House before he and his wife had returned home. But that was impossible. There was no way he knew she had been in the house; she was just being paranoid. But she blamed it all on Heather Donovan. Ever since her first encounter with Donovan, everything she once believed no longer made sense. Perhaps it had been a mistake to return to Frederickport.

TEN

When Brian returned to the police station, he found Heather with the chief in his office.

"Any luck?" Brian asked after walking into the room and closing the door behind him.

"If you mean, did I find Betty's ghost? Nope. No sign of her at the morgue or at her house. If she hasn't moved on, then maybe she's wandering around in our neighborhood. And I'm wondering if Max is wrong. Perhaps it was Betty he saw at Marlow House and not Olivia," Heather suggested.

Brian sat down on the chair next to Heather while saying, "They look nothing alike."

"He's a cat, Brian. He could be wrong. Don't all humans look alike?" Heather asked.

Brian shrugged, and the chief asked, "What did you find out this morning?"

"I spoke to Eden. She saw Betty leave early yesterday morning. Time matches with what Josephine told us. But Eden wasn't there when Betty returned. I found something interesting. It seems Becca and Betty had some sort of falling-out about a month ago."

The chief leaned back in his chair while folding his arms across his chest. Looking over his desk at Brian and Heather, he let out a sigh. "That's interesting. The cellphone we found in Betty's car, we got it open, and that phone call Josephine said Betty received before she left her house, it was from Becca."

"Makes sense since she was a couple of houses from Becca's house. She must have been going there, but why?" Brian asked.

"When are you going to talk to Becca?" Heather asked.

"Do you know her?" the chief asked.

Heather shrugged. "Just who she is. I've seen her on our street. We've talked a few times. More like very casual acquaintances."

"I was planning to go over there now," Brian said. "I thought I could drop Heather off at her house first if you're done with her." Both Brian and Heather looked at the chief.

"Yes. And I appreciate all your help, Heather."

"No problem." Heather looked at Brian. "You can drop me off at Marlow House instead of my place. I'll call Danielle first. I don't really feel like being home alone right now. Not with a potential killer who knows I'm a witness. I keep thinking about our conversation this morning. Both of us ignoring the elephant in the room. I don't believe she didn't see me when she was with Betty. She looked me right in the eyes, and we stared at each other for a few moments. It's beyond creepy."

"It makes little sense," the chief said. "All the evidence shows she was on that flight. Even the car dealer backs it up, and he had photos. She must have a doppelgänger out there."

"Right. With the same jacket," Heather scoffed.

"I'll be curious to see that security footage when it arrives," Brian said.

"If she was really on that flight, then she has a twin," Heather insisted.

AFTER BRIAN DROPPED Heather off at Marlow House, he drove up the street to Becca Hammond's. Yesterday when stopping by her house, she hadn't been home. While he had her phone number, he and the chief agreed it was best to catch her at home instead of giving her additional time to consider what she wanted to say to the police while on the way to the station. When he arrived, he found a car in her driveway. It hadn't been there the day before.

Dave Hammond answered the front door a few minutes later.

"Brian, hello," Dave greeted him. He opened the door wider and said, "I assume this is about Betty?"

"Then you heard?"

"On the radio when we were on our way home. Please come in." Dave stepped aside while holding the door open. Brian entered.

"From what we heard on the radio, no one's been arrested."

Brian shook his head. "No. It's still an active investigation. I was hoping I could talk to Becca."

Dave showed Brian into the living room and motioned to a chair. "I'll go get her. She's lying down. The news hit her pretty hard. But she'll want to talk to you. If there is any way she can help, she'll want to."

After Brian took a seat, Dave left the room to get his wife. A few minutes later, Becca and Dave returned. By Dave's words, Brian assumed Becca had retreated to her bedroom to cry, but her clear eyes gave no indication of tears.

"Hello, Brian," Becca said quietly. "Dave said you were here to talk to me about Betty?" Becca took a seat on the sofa, facing Brian, her husband by her side.

"Dave tells me you just found out about Betty this morning?" Brian asked.

Becca nodded. "Yes. Yesterday we left for Salem to attend my niece's wedding. We spent the night. Just got back in town, and on the way home, heard the news. I heard on the radio they found her body on our street."

"Yes. What time did you leave yesterday?" Brian asked.

"Early. Before six o'clock. The wedding wasn't until the evening, but we needed to get there early to help my sister," Becca explained.

"And you didn't see Betty yesterday morning? Either of you?"

Becca and Dave exchanged brief glances and then looked at Brian and shook their heads.

"Can you tell me about your falling-out with Betty?"

Becca frowned at Brian. "Falling-out? Who said we had a falling-out?"

"According to one of Betty's neighbors, you were in front of Betty's house about a month ago, yelling at her. And later, Betty said something to the effect that you two were no longer friends."

"Eden Langdon? Right?" Becca asked.

"That didn't happen?"

Becca shifted in her chair and looked at Brian. "Yes, I was upset that day. But I wasn't yelling. Eden has a tendency to exaggerate."

"Can you tell me why you were upset?"

"You certainly don't think I had anything to do with Betty's death, do you? You think I killed my friend and then traipsed off on my merry way to a wedding?"

"Honey, don't get so upset. I understand this is hard, but just answer Brian's questions," Dave urged.

Becca glanced at her husband, barely concealing a glare. After a moment, she looked back at Brian and said, "The library had an exhibit a while back. The lost art of letter writing, or something like that. I have—had—this antique letter opener that belonged to my grandmother. Betty thought it would be a great addition to the display. I really didn't want to loan it to the library. It's not that it's extremely valuable—but it had sentimental value. Betty kept nagging me about it. And finally, I agreed. I let her use it in the display. And then someone took it."

"I don't remember a police report," Brian said.

"Really? It was my understanding they were making one. But it doesn't surprise me. Betty begged me not to say anything about it, because it would make the library look bad. She promised she would get it back."

"If she made that promise, sounds like she had an idea who took it," Brian said.

Becca shrugged. "Yeah, that's kind of what I thought, too. But I was pretty pissed. I considered Betty a friend, but if she wanted something, she could be relentless. I think I was so pissed because she knew that I really didn't feel comfortable lending the letter opener for the display, but she just wouldn't let up. She didn't respect my no. And I was also pissed at myself for allowing her to bully me into doing something I didn't want to do. Honestly, I had this nagging gut feeling not to loan the letter opener to the library for the display. But I ignored the feeling because Betty kept bugging me. And yes, I told her how I felt after it disappeared. That's what Eden witnessed. After that, I avoided Betty. But I certainly wouldn't want something bad to happen to her."

"Can you tell me what you talked about yesterday morning?" Brian asked.

Becca frowned. "Why do you want to know what Dave and I talked about?"

"I didn't mean you and Dave. What did you and Betty talk about yesterday morning? Why did you call her?"

Becca frowned. "I didn't call her. And I didn't talk with her yesterday. Who said I did?"

"Yesterday morning, Betty was over at Josephine Barker's house, sorting through some boxes for the library, when she got a phone call and then left abruptly. The only phone call Betty received yesterday morning was from you. It lasted just under two minutes."

"No. That's not right. I didn't call Betty yesterday. And we certainly didn't talk on the phone," Becca insisted.

Brian pulled a small piece of paper out of his shirt pocket. He unfolded it, looked at it and then said, "Is your phone number…" He read a phone number out loud.

"Yes. That's my cellphone number. But I didn't call her. I'll prove it." Becca stood up, walked to the coatrack by the front door, and retrieved her purse. She brought it back to where she had been sitting, sat down, and pulled her cellphone from the purse. A moment later, she opened her phone app. Instead of handing the phone to Brian, she stared at her phone.

After a moment of silence, Dave asked, "What's wrong?"

"This makes no sense," Becca muttered. She looked up from her phone to Brian. "It looks like I called her yesterday morning, but I didn't. And we were on the road to Salem when this call was supposedly made."

"Can I look at it?" Brian asked.

Hesitantly, Becca handed the phone to Brian. Brian read aloud the time of the phone call.

"Becca's right. We were on the road to Salem when that call was made. That's too early to call anyone, especially someone you haven't talked to in a month. I drove yesterday, and Becca was in the car with me. She never made a call."

"Did you have this phone with you?" Brian asked.

Becca looked at Brian. "Yes. But I didn't call Betty."

"If the phone was with you, as you say it was, can you explain why it shows you called her at that time and were on the phone for two minutes?"

ELEVEN

"I didn't mean for you to stay home and babysit me," Heather told Danielle after she discovered Danielle and Walt had planned to go shopping before she called to ask if she could hang out. Heather sat on the parlor sofa with Danielle while Walt sat across from them, silently reading a book.

"Hey, it's okay. I don't blame you for not wanting to stay home alone with all that's happened since yesterday," Danielle said.

"Like you pointed out earlier," Heather began, "just because Olivia was with Betty an hour before we found the body doesn't mean Olivia had anything to do with the murder. But the fact she denies being with her when I saw her, and she looked right at me… we were looking straight into each other's faces, and now she pretends she wasn't with Betty. And to go to such an elaborate means to establish an alibi. One that's obviously bogus. If she wasn't involved in the murder, what is she hiding? She is hiding something."

"Are you certain the quilt jacket Olivia wore when she came over here to pick up the keys was the same jacket you saw her wearing when she was with Betty?" Danielle asked.

"Yes. Same fabric, same pattern. If it's not the same jacket, then Olivia's twin bought the same one."

"I don't think that's the case. When Olivia stopped here to ask if she could use our Wi-Fi, I commented on her jacket. She told me she made it herself. Sounded like it's a one of a kind. She said nothing about there being two of them."

"I knew it! Well, as soon as the chief gets those videos from the airline, that should prove what I'm saying was true. There was no way she was on that plane. I know what I saw," Heather insisted.

"The fact that she broke into Marlow House when we were gone doesn't make me feel terrific," Danielle said. "If she's not the killer, she witnessed something. There's no other reason to lie about being with Betty before her murder unless she was somehow involved."

"Exactly!" Heather agreed.

Walt closed his book and set it on his lap. He looked at Heather and Danielle. "I think it might be a good idea for me to go over to Heather's with her so I can have a little chat with Bella."

Heather looked at Walt and narrowed her eyes, wondering why he would want to talk to her cat. "You suspect Olivia was in my house, too?"

Walt shrugged. "You weren't home at the time. And frankly, considering it was you she ran into when she said she wasn't in town, makes me wonder why she would break into our house instead of yours."

Heather frowned. "That doesn't make me feel terrific."

Walt gave Heather a weak smile. "Sorry."

"I can understand why she might break into Heather's, but why break into our house?" Danielle wondered.

"Thanks a lot! If I wasn't going to have nightmares about this, now I am sure to!" Heather grumbled.

The doorbell rang.

WALT LEFT Danielle and Heather in the parlor while he answered the door. When he returned, Brian was with him.

"How did it go?" Heather asked Brian after he walked into the room.

"It was interesting," Brian said before taking an empty seat and recounting his conversation at the Hammonds' house.

"How did they explain the phone call?" Heather asked after he got to the part of the visit where Becca vehemently denied calling Betty, yet they found the call on her cellphone.

"Her husband, Dave, suggested it was a butt call," Brian explained.

"That sounds like a lame excuse. What are they hiding?" Heather asked.

Brian shrugged. "Perhaps nothing. Dave showed me a gas receipt from their trip. The gas station was a good thirty minutes from here, and according to that receipt, they were pumping gas at the same time the call was made. According to both Becca and Dave, she had been in her purse, trying to find their credit card that had fallen out of her wallet. Since her cellphone was also in her purse, it's possible during that time she accidentally called Betty and never realized it. Betty obviously answered the call. After realizing it was a butt call, she simply hung up. It's happened to me before."

"Yeah, me too," Heather reluctantly agreed.

"But didn't Josephine say Betty got a call before she left?" Danielle asked. "I thought that was the only call on her phone for Friday morning."

"It's possible it was a butt call and also the call Betty was talking about," Brian said.

"How do you figure that?" Walt asked.

"According to Eden, Betty felt bad about the estrangement with Becca. Maybe she got that call from Becca, thinking she was extending an olive branch, and decided to go right over to her house," Brian said.

"If it was a butt call, Betty would know. I can see Becca accidently making a call when getting in her purse. But someone had to hang up, and it wouldn't have been Becca if she didn't even know she made the call. Unlikely she also accidentally ended the call. Betty would have been the one to hang up, and that would mean she knew it was a butt call," Danielle said.

Brian nodded. "True. But Betty might have also seen it as an excuse to rush over there, under the pretense of checking to see if everything was okay, since Becca had tried calling her."

Danielle shrugged. "I suppose I can see that happening."

"Have you found any connection between Betty and Olivia other than Olivia going to work at the library? Did they have a history?" Heather asked. "If Betty went over to see Becca and instead ran into Olivia, was there something between them?"

"During Olivia's interview, she claimed she had never met Betty. And according to Josephine, Betty wasn't part of the interview process, so she hadn't met Olivia during any of the video conference calls. However, when Joe was interviewing Olivia, I was in the room next to the interrogation room with the chief, watching. I don't care what Olivia claims. She recognized Betty when she looked at that photograph. Yet it was more a look of surprise. I've been giving it a great deal of thought," Brian told them.

"If she was responsible for Betty's death, and the police are interviewing her, why would she look surprised when shown the photograph? Wouldn't she expect them to show her a picture of the victim? And then show no reaction, like she had never seen her before," Danielle asked.

"Exactly." Brian nodded.

"What are you suggesting?" Heather asked.

"I'd say Brian is suggesting that our neighbor recognized her from the photo. That she was with her an hour before her death, but she didn't realize Betty had been murdered, yet for some reason she doesn't want anyone to find out she was here during that time-frame," Walt suggested.

With a frown, Heather looked from Walt to Brian. "Is that what you're saying?"

Brian shrugged. "Something like that."

The next moment, snow fell from the ceiling.

Danielle looked upward. "Thank God!"

"It's about time," Heather said.

"This could be helpful," Walt added.

Frowning, Brian looked at the three, confused. "What?"

"Eva's coming," Danielle explained. "And hopefully Marie's with her."

The next moment, the two mentioned spirits appeared in the parlor. Eva, once a silent screen star with an uncanny resemblance to Charles Dana Gibson's Gibson girl, made a dramatic entrance. She floated down from the ceiling while snowflakes swirled around her, drifting to the floor, where they disappeared.

Marie, the image of a woman in her eighties—a slightly younger version than she had been at the time of her death—appeared with no fanfare, already standing in the parlor while Eva floated downward.

"Sounds like you missed us," Marie said after Eva stood by her side and all signs of snowflakes disappeared.

"A lot has happened since yesterday," Danielle told the pair.

Brian sat quietly and listened while Danielle filled the spirits in on what had been happening the last two days, with Heather and Walt occasionally adding bits of information.

Now sitting on imaginary chairs, the two spirits listened. Finally, Marie asked, "Are you sure she's not a ghost?"

"You mean our new neighbor?" Heather asked.

"If she could be at the airport one moment and here the next," Marie said, "that would explain a lot."

"You are forgetting Joe, Brian, and the chief all saw her," Danielle reminded her. "And do spirits photograph? There were the pictures of her, reportedly taken after she landed in Portland."

Marie shrugged. "Well, anything is possible."

"I shook her hand," Walt added. "When we first met, I shook her hand. It was solid."

"While it is possible for a spirit to appear as a living being, even to give the illusion of having a solid body, I doubt that's the case here," Eva said. "I don't believe she's a spirit from what you tell me. Sounds to me like there's something nefarious underfoot."

"Perhaps we should check her out ourselves," Marie said.

THE GHOST AND THE NEW NEIGHBOR

Danielle nodded. "I think that's a great idea."

THE FIRST THING Marie noticed when arriving at Pearl's old house, its new owner didn't flinch when the snow fell from the ceiling. Nor did she blink when Marie and Eva suddenly appeared before her. Instead, the woman, who they assumed was Olivia, sat on a folding chair and looked as if she were in deep thought, silently gazing across the room, looking right through the two ghosts.

Eva glanced around the sparsely furnished room. "What happened to all Pearl's furniture?"

"The trustee donated it to a woman's shelter," Marie explained. "Adam didn't feel they would get more for the house having it furnished, especially considering how dated Pearl's things were. He felt it would show better without it."

"Oh," Eva muttered, giving the room one more glance. She turned her attention back to Olivia, who sat on the chair.

Marie walked closer to the woman, stopping inches from her. Still, the woman did not flinch. Marie reached out and waved a hand in front of her eyes. Once again, no response. Curious, Marie used her energy to tweak the tip of Olivia's nose.

"What the…!" Olivia shrieked and leapt to her feet while grabbing her nose and rubbing it.

"What just happened?" Eva asked.

Marie giggled and told Eva what she had done.

"Tsk-tsk, Marie, was that necessary?" Eva scolded.

Marie shrugged. "I wanted to confirm she's a living human and not a sneaky spirit pretending she's unaware of our presence." While neither a spirit nor a living human could see Marie manipulate her energy, only a living human could feel a pinch from that energy.

"I suppose you have your answer. She is very much alive," Eva said.

Marie nodded. "I agree." She watched a confused Olivia nervously circle the room, still holding onto the tip of her nose.

73

Glaring with disgust at where she had been sitting moments earlier, Olivia walked from the living room to the kitchen, the spirits trailing behind her.

"There is something familiar about her," Marie noted.

"You've seen her before?" Eva asked.

"I'm not sure. There is something about her. I can't put my finger on it." Marie cocked her head slightly while studying Olivia. Something rang. But it was not a phone. Marie watched as Olivia walked to the counter and picked up an iPad. She opened it.

"What's that?" Eva asked.

"It looks like someone's calling Olivia," Marie explained.

Eva frowned. "That doesn't look like a telephone. It's certainly much larger than what Danielle uses."

Marie chuckled. "It's an iPad. I think someone's FaceTiming her." The next moment, they heard a voice on the iPad say, "Hello, Olivia!"

Resting her hands along the outer edge of the kitchen counter, Olivia looked down at the now open iPad lying on the tile surface. A woman's smiling face looked up at her from the iPad's screen.

"Hi, Shanice," Olivia greeted her.

"I just wanted to check on my baby sister. Find out how you were doing."

"I'm not really doing much. I wish my things were here so I could start unpacking."

Marie moved closer to the counter, focusing on the caller, who now asked Olivia questions about her new house. After studying the caller for a few moments, recognition dawned.

"I know who Olivia Davis is!" Marie exclaimed. "Or should I say, who Olivia Mallory is."

TWELVE

About ten minutes after Marie and Eva left for Pearl's old house, Marlow House had another visitor.

"I thought you were going crib shopping, and then I noticed the police car over here, and I wondered what was going on," Lily said after Walt answered the front door and led her to the parlor, where Danielle, Brian, and Heather sat.

Danielle explained to Lily what had been going on since they'd left Lily's house. When she finished the telling, she asked, "Did Kelly and Joe leave?"

"Yes. And guess what?" Lily took a seat on an empty chair. Instead of waiting for a response, she said, "Kelly isn't having a beach wedding in July. They've moved the wedding date to March."

"March? Joe never mentioned that to me," Brian said. Joe, who worked with Brian at the police station, had asked Brian to be his best man at his upcoming wedding to Lily's sister-in-law.

Lily looked at Brian. "They only came to that decision last night."

"I wondered if that might happen when she found out you were pregnant," Heather said.

Brian looked at Lily. "You're what?"

Lily looked from Brian to Heather. "You haven't told him yet?"

"Umm, no." Heather shrugged. "I've sort of been preoccupied since we had breakfast together."

"You're really pregnant?" Brian asked Lily.

Lily grinned at Brian and gave her still-flat belly a pat. "Yep. Due the end of July."

"Ahh, so that's why the change in wedding date?" Brian asked.

"We told Kelly they could still have the wedding at our place in July, but I understand. I don't think she wanted to risk the drama if I go into labor during her ceremony."

"Congratulations. Wow, Connor is going to be a big brother," Brian said.

"We're having a regular population explosion on Beach Drive." Heather glanced at Danielle's belly.

"So where are Kelly and Joe planning to get married?" Danielle asked.

"I suggested Pearl Cove. Ian and I offered to pay for it as their wedding gift."

Heather's eyes widened. "Wow, that's generous."

"Not sure if they're going to accept or not. But it would be a way for Kelly to sort of have a beach wedding. At least they'll have a great view of the ocean. Without worrying about the rain," Lily explained.

"And if she has it in March, chances are there will be rain," Heather said.

Their conversation stopped when Marie suddenly appeared, standing in the middle of the parlor.

"Marie is here," Danielle announced.

"Hi, Marie," Lily greeted her, even though she couldn't see the spirit.

"Eva stayed over with Olivia to keep an eye on her. But I wanted to tell you, I know who Olivia is. In fact, I've met her. Of course, she was only a child at the time," Marie explained.

Danielle frowned. "Really?" Danielle went on to tell Brian and Lily what Marie said.

"Years ago, Olivia and her sister, Shanice, lived in Frederickport with their parents, Elmer and Helen Mallory. I knew them, but we weren't especially close. Friendly, but not someone I socialized with. Elmer got a new job and moved his family to Texas." Marie paused a moment, and Danielle repeated her words for the non-mediums.

"When over at Pearl's…" Marie frowned and added, "I guess it's not Pearl's anymore. When I was over at Olivia's, she received a FaceTime call from her sister, Shanice. And it clicked. I figured that's who it had to be." Marie glanced at Danielle and waited for her to repeat for Brian and Lily what she said.

"Do you know anything about them?" Heather asked.

"Shanice's mother, Helen, was close to Esther Meek. After the Mallorys moved from Frederickport, the girls and Helen came every summer and spent a week with Esther. When the girls got older, Helen came alone. You know how teenagers are. They always want to stay home with their friends," Marie explained. When Danielle repeated what Marie said, she paraphrased, leaving out the name of the friend they had visited in Frederickport, and referred to her as Helen's Frederickport friend.

"I suppose you don't know anything about Olivia as an adult?" Danielle asked.

"A little. At least, what Esther told me over the years. While Helen and I had not been close and we didn't keep in touch after they moved, I would periodically ask Esther how they were all doing. Esther is a bit of a gossip, so she loved sharing all the details. The older sister never married, but Olivia married a pastor's son and became very involved with the church. It surprised Esther, because the Mallorys weren't churchgoers. Olivia had two sons."

"So she's a widow now?" Danielle asked, without repeating what Marie had told them.

Marie shook her head. "No. Esther told me that not long after the youngest graduated from high school, she divorced her husband. Her sons sided with the father and had nothing to do with their mother after the divorce. From what Esther said, it had been an abusive relationship. Apparently, Olivia's parents had no idea all that had been going on. They had moved to California for Elmer's job not long after their second grandson was born. They always felt their son-in-law was very controlling, but they were unaware of the abuse. After Olivia separated, she moved from Texas to live with her parents in California. She didn't have anything after the marriage ended. I got the impression she wanted out of the marriage and left with not much more than her clothes. At the time, she had no work experience outside the home. She had been a stay-at-home mother for all those years."

Heather updated Brian and Lily on what Marie had said so far. After the retelling, she asked, "If she was married all those years and raised the two sons, she should have at least gotten half of whatever the husband had."

Marie shrugged. "It doesn't always work that way. She stayed with her parents, and she had therapy. From what Helen told Esther, it was quite traumatic for Olivia. Not just leaving her marriage and having her sons reject her, but all the friends she'd had at her church, people who had become such an important part of her life, they all sided with the husband. After all, it was the woman's duty to stay with her husband. Ladies at the church told her she needed to find out what she was doing wrong to make her husband act that way. According to them, she had taken a vow, and it was her duty to obey her husband. They told her she needed to pray on it to save her marriage." Marie gave a snort and added, "Esther said she began questioning everything about her church. Looking at it critically and examining everything she had once believed. At least, what they had taught her to believe after joining her father-in-law's church."

"Sounds like Olivia was going through deconstruction," Heather said. Everyone glanced at Heather while Danielle repeated what Marie had said. After Danielle finished repeating Marie's words, Heather said, "I have some friends who've gone through deconstruction. They question what they learned in organized religion. Questioned the patriarchy."

"Elmer Mallory passed away a few years after Olivia's divorce. From what Esther told me, Olivia embarked on a spiritual mission of discovery. She dabbled in everything from Buddhism to paganism. I don't think Esther approved. Helen passed away a few years after her husband, and I assume they divided their estate between the two daughters. Which was good for Olivia if what Esther told me was true, that Olivia left her marriage virtually penniless. The Mallorys were well off. After Helen's death, Esther didn't stay in touch with the family, so I'm not sure what happened to them after that. It's entirely possible Olivia remarried, and she is a widow or divorced again."

"The other sister never married?" Lily asked after Danielle repeated Marie's last words.

"Not that I'm aware of. But it's certainly possible. She was more of a free spirit, according to Esther. She had several live-in relationships over the years, but no marriage or children. And while the parents never realized Olivia was in an abusive relationship, apparently her sister, Shanice, didn't care for the brother-in-law. In fact, after the oldest son was born, Olivia's husband had forbidden his wife to have anything to do with the sister, claimed she was immoral, and he wouldn't subject his family to that type of influence."

"Did Olivia do what her husband told her to do?" Heather asked indignantly. "Cut her sister out of her life?"

Marie nodded. "Yes. At least until she left him." Danielle then repeated all that Marie said.

"What did the parents think about that?" Heather asked. "You said they didn't realize he was abusive. That's freaking abusive."

"You have to remember, my generation was raised to accept certain behavior from husbands. They didn't recognize it as abuse, not as we do now," Marie explained.

"And in many fundamentalist churches today, that's still true," Danielle said. "Like in the church Olivia attended."

"I suspect her parents initially believed Olivia was happy in her marriage. It had been her choice to join her husband's church. It's not that they weren't Christians too. But some churches are a little more rigid when interpreting the roles of a husband and wife. Women typically vowed to love, honor, and *obey*. I also suspect Elmer and Helen didn't want to do anything to risk being cut off from their grandchildren."

After Danielle finished retelling what Marie told them, she said, "I guess that answers one question we had. No reason to do any more research on Olivia's siblings. She obviously doesn't have a twin."

Heather looked at Danielle. "Unless it's a sibling who might pass as a twin. I've known sisters who could pass as twins but are a few years apart in age."

Marie smiled at Heather. "No, I don't think that's the case in this situation. One thing I didn't mention. Shanice was adopted. She's black."

"What did Marie say?" Lily asked, once again hating being unable to hear both sides of the conversation and relying on a translator.

Heather looked at Lily. "Olivia's sister was adopted, and she's black. So no way is there a twin out there."

The next moment Eva arrived in the room, sans the snowflakes or fanfare.

"Eva is here," Walt announced.

"Did you learn anything else?" Marie asked.

Eva shrugged. "The conversation between the two was quite boring. And when it ended, she took that pad device back into the living room and used it to start watching a movie. Since it was not just a movie I'd seen before, it was also one I didn't care for, I decided there was really no reason for me to stay over there."

Danielle repeated for Brian and Lily what Eva said.

"I'm wondering if we should have a little talk with this friend of the mother. Marie, does she still live in Frederickport?" Brian asked.

"Tell Brian no. She moved a couple of years ago."

After Danielle repeated Marie's answer, Brian asked, "Do you have her number? We could call her."

"I'm afraid Esther and I drifted apart several years before my death. I'd heard she moved to Florida."

Again, Danielle repeated Marie's words.

Brian frowned. "You said Esther? What was her last name?"

"Esther Meek," Danielle said, remembering what Marie had said earlier.

"Esther Meek? Are you sure?" Brian asked.

Marie frowned. "Yes. Why?"

"What is it, Brian?" Heather asked.

"Betty Kelty was renting her aunt's house. Her aunt who moved to Florida. Betty Kelty was Esther's niece," Brian explained.

THIRTEEN

When Lily returned from Marlow House Saturday afternoon, she found Ian sitting at the breakfast bar, with Connor sitting nearby in his highchair. The two ate cold cheese sandwiches.

"What's for lunch?" Lily asked as she stepped up to the breakfast bar. Connor held out his sandwich to Lily, offering her a bite. She eyed the unappealing half sandwich, squished and clenched in the little fist, the soft wheat bread now smashed and flattened, with cheese and mayonnaise escaping from between the two half slices. She pretended to take a bite and then sat next to Ian at the breakfast bar.

"Want half my sandwich?" Ian offered.

Lily rested her elbows on the countertop and sighed. "No, thanks. I'm going to make something in a minute."

"Mom called; she wants me to come over. Says there's something she needs to talk to me about. Claims it's important and can't wait. I promised her I'd come over when you got back from Marlow House." Ian took a bite from his sandwich.

Lily groaned. "Do I have to go with you?"

After Ian swallowed, he said, "No. Mom wants to talk to me —alone."

Lily arched her brows. "Alone? What do you think is going on?"

Ian shrugged. "Only way to find out is to go over there. It might be something about the house. The other day she was complaining about the fencing Dad wants to use."

"Gosh, what does your mom expect you to do about it?"

Ian shrugged and then asked, "Is everything okay across the street?"

Lily told Ian all that had been said at Marlow House. When Lily finished her telling, Ian, who had eaten his entire sandwich, picked up a napkin and wiped his mouth before saying, "So there is no twin?"

"Apparently not. And according to Danielle, when she commented on the quilt jacket, Olivia claimed she made it herself. And Heather swears that's the same jacket the woman had on when she was with Betty yesterday morning. So if it is a one-of-a-kind, homemade jacket, it can't be some coincidental doppelgänger."

"The woman is obviously lying about when she arrived in Frederickport. Once the chief has a look at those videos, her claim to have been on that plane won't stand up, especially not with Heather swearing she saw her that morning."

"That's what's really weird to me. The way this Olivia person can blatantly lie about it, and she knows Heather was there. I can't believe how she talked to Heather this morning and pretended like nothing happened. That is freaking weird, if you ask me."

IAN DIDN'T HAVE to ring the doorbell at his parents' rental house. As he stepped onto his parents' front porch, his mother opened the door.

"What took you so long?" June asked.

"I told you, I had to wait for Lily to come back from Marlow House so she could watch Connor." Ian followed his mother into the entry hall.

June shut the door behind them. "Lily is certainly lucky to be able to pick up and go whenever she wants, knowing she has a built-in babysitter."

Ian chuckled. "I don't babysit my son. I'm his father. It's called parenting."

"And when a mother doesn't work outside the home, it's her job to take care of the children." June made her way into the living room, Ian trailing behind her. She took a seat on a recliner and motioned to the other recliner for her son.

Instead of commenting about a mother's job, Ian asked, "Where's Dad?"

"He had to go to the hardware store. I told him to take his time. I wanted to talk to you without him here."

Now sitting on a recliner, Ian eyed his mother curiously. "What about?"

"While I am delighted to have another grandchild, I simply don't understand why you two couldn't have simply waited a few months and not ruined your sister's big day. Was this Lily's idea?"

Ian frowned. "You mean getting pregnant?"

"Of course. What do you think I mean?"

"We told you last night. It wasn't planned. These things happen."

"And you couldn't have been a little more careful? You already promised to host their wedding, and now everything is ruined. This was incredibly selfish of you. But I suspect this was Lily's doing."

Ian leaned back in the recliner and propped one leg over the opposing knee. "No, I distinctly remember it was my idea. That's if she got pregnant the night I suspect."

June frowned. "I thought you said you weren't trying to get pregnant?"

"We weren't. But I was the one who initiated sex when she got pregnant." Ian grinned. "I gave her a glass of wine, told her she was beautiful, reminded her our son was asleep…"

"Ian, please!" June gasped. "This is not an appropriate conversation to have with your mother. Or with anyone!"

"Mom, you are the one who started this conversation," Ian reminded her, the humor gone from his voice.

"I did not bring up the topic of your sex life," June snapped.

"You do understand how babies are made? Don't you?"

June glared at Ian. "Why are you being like this?"

"I'm trying to figure out the point of this conversation. You seem to be upset that Lily's pregnant, and instead of accepting it as something natural that happens in a healthy marriage, you're suggesting this was some scheme by my wife to ruin Kelly's wedding, which is absolutely ridiculous. Birth control is not a hundred percent. We would have preferred our second child to come a little later. What exactly do you want us to do? Have an abortion?"

"Of course not! Don't even suggest that to Lily!"

"Don't worry, Mom. While Lily and I support a woman's right to choose, we both agree that the only time we'd consider abortion would be if it was an unviable pregnancy or if it endangered Lily's life. We are more than willing to welcome our next baby with all the love we welcomed Connor, even if it's not convenient. Are you?"

June stared at her son and sputtered, "Of course. Don't be ridiculous."

"Then I'm not sure why we're having this conversation."

"Are you aware your sister stopped by this morning after going to your house? She told me they want to move the wedding date to March. March. That is only two months away. There is no way we can plan a wedding that fast. Especially now that we have to find a new venue."

"Lily suggested having the wedding at Pearl Cove. They do events mid-week such as weddings."

"Yes, she told me that. I understand Lily was quick to spend your money."

Ian sat up straight in the recliner, placed both feet firmly on the floor, and leaned toward his mother, his expression stern. "If you don't stop speaking disrespectfully about my wife, this conversation is over. And Lily, Connor, and I may not be able to make the next family dinner."

June's eyes widened. "I wasn't being disrespectful."

"Yes, Mother, you were. First of all, I think Lily's offer to pay for Kelly and Joe's wedding was most generous. And I love her for it.

Plus, you seem to forget Lily did not come into our marriage as a pauper. And even if she had, we're married now. Lily and I are a team. I trust her. I love her. You know as well as anyone I didn't jump into marriage. It took me a long time to find a woman I wanted to make a life with. And now that I've found her, I will not sit back and say nothing while my mother—my mother, whom I do love very much—makes snide remarks about my wife."

"I'm sorry if it came out that way," June sputtered.

"Mom, do you know the three main reasons people get divorced?"

June shrugged in response.

"It's sex, money, and in-laws. I know you don't want to hear it, but Lily and I have a great sex life. In fact, that's why we're having an unplanned baby." Ian grinned before continuing, "The next is money. As you are aware, money is not a problem for me. I'm blessed. Many people aren't as lucky. And Lily, well, she isn't with me for the money, because the settlement from the Gusarov estate set her up for life. So that means the biggest threat to our marriage is possible in-law problems. Now, I get along terrific with Lily's parents. Her mother adores me, and I get along well with her father. So that only leaves you and Dad. Do you want to be the one responsible for my marriage breaking up?"

"Of course not. How can you even suggest such a thing? I would never want to cause you marriage problems!"

"And I wouldn't want that either. Which is why I'm willing to limit the time we spend with you if you continue this pattern of criticizing my wife."

"I don't criticize Lily! I... I sometimes make suggestions, but that's because I care about you."

"No. What you call suggestions are criticisms of our marriage. For one thing, you are constantly bringing up the fact Lily is not working outside the home, and you take issue with the fact I watch Connor while she spends time with her girlfriends."

"I simply care about you," June insisted. "I know how hard you work. And how much work it is to take care of an active toddler. I don't understand why Lily doesn't understand that she shouldn't be expecting you to watch Connor whenever she feels like running off."

Ian leaned back in the chair and let out a sigh. "Can you even hear yourself, Mom? I'm serious. I should record you and play it back. Maybe then you would understand what I'm talking about. But I doubt it."

"You are mad at me because I worry about you?" June asked with a pout.

Ian studied his mother for a moment before answering. Finally, he said, "Mom, if you want me in your life, you need to respect my marriage. And you need to respect me. Or at the very least pretend you do."

"Don't be silly! I respect you!"

Ian shook his head. "No. No, you don't. Do you have any idea how insulting it is when you act as if I'm not capable of taking care of my son?"

"I never said you were incapable."

"You act like it when you make comments about how Lily should watch Connor, or insist on coming to our house and watching him when I'm working. If I needed help, I would ask." Ian couldn't tell his mother that he often had help with Connor when he was home working and Lily was elsewhere. But he doubted his mother would understand about Marie's ghost being his son's favorite babysitter.

"I simply want you to know I am there for you," June insisted.

"I do. But you need to understand, I feel blessed that I can be part of my son's daily life. That when he looks back at his childhood, he will remember both of his parents present. Most people don't have the luxury Lily and I have. Hell, in most families, both parents have to work to put food on the table. And in case you haven't noticed, Lily is a wonderful mother. And when this new baby comes, I imagine we will ask you for help. But I won't ask, not if you continually slip in snide remarks about my wife, like suggesting she got pregnant just to screw up Kelly's wedding."

After a moment of silence, June asked in a small voice, "What do you want me to do?"

"To begin with, no more comments about Lily going back to teaching. When that time comes, if it does, that will be something she and I discuss between us. And ultimately it will be her decision. And if Lily wants to take off with her girlfriends for an afternoon and leave Connor with me, that's between Lily and me. You don't need to rush over to our house and offer to watch Connor, and whatever you do, don't reprimand Lily for leaving Connor with me. In fact, don't reprimand Lily for anything."

FOURTEEN

After Lily returned home, Walt and Danielle decided to go shopping for cribs, as they had originally planned to do. Brian returned to the police station, and Heather returned to her house with Marie and Eva. Heather still did not feel comfortable staying at her home alone, not with a killer on the loose and Olivia Davis living next door.

"I never thought I would miss Pearl as a neighbor," Heather told Eva and Marie. The three sat together in Heather's living room, with Bella curled up on the sofa next to Heather and the two spirits sitting on nearby chairs. "Pearl could be a pain, but at least I never worried about her murdering me. Heck, I'd even take Kelly as a neighbor over this Davis woman."

"I'm curious, Heather," Eva began. "You say you saw Olivia an hour before you and Chris found the body. But she denies being in Frederickport at that time."

"She's obviously lying," Heather said. "She claimed to be on a flight and showed the police some bogus flight information."

"But what does she say about it?" Eva asked.

Heather frowned. "I told you, she claimed to be on a flight at the time of the murder."

"Yes, I understand that. But what did she say about the fact you saw her with the murder victim an hour before you found the body? Didn't you say you two looked each other in the face?"

"Yes. We stared at each other for a few moments, and then I got a phone call from Chris, and when I looked back over there, they were already walking up the street. That's why I don't want to be here alone. She knows I saw her and that she's lying. If she killed Betty, she'd also have a motive to kill me. I'm the only witness who can place her here before the murder."

Eva let out a sigh. "Yes, I understand that. But what did she say when you confronted her about it? When you reminded her of your encounter yesterday morning?"

"Confronted her? I don't want to give her a reason to knock me off. Why would I confront her?"

"I understand what Eva is saying." Marie spoke up. "In fact, I wondered about that myself. Aren't you curious how she might respond?"

"You really think it would have been a smart idea for me to confront her about it when she showed up in my front courtyard this morning? Just the two of us? I didn't know how she was going to react. And if I'd had Brian with me, all she would do is deny it. It would be her word against mine. Sure, the chief and Brian believe me, but what she showed them about being on that flight, there is no way for the chief to hold her. It's her word against mine, and she has the paperwork to back up her claim. Perhaps she had nothing to do with the murder, but she was here. She is hiding something. And when the police get that security footage back, proving she was not on that flight, then my testimony will be useful."

"Let's find out what she's hiding to help solve this murder," Marie suggested.

Eva smiled. "You want Heather to go over and confront her?"

"We should all go over to her house," Marie clarified. "You, me, and Heather."

Heather frowned. "I don't want to go over there. Why would I do that?"

"She won't know you have... spiritual bodyguards. When we go over there, you ask her point-blank why she is lying about when she arrived in Frederickport. Tell her to drop the act, that you both know she was here. Either she will break down and tell you why she lied, or if she was involved in the murder, she'll probably try to kill you too." Marie flashed Heather a smile.

"Gee, that sounds like fun," Heather grumbled.

"It sounds like a good idea," Eva said.

Heather considered the suggestion a few moments before standing. "Fine, let's get this over with. Hopefully, this will speed things up, and if she doesn't kill me, maybe she'll tell me why she lied, and hopefully whatever she's hiding will help the police solve this murder."

Ten minutes later, Heather stood on Olivia's front porch, Eva and Marie by her side. When Olivia opened the door a few minutes later, she didn't invite Heather in. Instead, she stood behind the door, as if reluctant to open it wider.

"Yes?" Olivia greeted her, still shielding herself with the door.

"Hi. Remember me, your neighbor? I was wondering if we could talk a minute?" Heather asked.

Olivia studied her for a moment and reluctantly opened the door wider. "Umm, you can come in. I'm afraid my furniture hasn't arrived yet, so all I can offer in the way of seating is a folding chair."

"That's fine. I'm not staying long." Heather walked into the house, followed by the two spirits. Or, as Heather liked to think of them in that moment, her two guardian angels.

After Olivia shut the front door, she motioned Heather to the living room. Silently, Heather followed her neighbor, and a moment later she took a seat on one folding chair, with Olivia on the other.

"What did you need?" Olivia asked.

"Why did you tell the police you arrived in Frederickport after I found Betty Kelty's body?"

Olivia frowned at Heather. "What?"

Heather let out a sigh. "Yesterday morning, remember? It was early in the morning, and you stepped out your front gate with another woman. You turned, and we looked at each other. You stared right in my face. And then you and that other woman walked up the street together. That other woman was Betty Kelty, and she's the one who was murdered."

Olivia stared at Heather but did not respond immediately. Finally, she said, "I have no idea what in the world you're talking about. I was on a flight at that time. You're confused."

"I am not confused!" Heather blurted. "We looked right at each other!"

"It must be someone who looks like me."

"No. It was you. You wore that quilt jacket you have."

Olivia continued to stare at Heather. Finally, in a calm, low voice, she said, "I'm sorry. You are mistaken. I was on a flight at the time when you say you saw me."

"I already told the police everything," Heather blurted.

Olivia cocked her head slightly and absently licked her lips while her gaze never left Heather. "And I told the police I was on that early morning flight during that same time. I'm sure they understand it is a case of mistaken identity on your part. You seem quite sincere in your claim you saw me early yesterday morning. But I can assure you, I was up in a plane, not in Frederickport. I've already given the police my flight information to verify where I was early yesterday morning."

"The police have requested the security video from that flight, and when they get it, they'll find you weren't on it. So why are you lying about it? Did you have something to do with Betty's murder?"

"You're getting brave," Marie said with a chuckle. "A bit like poking at a wild animal while knowing someone is there to subdue the animal if it attacks."

"I imagine they told you that after you claimed to have seen me yesterday morning. But I never met Betty Kelty. I am very sorry for her tragic death. And frankly, I'm not thrilled that someone murdered a woman only a few houses from my new home. I'm sure it's worse for you, considering you found the poor woman."

"If you really had nothing to do with her death, why don't you admit you were here with her and explain to the police why you're lying? I'm not sure why you keep insisting you weren't here yesterday morning. We both looked at each other. Do you have poor eyesight? When you looked at me, is it possible you didn't see me?"

"I have perfect eyesight."

Heather glared at Olivia. "Once they get that security footage and realize you didn't get on that plane, you're going to have to explain to the police why you lied. Because I will swear you were with Betty before she was murdered."

"When the police get that footage and it's confirmed that I did, in fact, board the plane as I claim, I do not expect an apology from you. Because I can tell you sincerely believe what you're saying. You are most passionate in your belief, and if I were in your position and sincerely believed I saw someone with a murdered woman right before her death, and that person denied it, I too would be upset, as you are now."

"I saw you," Heather insisted.

Olivia smiled at Heather. "I understand you sincerely believe that."

Heather frowned at Olivia. "Is that all you have to say?"

Olivia shrugged. "There is nothing else I can say. But perhaps we should simply agree to wait for that security footage, and after the police view it, you'll realize I was telling the truth."

Heather stood up. "Okay. And when it shows you weren't on that plane, I wonder what your story will be then."

Olivia flashed Heather another smile and stood. "I take it you're going now?"

"I have nothing else to say."

Marie looked at Eva. "One of us should stay here and watch what she does when Heather leaves."

"You go with Heather," Eva told Marie. "I'll stay and see what she does."

"Of course, she might try attacking Heather before we get to the door," Marie quipped.

"SHE'S TRYING TO GASLIGHT ME," Heather told Marie after Olivia walked her to the front door, let her leave without attacking her, and closed the door after they went outside. Heather and Marie walked together toward the sidewalk.

"And she is doing an excellent job of it," Marie said.

"Hell, if it weren't for that darn quilt jacket of hers, which is supposedly a one of a kind, I'd be wondering if we should look for someone who looks like Olivia, not who is Olivia," Heather grumbled as she walked down the sidewalk toward her house.

Thirty minutes later, Heather sat in her living room on a recliner while Marie sat on the sofa, the two discussing what had been said at Olivia's house. Snowflakes began falling from the living room ceiling, and the two women stopped talking, looked up, and waited for Eva's arrival.

"What did she do?" Marie asked Eva when she appeared in Heather's living room. All traces of snowflakes vanished.

"Her demeanor changed the moment Heather walked out the door." Eva took a seat on the sofa next to Marie.

"How so?" Heather asked.

"She didn't look as calm as she had been when talking to you."

"Did her expression change to something maniacal? Is she preparing to come over here and slaughter me in my sleep?" Heather asked.

Eva chuckled. "She looked troubled—disturbed. But not homicidal."

"Shouldn't you stay over there and see what she does next?" Heather asked.

"As I said, she looked troubled. After she closed the front door on you, she walked to her window, pulled back the blind and watched as you walked away. She returned to the living room and got into her suitcase."

"Why did she go into her suitcase? She took something out, didn't she? I bet it was a gun!" Heather gasped. "She is coming over here to shoot me!"

Eva smiled at Heather. "I don't think she's going to shoot you with a book."

Heather frowned. "A book?"

"Yes, she took a book out of her suitcase and then went to that blow-up bed she has set up in her living room. She lay down and started to read. After watching her for a while, I decided to come over here."

FIFTEEN

B aby Boutique was the only shop of its kind in Frederickport. It was where locals shopped for baby shower gifts and designer infant wear. While its nursery furniture inventory was minimal, because of the limited space and the cost of stocking a wide selection of furniture, the store offered an assortment of catalogs for their customers to browse through and place orders.

Before coming to the shop, Danielle already had a good idea what they wanted. She had been doing her homework. She found what they had been looking for in the second catalogue they looked through, and with Walt in agreement, they stood at the front counter, placing their order. Danielle wrote a check for the deposit, and Walt provided the information for the order form. Their purchase included a dresser that doubled as a changing table, two cribs, and a matching rocking chair.

Danielle had just put away her checkbook and finished thanking the clerk for helping them when the bell hanging over the front door made a tinkling sound. When Walt and Danielle turned from the counter, preparing to leave, they saw Josephine Barker, the local library's retiring head librarian. She had just come into the shop.

"Oh, it's the Marlows." Josephine grinned.

"Hello, Mrs. Barker," Walt greeted her.

Josephine grinned at Danielle's expanding belly and said, "Shopping for the big day?"

"We ordered some nursery furniture," Danielle said.

"How fun! I'm here to pick up a baby gift for my niece. They have such adorable clothes!"

"I was so sorry to hear about Betty," Walt told Josephine. "She was such a nice person, always so helpful."

Josephine turned a sad smile to Walt before saying, "It's tragic. And from what I understand, they don't seem to have any leads on her murder. The killer is still out there."

"We met the new librarian," Walt said. "She's our new neighbor."

Josephine nodded at Walt. "Yes, I'm aware of that."

"What is she like?" Danielle asked.

Josephine looked at Danielle. "I don't really know Olivia. Not personally, anyway. I handled her interview. While she hadn't been a librarian for as long as many people her age, she had excellent referrals. In fact, she initially applied for the head librarian position, but we ended up giving it to Betty. We prefer hiring from within."

"And now?" Walt asked.

Josephine shrugged. "I'm fairly certain she'll be taking the head librarian position; she's more than qualified. And I'll stick around so I can help her get settled in and hire another librarian now that Betty's gone."

"Did Olivia know Betty?" Danielle asked.

"Not that I'm aware of. She wasn't part of the interview process. Betty heard the name of the new librarian, and if she recognized it, she never said anything to me about it."

"The strange thing, one neighbor swears she saw Olivia yesterday morning with Betty. They were leaving Olivia's front yard. And then an hour later, Betty's body was found up the street," Danielle said.

"Yes, I heard that. When I stopped by to welcome Olivia to Frederickport, she told me someone claimed to see Betty with a woman who looked like her. But Olivia told me she was in flight at the time," Josephine explained.

"The person who claimed to have seen her insists she was wearing a quilt jacket like the one Olivia wears," Danielle said.

"WHAT WAS THAT ALL ABOUT?" Walt asked Danielle after the two left Baby Boutique and got into the Packard. "You aren't normally so…"

"Gossipy?" Danielle finished for him.

"Something like that."

"Yeah, I felt like a big gossip in there. But I wanted to find out if Josephine was aware of any connection between Betty and Olivia."

"And you had to do that by telling her someone claimed to have seen Olivia with Betty before her murder?"

"I was hoping if I got all gossipy, Josephine might remember something she hadn't considered before and say something to us."

"Which she didn't."

"Yeah, I got zip." Danielle sighed.

Walt turned on the ignition and asked, "Where to now?"

"When we drove past Adam's office, I noticed his car parked out front. Can we stop by?"

"You want to pick his brain on our new neighbor?" Walt asked as he pulled the car out into the street.

WHEN WALT and Danielle walked into the front offices of Frederickport Vacation Properties on Saturday afternoon, they found both Adam and Melony sitting at Leslie's desk, eating pizza.

"Does Leslie know you're eating on her desk?" Danielle teased as she and Walt walked all the way into the office.

"Nah, she's home sick," Adam said. "How are you guys doing? Any news on the killer?"

"Not really," Danielle said, taking a seat on an empty chair.

"Want some pizza? Or does it smell gross to you?" Melony asked.

"I think that phase of my pregnancy is behind me," Danielle told her. "Food smells don't really bother me anymore."

Adam set a slice of pizza on a napkin and held it up. "You guys want some?"

"No, thanks," Walt and Danielle chorused.

Adam set the napkin with the slice on the desk before him and pointed to an empty chair. "Make yourself comfortable, Walt. Your wife already has."

Walt chuckled and sat down on the offered chair.

"Don't pick on Danielle," Melony chided Adam.

"Yeah, I got two kids in here." Danielle patted her belly.

Adam cringed. "I still can't believe you're having twins."

"I'm getting used to the idea myself," Danielle said. She eyed the slice of pizza Adam had offered and said, "On second thought, that looks good."

Adam chuckled, handed Danielle the slice, and asked Walt again if he wanted some, which Walt declined.

The next moment, a man stepped into the office. He looked familiar to Danielle, but she couldn't place him. "Lunchtime?" the man asked as he walked toward Adam and Melony while flashing a smile to Walt and Danielle.

"Want some?" Adam offered.

"No, thanks, I brought you these." The man reached out and handed Adam a set of keys.

Adam took the keys and said, "Have you met Walt and Danielle?"

He smiled at the couple in question and said, "We haven't met, but I know who they are."

"Let me introduce you. Walt, Danielle, this is Kenny Chandler. He's been doing some handyman work for me," Adam explained.

They chatted a few moments before Kenny said his goodbyes. After he left the office, Danielle asked, "Is Bill still working for you?"

"Yeah. But I needed some extra help because Bill's been super busy. I'm not the only one he works for."

Danielle gave a nod and said, "I wanted to ask, what do you know about our new neighbor?"

Adam shrugged. "Not much. I heard she's the new librarian. But aside from that, I don't really know anything about her. I only talked to her once, when she called me from the airport yesterday morning to ask me about picking up the keys. She called me because she couldn't get ahold of that yahoo agent of hers."

"What time was that?" Danielle asked. Adam told her the time, which coincided with Olivia's story.

"Are you sure she was at the airport?" Danielle asked.

Adam shrugged. "It sure sounded like it."

Walt looked at Adam. "What do you mean?"

"When she called me, she introduced herself. Told me she had arrived earlier than planned, couldn't get ahold of her agent, and wanted to find out where she could pick up the keys. Right after she asked, I heard an announcement in the background." Adam paused before saying, in a high-pitched squeaky voice, "Flight 1969 arriving at gate B3."

Melony looked at Adam and arched a brow. "I swear that's how you sounded before you went through puberty."

Adam frowned at Melony. "Oh, shut up."

Melony laughed.

"Was that really the flight number and gate?" Danielle asked.

Adam turned his frown to Danielle. "Yeah, why? It was also a flight from Vegas."

"No reason," Danielle said.

"Anyway, I asked her if she was at the airport, which was kind of a lame question, considering what I heard in the background. She told me her plane had landed about ten minutes earlier, and after she got her car, she planned to drive into Frederickport. That was about the extent of the conversation. Oh, and I told her to pick up the keys at Marlow House."

"Perhaps we should just go to Vegas," Melony blurted. Everyone looked at her.

"What made you think of Vegas?" Adam asked.

"You mentioned it, like, one second ago," Melony reminded him.

"Oh, you're talking about getting married in Vegas?" Adam asked.

Melony nodded. "Sure, lots of people get married there."

"Wait a minute, you guys aren't thinking of eloping to Las Vegas?" Danielle asked.

Melony looked at Danielle and shrugged. "Considering our age, I'm not sure I would call it eloping. But Adam and I have been trying to figure out what we want to do. And one thing we both agree on, we don't want a big wedding. It's not like we have any family who'll be there."

Danielle looked at Adam. "What about your parents? Your brother? Don't you want them there?"

"Honestly? Not really," Adam said. "Anyway, my brother took that teaching job in London, so no way he'll come."

"And Adam's parents already informed him they probably won't be able to make it," Melony added.

Walt and Danielle looked at Adam, who only shrugged.

"It's because of who he is marrying," Melony said. "They never liked me, anyway. Ever since I talked their son into running away with me when we were kids."

"You didn't talk me into it," Adam argued.

"Yes, I did. It was my idea." Melony looked back at Walt and Danielle. "Ever since, they never had a great opinion of me. It doesn't help that I'm divorced. But I think the cherry on top of their pie of disgust, my part in changing Marie's will. Now they view me as the person responsible for stealing Warren's rightful inheritance. And now that I'm marrying Adam, the one who got that inheritance, I'm the gold digger."

Adam reached out and patted Melony's knee. "But you're my gold digger."

Melony leaned toward Adam and kissed his lips.

"But you guys shouldn't get married in Vegas. You need to be married here, in Frederickport," Danielle insisted. "With your friends."

"I'm not good at planning this type of thing," Melony confessed. "And it certainly isn't Adam's forte. Now, if you need someone to defend you for murdering someone, I'm your person. But when it comes to planning a wedding, even a small one." Melony shrugged. "If not Vegas, I'm okay with going down to city hall."

"You are so romantic." Adam chuckled.

"Let me plan your wedding," Danielle blurted. "Something small, with your friends. At Marlow House. And it will be our treat. Consider it a wedding gift."

Melony looked at Danielle and smiled. "That is so sweet. But we can't have you do that. You're pregnant, girl. That's too much."

Danielle shook her head emphatically. "I want to. I also want to do this for Marie. She would love this."

Adam smiled at Danielle. "Yes, she would have loved that." What Adam didn't know, his beloved grandmother, Marie, hadn't moved on, and would attend the wedding at Marlow House if he and Melony accepted Danielle's offer.

"I think it's a great idea," Walt chimed in. "I'll help Danielle, and so will Joanne. Danielle loves doing this sort of thing, and once the babies come, she won't be able to entertain as much as she enjoys, at least not for a while."

"A wedding at Marlow House?" Melony said aloud, letting the idea sink in.

"I'd rather do that than Vegas," Adam admitted. "And I would like our friends there."

"You will need to pick a date. FYI, Joe and Kelly have moved their wedding to sometime in March. So you might want to get married in February. Maybe Valentine's Day?"

"But you got married on Valentine's Day," Adam reminded her.

"It's a day for all lovers," Danielle insisted.

Melony picked up her phone and opened her calendar app. "Valentine's Day falls on a Thursday. We should probably have the wedding on a weekend. But Saturday would be good." She looked at Adam. "What do you think, a February wedding at Marlow House?"

WALT AND DANIELLE sat in the Packard, preparing to go home after leaving Adam and Melony. Sitting quietly on the passenger seat, Danielle pulled her cellphone from her purse and started surfing. A moment later, Walt laughed.

Danielle looked up from her phone. "What's so funny?"

"You and Lily. You're both pregnant, and you have both agreed to plan a wedding."

Danielle grinned and looked back at her phone. "Yeah, I guess that is sort of funny."

Walt turned the ignition on, and when he was about to pull out into the street, Danielle blurted, "Holy crap!"

Walt looked at Danielle. "What?"

"I just checked yesterday's flights from Vegas. Flight 1969 did arrive at gate B3 at the time Adam talked to Olivia on the phone."

SIXTEEN

"**Y**ou make pretty good french toast," Heather said before taking a second bite of her breakfast. She sat with Brian at her kitchen table on Sunday morning.

"It tastes a lot better with your sourdough bread than when I make it at home."

Heather wrinkled her nose. "That's because you use that boring white sandwich bread. I don't know how you can eat that stuff."

Brian shrugged and poured more syrup on his french toast. "So who's all going to be there tonight?"

"Besides us, it's going to be Lily, Ian, Walt, Danielle, Mel, Adam, the chief, and Joe and Kelly. I could kinda do without Kelly, but whatever."

"What about Sunday dinner at Ian's parents?" Brian asked.

"They already did their weekly dinner on Friday. His parents have other plans tonight. In fact, when Lily first asked me, I almost said no, because I figured they'd be coming too. I can deal with Kelly, but I really don't want to spend an evening with June and John. John's not so bad, but that woman drives me nuts. Actually, when I'm around her, I start feeling sorry for Kelly."

Brian chuckled. "Why's that?"

"She's so annoyingly controlling. Ian's way of dealing with his mom is with humor, and then he does what he wants, but Kelly pretty much just takes it."

"I've noticed that too. You didn't mention Chris. Isn't he coming?"

Heather smiled. "No. He's going to a concert tonight in Portland."

"Who's he going with?"

Heather shrugged. "One of the women he's been dating. I really can't keep up with his social life. I keep asking him when he's going to bring one here to meet us."

"He must not have met a woman he cares about enough to meet his friends."

"I suppose." Heather picked up a napkin and wiped syrup off her lips.

"Is the chief bringing his boys?" Brian asked.

"No, they're staying with his sister. In fact, Connor's going over there too. Evan thinks he's babysitting him." Heather chuckled. "But it's more a playdate with Aunt Sissy's supervision."

When Brian and Heather finished their breakfast, they both got up to clear the table. Brian started doing the dishes, and Heather announced she was taking out the trash.

"You want me to do that?" Brian asked from the sink.

Heather flashed Brian a smile and said, "No. I find something incredibly sexy about a man doing dishes. I'll take the trash out."

Brian laughed at Heather's comment and turned his attention back to the dishes while Heather pulled the bag of trash from the trash can, tightened its cord, and headed for the back door.

WHEN HEATHER first moved to Frederickport, the disposal company picked up the garbage each week on Beach Drive. But after upgrading the trash receptacles, the pickup along her side of Beach Drive was now off the alley. Heather preferred the change.

She had hated dragging her cans from the back of her house to the street each week.

Along the back property line separating her yard from Olivia's stood a hedge of arborvitae, each reaching about seven feet tall. At one time, it served as a privacy wall, yet several trees had been removed after turning brown, leaving a gap. Heather kept her trash adjacent to the gap, while Pearl's trash bins had been pushed against the other side of the arborvitae hedge. Since moving in, Olivia had not moved the bins.

Heather didn't give her neighbor's trash bins any thought as she approached her own, believing she was alone outside. But just as Heather reached her bin and was about to open its lid, she looked through the gap in the arborvitae and saw Olivia standing on the other side of the hedge, looking down at her own trash bin, with something in her hands.

It looked as if Olivia was about to drop something in the trash can, but then she moved one hand upward, unfurling what looked like a bloody rag. Heather let out a gasp and dropped her trash bag to the ground. Olivia turned abruptly in Heather's direction. In her right hand she held a bloodstained knifelike tool, and in the other a bloody rag. The two women stood just a few feet apart.

Heather's eyes widened at the bloody objects in her neighbor's hands. She took a step back, away from Olivia, never taking her eyes off her.

"These were in the trash," Olivia blurted.

"What is that?" Heather demanded.

"I don't know. I was bringing my trash out, opened the bin, and saw this on top of some stuff I'd put in there earlier. I reached in, pulled it out. It looks like blood," Olivia stammered.

Heather wasn't sure if Olivia was waving the knife around to show her the blood, or to threaten her. "Uh, yeah, it does. Please stop waving that knife."

"It's not a knife." Olivia shoved the object toward Heather as if to show it off or take a jab at her.

Heather quickly stepped back away from her neighbor. "I said stop waving that thing at me!"

Olivia immediately dropped her hand with the knife to her side.

Heather was about to call for Brian when she heard his voice ask, "What's going on out here?"

Olivia stared at Brian as he approached them. When he got to Heather's side, she said, "You're that police officer."

"Yeah, he's also my boyfriend," Heather snapped, moving closer to Brian. "I think she has the knife that killed Betty. It's covered in blood, and so's that rag."

Olivia looked down at the objects in her hand.

Taking hold of Heather's wrist, Brian drew her behind him without taking his eyes off Olivia. "I want you to set those on the ground, please, and take a step back."

Still holding the bloody objects in her hand, Olivia looked up at Brian and frowned.

"Now!" he barked.

Olivia jumped at the harsh command and immediately complied. After dropping the objects, she stepped back nervously, away from the bloody items and away from Brian and Heather.

"Can you explain where you got those?" Brian asked.

"I was bringing my trash out." She then pointed to something on the ground. Brian hadn't noticed it before, but when he stepped closer to the opening in the hedge, he spied a full trash bag, its top tied together, sitting on the ground, leaning against the bin. "I was just getting ready to put my trash in the bin when I noticed a rag sitting on top of the stuff I'd put in the bin earlier. I wondered what it was, so I pulled it out. It looks like blood, but maybe it's red paint, I don't know. It's not mine. I don't know who put it there. But if you think they're from the murder down the street, please take them."

Brian glanced around and then asked Heather to run into the house and grab some small plastic storage bags. Heather returned a moment later and handed Brian several gallon-sized plastic bags. The two women watched as Brian leaned down and carefully picked up the items Olivia had dropped, slipping each one into a separate baggie after using one as a glove to prevent him from touching the items.

"You think that's the knife that killed Betty?" Heather asked.

"It's not a knife," Olivia argued.

Brian stood while examining the contents in the baggies. "She's right. It isn't a knife. It looks like a letter opener."

Heather leaned closer to the baggy and took another look. "The tip is sharp like a knife, and that sure looks like blood."

Olivia began to cry. Startled by the sudden burst of tears, Heather and Brian looked up to Olivia, who now stood in her driveway, wailing.

Before they asked her why she was crying, a voice on the other side of Olivia's driveway called out, "What's going on over here?" It was Walt.

Olivia didn't answer; instead her crying intensified. Concerned, Walt walked to her and was surprised when Heather and Brian stepped through the opening in the hedge.

Walt walked toward the three. "What's wrong?" He looked at Brian and Heather for answers.

"I think she might have found the murder weapon," Heather said. "Either that, or she was about to get rid of it."

Olivia swiped the cuff of her sweater's right sleeve over her tear-stained face and glared at Heather. "I don't care what you think you saw the other day. But I did not kill Betty Kelty. I never met the woman!"

"But I saw you with her," Heather hissed. "And it looks like I caught you with the murder weapon!"

OLIVIA HAD AGREED to go with Walt and wait with him at Marlow House while the responders Brian called processed the scene. If the letter opener proved to be the murder weapon, Brian didn't want any evidence destroyed, such as possible fingerprints on the trash bin.

While Danielle would rather not serve breakfast muffins and hot tea to a potential killer, at least she felt relatively safe. She wasn't alone in the kitchen with Olivia, both Marie and Walt were there, and should her new neighbor decide to grab a nearby knife and do to her or Walt what she might have done to Betty, either Marie or Walt could stop her.

"I should never have moved here," Olivia said, once again breaking into tears. The muffin sitting on the plate Danielle had served her remained untouched.

"Why did you choose Frederickport?" Danielle asked.

Olivia looked up and dabbed the tears from her face with a napkin. She smiled weakly at Danielle. "My family used to live here. I was really little at the time. I don't remember actually living here. But I do remember visiting each summer. My mom and my sister and I would come and stay with one of Mom's good friends. About five months ago, I sold my house in California and was staying with my sister, trying to decide where to move. On a lark, I looked at job openings in Frederickport and saw there was an opening in a library. I thought it was fate. Boy, was I wrong."

"Who was your mother's friend?" Danielle asked, already knowing the answer.

Olivia smiled softly and said, "Esther Meek. But she doesn't live here anymore."

"Yes, she moved to Florida," Danielle said. "She was Betty Kelty's aunt. Betty was living in her house."

Olivia stared at Danielle, and the next moment, she fell to the side and tumbled from the kitchen chair. She would have hit her head when falling, but Walt caught her in time, using his energy to ease her to the floor.

Danielle rushed to Olivia's side, leaning down to her body. She felt for a pulse and then looked up at Walt. "I think she fainted."

SEVENTEEN

On Saturday, Lily made a reservation for a party of eleven at Pearl Cove. When she and Ian arrived at the restaurant Sunday evening, the hostess showed them to a round table for twelve. Joe and Kelly arrived next, and Kelly sat next to her brother, with Joe on the other side of her. Brian and Heather arrived at the same time as Walt and Danielle. Brian took a seat next to Joe, with Heather on his right, and Walt next to Heather. Just as they sat down, the chief arrived. He sat next to Danielle. The last to join the dinner party were Melony and Adam. Melony sat next to the chief, with Adam to her right, and Lily sitting on the other side of Adam.

The entire dinner party arrived within minutes of each other, creating a noisy entrance, with chairs pushed around, hello hugs, and several conversations going on simultaneously. The hostess had handed each of them a menu when initially seated, so some were looking at their menus, while others had already set theirs on the table when the server arrived a few minutes later to take their drink order.

The server returned with their drinks ten minutes later. After distributing the beverages, she took their dinner orders and left the table. When she did, Brian started filling Joe in on what had happened that morning at Heather's house. Since Joe and Kelly had been in Astoria most of the day, this was the first Joe was hearing about the bloody rag and letter opener. Brian had just started telling Joe the story when Kelly overheard, stopped talking to her brother, and turned toward Joe to listen to what Brian had to say. By the time Brian finished the telling, everyone at the table was quiet and listening.

"And it really was the murder weapon?" Kelly asked.

"It matched the blood of the victim," the chief told her. "And according to the coroner, it looked like the weapon that could have killed her. Not sure if the killer knew what he was doing or if it was a lucky shot. Of course, not lucky for Betty."

"What do you mean?" Lily asked.

The chief looked at Lily. "The letter opener hit at just the precise angle to do maximum damage. Had the killer been off an inch either way, with just a slight change in angle, it wouldn't have killed her."

"Did you find any other fingerprints at the scene?" Melony asked.

"None that shouldn't have been there," the chief said.

"And no one saw who put it there?" Kelly asked.

"Oh, come on, we know who put it there," Heather scoffed. "Before, I was willing to believe our new neighbor just didn't want to admit she was in town already because she had some reason that had nothing to do with the murder. But now, she's caught with the murder weapon. Come on, people."

Kelly turned to the chief. "Why haven't you arrested her?"

"Because she has a credible witness who claims she was in Portland at the time of the murder," the chief said. "And they even sent me photo verification."

"There is Photoshop," Kelly said.

Heather looked at Kelly. "Exactly what I say!"

"While I believe Heather, at this point, it's Heather's word against Davis's. And since we can't find a connection, much less a viable motive, between Olivia and the victim, it's too early to make an arrest. It's like there are two women out there who look exactly alike and even dress alike. But one was in Portland while the other one was in Frederickport," the chief explained.

"Maybe she has a twin?" Kelly suggested.

"No, she doesn't have a twin," Danielle said. "She has a sister, but she's not a twin. However, when she was at our house this morning, while the police processed the area where they found the murder weapon, we learned there was a connection between Betty and Olivia other than they were both going to be co-workers. It seems Betty's aunt, the one Betty rented the house from, she was a good friend to Olivia's now deceased mother. In fact, growing up, Olivia and her sister would come to Frederickport with their mother and stay with Betty's aunt each summer."

"Did Betty and Olivia know each other back then, as kids?" Lily asked.

Danielle shrugged. "I asked her that question after she came to."

"What do you mean, came to?" Adam asked.

"She fainted in our kitchen," Walt said.

"Fainted?" several at the dinner table chorused.

Danielle then recounted the events in the kitchen that led up to Olivia fainting, leaving out the part where Walt's telekinetic powers softened her fall. She then said, "Anyway, after she came to, I asked her if she remembers if she had ever met Esther's niece. She claimed she never had."

The chief took a sip of his drink but said nothing. Danielle had called him earlier and told him about the connection between Olivia and Esther. He had then called Esther in Florida, who remembered Olivia, yet hadn't seen her since she was a teenager. Esther couldn't recall if Olivia had ever met her niece during one of her visits.

"I assume you've requested video surveillance tapes from the airport and airline?" Melony asked.

The chief nodded. "Yes. I should get them tomorrow."

"So once you prove she wasn't on that flight, you can arrest her?" Kelly asked.

"It will just prove she lied about when she arrived—and that she could get the car dealer to lie for her. But we have a long way to go before we can bring murder charges against anyone. So far, we have no motive. Plus, once we prove she was not on that flight, we have no idea what she'll decide to tell us. Perhaps she saw something that morning, and for whatever reason, she doesn't want to tell us. Or she is afraid. It could be anything." The chief gave a shrug.

Adam looked at his fiancée. "Hey, Mel, maybe you should go over there and introduce yourself. Sounds like she may need a good lawyer."

"I was thinking the same thing," Melony said with a chuckle.

"Oh, come on, you guys!" Heather grumbled. "If she killed Betty, the last thing I want is Mel as her attorney!"

"Why?" Adam asked.

"Because Mel is too good an attorney, and I don't want to live next door to a killer!" The other residents of Beach Drive agreed with Heather.

THEY WERE STILL DISCUSSING the murder when Marie appeared, standing behind her grandson, Adam. The only ones at the table aware Marie had arrived were the three mediums, Walt, Danielle, and Heather.

"Eva is with Olivia," Marie told the mediums.

The other people at the table, unaware of the new arrival, continued talking, but Walt, Danielle, and Heather kept looking Marie's way, listening to what she had to say.

"Olivia is watching a movie on her iPad, and Eva wanted to watch it too, so she told me to go ahead and come here, and she would come get me if necessary."

Adam, who had been listening to Ian say something, glanced toward Walt and Danielle and noticed them staring at him. He stared back, but when they didn't change expression or say anything, he frowned. Adam didn't realize it was Marie they were looking at, not him. Finally, he blurted, "What?"

Everyone at the table stopped talking and turned to Adam. Even Walt and Danielle turned their attention from Marie to him.

When Melony frowned at Adam, silently asking him what was up, he glanced at her and then looked back across the table at Walt and Danielle. He shrugged and said, "The way Walt and Danielle were looking at me, I thought they wanted to ask me something."

Walt and Danielle exchanged quick glances and then looked back at Adam. "We were staring at you?" Danielle asked innocently.

"I know what this is about," Melony cheerfully announced.

Walt arched his brows, curious to know what she meant.

"I bet you were wondering if we made our final decision yet. And the answer is yes if you're sure it won't be too much trouble," Melony explained.

Marie looked at Melony. "What's she talking about?"

Danielle grinned. "Great! Did you set a date?"

"Date for what?" Lily asked.

Melony turned to Lily. "Adam and I set the date for our wedding. It's going to be small, but all of you are invited. It's going to be the Saturday after Valentine's Day at Marlow House."

"Marlow House?" Kelly repeated.

Melony turned a smile to Kelly. "Yes. Danielle has so graciously offered to host our wedding at Marlow House."

"Wonderful!" Marie looked at Danielle. "You never told me!"

"I'm going to be Mel and Adam's wedding planner," Danielle said primly.

"I need a wedding planner." Melony laughed. "I'm not good at entertaining, much less planning a wedding."

"I'll help!" Heather offered.

"Me too!" Marie chimed in.

"Wow, another wedding at Marlow House," Kelly muttered.

Melony looked at Kelly. "You have a wedding to plan yourself. But you have a mother to help you."

"Uh, yeah," Kelly muttered.

"Since we're talking weddings, this might be a good time to announce to everyone"—Joe turned to Brian—"we've changed our wedding date to March. Actually, we changed the month. We haven't settled on the actual date yet."

"Right after us!" Melony grinned. "I assume you're not having an outdoor wedding at Lily and Ian's now."

Kelly shook her head. "No. We decided we didn't want to wait until summer. But we're still trying to work out the location."

"Wish you'd consider my suggestion," Lily said. "And since we're here now, I could ask them for a copy of their events menu."

"Oh, are you talking about getting married here?" Melony asked. "Because if you are, I think that would be a great choice. In fact, Pearl Cove would be my second choice for a wedding venue."

Adam looked at Melony. "I thought your second choice was Vegas?"

Melony looked at Adam and said with a cheeky grin, "Only if we can get an Elvis impersonator to marry us."

EIGHTEEN

I t was not the meow that woke Danielle. It was having to go to the bathroom. Reluctantly, she opened her eyes and looked up at her bedroom's dark ceiling. Next to her, Walt continued to sleep. She heard his steady breathing. Moving slowly so as not to wake her husband, Danielle slipped out of bed. She glanced at the window facing Beach Drive and spied Max hidden behind the curtain as he sat on the windowsill, looking out through the glass pane, with only his black tail visible; it swished back and forth. He let out another meow.

Instead of going to the bathroom, Danielle hurried toward the window. If Max continued meowing, he was sure to wake Walt. Once at the window, Danielle pushed the curtain to one side, intending to move the cat. Yet, before she picked him up, her glance moved to the glass pane and to what had captured Max's attention.

"Holy crap!" Danielle blurted, now pressing against the window and looking out into the early morning. Max let out another loud meow.

"What is going on over there?" a sleepy Walt grumbled from the bed.

"Someone just flew by the house!"

"What?" Walt sat all the way up in bed and rubbed his eyes. He looked across the room and saw Danielle at the window, a hint of morning sunshine streaming into the bedroom.

"I'm serious. Someone just flew by the window, but whoever it is, they're gone now." Danielle turned to Walt. "I wonder if that was Marie."

"What are you talking about?"

"I've got to pee," Danielle blurted before dashing to the bathroom, leaving Max behind.

When Danielle returned from the bathroom, she found Walt sitting on the side of the bed with Max.

"I'm sorry I woke you," Danielle said.

"You do understand, I don't have to know what you're doing when you go to the bathroom."

Danielle giggled. "Sorry. Too much information?"

"By the way, Max verified your story. But it wasn't Marie."

Danielle took a seat on the side of the bed with Walt and Max. "What do you mean?"

"When you were in the bathroom—doing whatever you were doing—Max told me someone flew by the window. Whoever it was was flying around the neighborhood. When he or she flew by the window, Max glimpsed their face, and he's fairly certain it wasn't Marie or Eva."

"If it wasn't Marie or Eva, what did I see?" Danielle asked.

"My guess, another spirit. I might suggest you were dreaming while sleepwalking, but since Max saw it too…" Walt gave a shrug.

Danielle stood up and walked to the window. Once again, she pulled the curtain to the side and looked out. Early morning sunlight gradually replaced the darkness. "She's up early. I wonder if she saw it, too."

Walt got off the bed and walked to Danielle. "Who?"

Still standing at the window, the drapes pushed to one side, Danielle nodded toward Beach Drive. "Heather. It looks like she's walking to Chris's house. If it weren't so early, I'd say she's going to hitch a ride to work with him; her car is still in the shop."

HEATHER USED her key to let herself into Chris's house. She didn't want to wake him. The moment she opened the door, Hunny greeted her, tail wagging.

"Hey, girl," Heather said as she shut the door behind her and gave the dog a pat.

"You want some coffee?" Chris called out from the kitchen. "I also have tea."

Heather headed toward the voice, Hunny by her side. When she walked into the kitchen, she found Chris standing by the sink, filling the coffeepot with water. Barefoot, he wore only boxers.

"Aren't you cold?" Heather asked.

"Not really." Chris poured the water from the coffee pot into the coffeemaker. He looked at Heather and asked, "Did you want some coffee, tea?"

"Thanks, but no. Maybe after I get back from my run. I don't like to drink coffee or tea before I go running. So how was the concert? I figured you'd still be sleeping."

Turning to face Heather, Chris leaned back against the counter as he waited for the coffee to brew. "I left early."

"Why? Did something happen?"

Chris shrugged. "It's just that I should know better."

Heather frowned. "What do you mean? What happened?"

"I've become friends with a bartender at one of the places I go to when I'm in Portland. He introduced me to the woman I asked to the concert. When I first met her, I thought she was gorgeous— model movie-star looks."

Heather grinned. "Is she as pretty as you?"

Chris rolled his eyes and let out a sigh. "Stop objectifying me. But yeah, she's pretty hot. At first glance, anyway."

Heather frowned. "What do you mean?"

"It's just never a good idea asking someone out—someone you'll have to spend a few hours with—if you don't know anything about them aside from how they look."

"People do that all the time on blind dates."

"Yeah, I suppose. But the next time, I'll take them to coffee so it's easier to cut it short."

"Now you have me curious. What was wrong with her?"

"Hmm, let's see, the first red flag, there were a couple of plus-size ladies enjoying the concert. Actually, they seemed like they were having a lot of fun. My date proceeded to make snarky comments about them, how they obviously couldn't find real dates because of their size. I was grateful they were far enough away that they couldn't hear what she was saying."

"Sounds lovely," Heather said dryly.

"And then there were remarks about a biracial couple, and how the white guy was betraying his race by dating that—well—I won't say what she called her."

"Oh, my god! What a bitch! What did you do?"

"I told her I was feeling sick, and that I had to go. And that I hoped she could find her way home."

"You left her there? Good for you! What did she say?"

Chris smiled. "She asked what was wrong with me. I said, 'You.' And then I turned and left."

"I'm proud of you."

Chris shrugged. "Life is too short to spend with ugly people."

Heather giggled.

"So how was your evening at Pearl Cove last night?"

Heather proceeded to tell Chris all that had happened the night before. After she finished the telling, she glanced at the kitchen clock and said, "I should probably get going if I want to get a run in before work. Thanks for letting me take Hunny with me."

"No problem. Hunny will enjoy it. Did Brian go home already?"

"He was just getting up when I left and said something about interviewing Becca Hammond again."

AFTER LEAVING Heather's on Monday morning, Brian drove straight to Becca Hammond's house. He hoped to catch her before she left for work, because he would rather not talk to her at the grocery store.

Brian understood it was probably a long shot, but he had to ask Becca. Ever since finding the bloody letter opener, he kept thinking about the other letter opener, the one that had caused the rift in Becca and Betty's friendship. Could it possibly be the same one? The one they found yesterday looked like an antique, and Becca's was an antique. He had mentioned something to the chief and Joe about it the night before, and while both said it wouldn't hurt to ask, they didn't expect it to be the same letter opener.

"Officer Henderson," Becca greeted him when she opened the door for Brian.

"I'm sorry to stop by so early, but I was hoping I could catch you before you go to work."

"Well, if you wanted to talk to my husband, I'm afraid he already left for work. As for me, I don't work today."

"You are the one I need to talk to," Brian said.

Becca opened the door wider. "Come on in. Would you like a cup of coffee?"

Five minutes later, Becca and Brian sat at her kitchen table, each with a cup of coffee. Brian handed Becca his cellphone to show her a picture he had on it. "By any chance, is this the letter opener you had stolen?"

Setting her coffee cup on the table, Becca reached over and took Brian's cellphone from his hand. She looked at the image on its display. "Oh, my God! You found it!" Becca looked up at Brian and grinned. "I can't believe you found it. Who had it?"

Brian let out a heavy sigh and took the phone back from Becca. "So it really is yours?"

"It certainly looks like it. Where is it?"

"Becca, it appears your letter opener was the murder weapon. Someone used it to kill Betty."

Becca stared dumbly at Brian. "No. That's not true. That doesn't make any sense."

"Yesterday, a resident of Beach Drive found it in their trash bin. It was wrapped in a bloody rag, and the letter opener had traces of dry blood on it. We tested it. The blood matches Betty's. And according to the coroner, it appears to be the weapon used to kill her."

Becca shook her head. "I don't want it back. Do whatever you want with it. I don't want it."

"We couldn't give it back to you right now, anyway. It's evidence in a murder investigation. But I need to find out who had access to that letter opener before it disappeared."

Becca considered the question for a moment and then shrugged. "I suppose anyone who was at the library that day. But I have no idea who that would be. I really don't know. You could ask Josephine what library staff was on duty. But since she was on vacation when it was taken, I doubt she'd be much help figuring out who else was at the library during that time. You could ask Kenny. He was there. I saw him and Betty exchanging heated words about the display."

"Kenny?" Brian frowned.

"Yeah, he was the janitor at the library. But he quit right after the letter opener fiasco."

WHEN BRIAN ARRIVED at the police station on Monday morning, he found the chief and Joe standing at the front desk.

Joe greeted Brian with, "You will not believe this."

Brian returned with, "You will not believe this. The letter opener we found yesterday was the same letter opener taken from the library. It belonged to Becca Hammond."

Joe frowned. "You're kidding me?"

"I'm just trying to figure out how Olivia Davis got her hands on the stolen letter opener before she used it to kill Betty," Brian said.

"She didn't kill Betty," the chief said.

"Then why does she keep lying about when she got into town? Why is she saying she didn't see Betty right before she was murdered? We just need to figure out how that letter opener fits into all this," Brian said.

"Brian, you are not listening. Olivia couldn't have killed her," Joe said.

Brian frowned at Joe.

"We got the surveillance videos this morning. Olivia got on that plane, just as she told us. I don't know who Heather saw Friday morning, but it was not Olivia Davis. She was telling the truth," the chief explained.

NINETEEN

Heather stood in disbelief, looking down at the computer monitor on the police chief's computer. Chief MacDonald, who sat behind his desk, had rolled his chair slightly to the right so Heather could have an unobstructed view. Sitting on the other side of MacDonald's desk, in the two chairs facing him, were Joe and Brian, who silently watched Heather.

"I can't believe this!" Heather finally blurted. She looked up at Brian and asked, "How is this even possible? I know what I saw."

Brian shrugged. "Whoever you saw Friday morning, it definitely was not Olivia Davis. As you saw in that video, she boarded that plane when she said she did."

"This is crazy," Heather muttered as she began pacing behind the chief's desk.

"Heather, let me ask you something," Joe began.

Heather stopped pacing and turned to Joe.

"First, everyone in this room knows you saw a woman with a distinct hair color like Olivia's wearing a quilt jacket early Friday morning. You told us all before Olivia Davis ever arrived in Frederickport."

"And?" Heather frowned.

"When you saw the woman that morning, how long did you actually look at her face?"

Heather shrugged. "I don't know. I looked up, saw someone coming out of the yard. The next moment, the one I thought was Olivia looked me in the face. I know our eyes met. Then my phone rang, and I looked away to answer the call. When I looked back, they were already walking up the street. That's when I noticed the quilt jacket."

"How far were you from them?" Joe asked.

"I told you, when I first saw them, I was just leaving out my front gate, and they were leaving out the front gate of Pearl's yard. I don't know how many feet that is."

"And after you answered the phone call and when you turned back and noticed the quilt jacket, how far were they up the street?"

Heather considered the question a moment and then said, "They were just past Marlow House."

Joe let out a sigh. "I think I know what happened."

"I would like to know, too," Heather grumbled.

"You obviously saw someone with the same hair color as Olivia Davis. And that person was wearing a quilt jacket. And later, when you first saw Olivia Davis, your mind played tricks on you, making you believe it had to be the same woman, because they were similar in looks and were wearing a similar jacket."

"But from what Olivia told Danielle, her quilt jacket is a one of a kind. She made it," Heather reminded him.

"But that's your mind playing tricks on you. It's making you think it was the same jacket because of the other coincidences. Can you honestly say they were wearing the exact same jacket? That's a considerable distance from your front gate to Marlow House. I don't know how you could have distinguished the fabric patterns of the pieces making up that jacket."

Heather stared at Joe. After a moment, she closed her eyes, let out a sigh, and opened her eyes again, returning her gaze to Joe. She shook her head. "I honestly don't know anymore."

"I also bet that when you try to remember that encounter with our mystery woman, your brain fills in the face with Olivia's. After all, they are undoubtably similar, and after you first met Olivia at Marlow House, you were convinced it was the same woman."

"I'M glad you could get away," Danielle told Lily. The two friends sat together at a booth in Lucy's Diner. The server had just brought their beverages, taken their lunch order, and left the table.

"I figure I might as well enjoy spur-of-the-moment lunches with girlfriends while I can. Before long, the two of us will each be occupied with not one, but two little demanding humans!"

"I still can't believe you're pregnant, too," Danielle said.

Lily grinned. "I was shocked myself. I thought we were being careful. But you know what they say, no birth control is a hundred percent. But after this baby, Ian has agreed to get snipped."

They chatted a few minutes more about their pregnancies and then shifted the conversation to the reason for their afternoon meeting.

"I just figured, since we both had weddings at Marlow House, it will be easier for me to put together a list of what I need to do for Mel's wedding if you help me. You'll probably remember things I forgot."

"I think it's a great idea."

"While Mel insists she isn't good at planning social events, she already got a list to me this morning on things she wants to do."

"Such as?" Lily asks.

"She says she absolutely does not want me to prepare the food. She thinks that will be too much for me, considering the pregnancy."

"I agree with her. Does she have any idea where she wants to get the food?"

Danielle nodded. "Yes. She's going to use Pearl Cove's catering service and wants to order a wedding cake from Old Salts. She wants the double fudge chocolate cake."

"In a way, you'll be making the wedding cake," Lily teased. Old Salts used Danielle's double fudge chocolate cake recipe, yet they called it Marlow House's Double Fudge Chocolate Cake. It had become a favorite with their customers.

"Is this where all the Housewives of Frederickport hang out?" A familiar voice interrupted their conversation. Danielle and Lily looked up to Heather standing over their booth.

Lily arched her brows. "Housewives of Frederickport?"

Heather shrugged. "As opposed to us working girls. Can I sit down while I wait for my order?"

"Oh, sure," Danielle said before scooting down the bench to make room for Heather.

Heather sat down in the booth and dropped her purse to the floor by her feet. "I'm just picking up something to take back to the office for Chris and me."

"So you got your car back?" Danielle asked.

"No. I'm picking it up after work. Chris loaned me his car. But I already spent most of my lunch hour at the police station. Thankfully, I have a boss who won't get pissy if I eat at my desk when I'm on the clock."

"Did you get arrested again?" Lily teased.

"No. But I should probably be committed to an insane asylum," Heather said before telling Danielle and Lily what had happened at the police station.

"So that woman you saw really wasn't our new neighbor?" Lily asked.

Heather shrugged. "Apparently not. I'm totally baffled. I suppose Joe's explanation makes sense."

"Joe is always good at coming up with a reasonable explanation for an unexplainable event," Danielle snarked.

"Do they have any leads?" Lily asked.

"The murder weapon was an antique letter opener that belonged to our other neighbor Becca Hammond," Heather said.

"Becca is a suspect now?" Lily asked. "Just when we stop worrying about one neighbor, another one becomes a suspect?"

Heather shook her head. "No. Becca loaned the letter opener to the library a month or so ago, to be used in a display. Someone stole it. They have no idea who took it. It could have been anyone.

Whoever took it, that's probably who killed Betty. Unfortunately, the library doesn't have a security camera set up."

"Unlike the airport," Danielle quipped.

Heather let out a sigh. "I tell you what; do you want to know one thing I'm thankful for?"

"What?" Danielle asked.

"Imagine if I went to the police after Olivia picked up the keys and told them she was the one I saw with Betty. And then they get the videos from the airline and think I made it all up."

"YOU KNOW, HEATHER IS RIGHT," Lily told Danielle after Heather left the restaurant with her to-go order and headed back to work. "People would start questioning her motives. They might even consider her a suspect, but at the very least, they would question her character. Not very nice to make up such potentially damaging stories about someone she doesn't even know. And imagine if they had charged Olivia with murder, all based on what Heather saw. If not for the video they got from the airport, they could convict Olivia of murder."

Danielle didn't have time to comment; for the next moment, the server came with their food. By the time the server left the table, someone else had arrived.

"I thought that was your car out there," Kelly told Lily when she walked up to their booth.

"You here for lunch? Want to join us?" Lily offered.

Kelly glanced briefly at the food just served and said, "I'm not really hungry, but I wouldn't mind just sitting down for a minute and getting something to drink, if that's okay."

"Sure." This time it was Lily's turn to scoot down the booth, making room for another person.

"I was just at Adam's office," Kelly explained. "Checking on new listings."

"Still looking for a house?" Danielle asked.

Kelly let out a sigh. "Yeah. But there's not much on the market right now."

"Have you decided on the wedding?" Lily asked. "Last night you sounded like you and Joe might accept our offer."

Kelly looked at Lily. "Joe and I talked about it last night after we got home from dinner. Pearl Cove would be an amazing venue, but we feel a little funny having you guys pick up the tab."

"We told you, we want to do this for your wedding gift. You are Ian's baby sister. He adores you. He wants to do this for you."

Kelly stared at Lily for a moment. Finally, she broke into a slight smile and said, "That's really sweet of you to say."

Lily grinned. "Hey, it's true."

Kelly took a deep breath before saying, "This morning, before I went to Adam's, I stopped by my parents' house. I wanted to talk to Mom about your offer and how Joe and I were seriously considering it. I wanted to see what she'd say."

"And?" Lily asked.

"Mom started crying."

"Crying? Why?"

"I have no idea. She just started crying. I asked her what was wrong. She wouldn't say. She just made me promise not to tell Ian." Kelly paused and looked at Lily. "But I didn't promise not to tell you. So when you tell Ian, can you ask him why Mom was crying?"

TWENTY

Olivia had hoped the movers would arrive on Monday morning. And they might have if the moving van hadn't experienced engine problems. She received the call shortly before noon, telling her they would not be arriving until after three that afternoon. It would give them less than two hours to unload before sunset. Olivia was not happy.

Two hours before the movers' arrival, Olivia decided she might as well go to town and buy some groceries. This way, she wouldn't have to go tomorrow, and she could stay home and concentrate on unpacking and settling into her new home.

After grabbing her purse and cellphone from the kitchen counter, she exited through the side door and headed toward her driveway off the back alley, where she had parked her car. When she reached her vehicle a few moments later, she found something sitting on its roof, looking at her—a black cat with white-tipped ears.

"Well, hello," Olivia greeted the feline. "I hope you haven't scratched my new car."

The cat meowed, stood up, and then leapt down to the driveway.

Olivia moved closer to the vehicle and inspected the area where the cat had been sitting while he walked between her feet, purring and rubbing against her ankles.

Standing on tiptoes, she ran her fingertips over the paint and was relieved to find no scratch marks. While still on tiptoes, she looked down at the cat weaving between her feet and rubbing against her.

"So you want to make friends?" No longer on her tiptoes, Olivia leaned down to pet the cat, but he ran under the car, out of her reach.

"Playing hard to get?" Olivia said with a chuckle as she knelt and peeked under the car. "You really can't stay under there. I need to go." The cat, now lying under the car, his tail swishing back and forth, made no attempt to move. Instead, he let out a meow. "Come on, you don't want me to run you over, do you?"

When the cat refused to budge, Olivia stood up, fished her car keys out of her purse, and opened the passenger door. She tossed her purse inside the car, onto the passenger seat and then slammed the door shut, assuming the sound of the door would scare the cat away and out from under her car. It did not.

"Seriously?" Olivia muttered, now circling the car, trying to figure out the best way to get the cat to move. "Come on, kitty. I think you belong to the Marlows, and I don't want to run over my neighbor's cat on my first week in the neighborhood." She slapped her hand along the car a few times, making a loud sound and hoping that would scare the cat. Yet he refused to come out from under the car.

Once again, Olivia leaned down, this time getting on her knees and crawling partway under the car toward the cat, all the while saying, "Go on, shoo, go on…" Something attached to the underside of her car caught her attention. Olivia's eyes widened. At that moment, she thought she was going to die.

She didn't die, but she managed to get out from under the vehicle, and she knew she needed to call the police before something happened. But then she realized she had put her cellphone in her purse, and that purse currently sat in the car with the door closed. She could not risk reopening the door. She had been lucky the first time.

Without hesitation, Olivia ran from her driveway, down the side of her house, to the sidewalk, and then up the street to the front door of Marlow House.

WALT SAT IN THE PARLOR, writing notes for his book, when he heard the doorbell ring, followed by pounding. Since Danielle was still in town with Lily, and Joanne was off today, Walt knew the door would not answer itself. The person seemed rather anxious for someone to answer, considering the relentless pounding, followed by another ring and more pounding.

Curious, Walt dropped the pad of paper and pen he had been using onto a nearby table and stood. He made his way to the front door; all the while, the pounding and intermittent ringing of the doorbell continued.

Before answering, he looked through the peephole and found their new neighbor, Olivia Davis, on the front porch, frantically slamming both of her fists against the door.

When Walt opened the door, the unhinged neighbor, primed to knock, involuntarily fell forward and might have landed on the floor, had Walt's telekinetic powers not pushed her back onto her feet, steadying her. Olivia seemed oblivious to the fact she had almost fallen, or that something had intervened.

Visibly relieved to see Walt, Olivia grabbed hold of his wrists. "It's a bomb! You need to call the police!"

WALT AND OLIVIA stood together in one of the upstairs bedrooms of Marlow House, looking out its south-facing window at Olivia's backyard and glimpsed what they could of her driveway off the alleyway. Joe and Brian had been the ones who initially answered the call, and the fact they showed up instead of someone more skilled in handling explosives told Walt they didn't take his call seriously.

"Olivia Davis from next door is here. She's quite upset and insists someone has put a bomb under her car," Walt had told them.

After they had arrived, Joe had said it would probably be best if they both wait at Marlow House until they checked it out, to which Olivia was more than happy to comply.

If the situation weren't so serious, Walt might have laughed at the way Brian and Joe approached the vehicle with no apparent concern, only to see them race from it seconds after peeking under the car. Brian wasted no time whipping out his phone and placing a call. He then made a second call to Walt and said, "She was right. It's a bomb. We need to clear the neighborhood."

LILY AND DANIELLE were just about ready to pay their bill at Lucy's Diner when their husbands walked in unexpectedly. Connor and their new neighbor were with them.

"What are you guys doing here?" Lily asked when they walked up to the table, Connor in Ian's arms.

"Scooch over," Ian told his wife as he handed her their son. "The bomb squad is at Olivia's house."

"Bomb squad?" Danielle squeaked as she moved down the bench, making room for Olivia, while Walt dragged a chair from an empty table and placed it at the end of the booth.

"Someone put a bomb under Olivia's car, and they're trying to remove it," Ian explained as he sat down, his son wiggling between him and Lily. Connor tried to reach his mother's abandoned lunch plate.

Lily shook her head in disbelief while absently handing her son a french fry from her plate. "I'm not sure what I'm more confused about. The fact someone put a bomb on our neighbor's car, or that Frederickport has a bomb squad."

"I have no idea if it is an actual bomb squad, or if they're from Frederickport," Ian admitted. "But Brian and Joe are there, and according to Walt, they're staying back while the professionals do what they do."

Danielle looked at Walt. "You were over there?"

Walt shook his head and then explained what had happened. When he finished the telling, Lily and Danielle looked to Olivia, who had not spoken a word since arriving and seemed unnaturally pale.

"Are you okay?" Danielle asked her neighbor.

Olivia gave a pitiful shrug. "I don't know. I move all the way to Oregon, foolishly believing returning to my childhood home will somehow give me the new beginning I need. Right before I get here, a woman who is supposed to be my new boss is murdered on my street. A neighbor, a woman I have never met before, insists I was with the murdered woman an hour before she was killed. Someone puts a bomb on my car, and my movers are supposed to get here in less than two hours, and who knows if I will even have a house in two hours? And if my house is still there, but the police aren't finished, how much is it going to cost me to pay the movers to stick around after three?"

Before anyone could respond to Olivia's emotional rant, Walt's cellphone rang. He glanced at his phone before answering. "What's going on, Brian?"

Everyone at the table fell silent and waited for Walt to finish his phone call.

"We can go home," Walt announced after he ended his call. He looked at Olivia and added, "Your house is still there, so is your car. And it's not three yet, so we can get you back before the movers arrive."

"What happened?" Danielle asked.

Walt looked at Danielle. "It was a bomb wired to go off when Olivia turned on the ignition."

"Oh my god, someone really was trying to kill me!" Olivia gasped.

"While it was a bomb, and they wired it to explode when you

turned on the ignition, whoever our bomber is, he's a novice, according to Brian. It wouldn't have gone off. In fact, it wouldn't have worked at all, because the bomber didn't have the wiring right," Walt explained.

"I thought you said he had it wired to explode when she turned on the car?" Danielle asked.

"Yes, they could tell what the intent was. How it was supposed to go off," Walt said.

IAN HAD DRIVEN his car to Lucy's Diner, as it had the car seat for Connor. When they drove back home, Lily drove her car with Walt and Danielle while Olivia went with Ian and Connor. When they got back to Beach Drive, the street was no longer blocked off. Minutes after Ian dropped Olivia at her house, the moving van arrived early.

Lily pulled up to the front of Marlow House and let Walt and Danielle off before pulling into her driveway across the street.

"There was something I didn't tell you at the diner," Walt told Danielle as the two made their way up the walkway to the front door of Marlow House.

"What's that?"

"The only reason Olivia saw the bomb, she was looking under the car, trying to get a cat to move. That cat was Max."

"Max was there?" Danielle stood on the front porch with Walt as he unlocked the door.

"Yes. Only black cat with white-tipped ears I know. And I'm curious to find out what he might have seen before Olivia came outside." Walt opened the front door and stepped to one side, letting his wife enter first.

Danielle started to walk inside but paused a moment and turned to Walt. "You think he might have seen the bomber?"

"I'm thinking it's possible. Perhaps he saw someone fooling with her car. He was curious and went to investigate. He obviously didn't know it was a bomb, or he would have come to me instead of sticking around. I doubt he even understands what a bomb is. And when Olivia came out to leave, Max was still there, sitting on top of her car. Maybe he went under the car because he wanted her to see what someone had put there. Max isn't stupid. And while dogs are often credited with saving their humans, cats are fully capable of doing the same. We both know Max is."

TWENTY-ONE

Walt and Danielle entered Marlow House minutes before it started to rain. It had been chilly outside, and Danielle appreciated the indoor warmth. She had just removed her jacket and placed it on the coat rack with her purse when her cellphone rang. She stayed in the entry hall to answer the call while Walt searched for Max.

"What the hell is going on?" came Heather's voice when Danielle answered the phone.

"I take it you heard about our little bomb scare?" Danielle asked.

"Brian called me. I can't believe someone put a bomb on Olivia's car! What the hell is happening?"

"I have no clue, but Walt is looking for Max to find out if he knows anything." Danielle then told Heather about Max's involvement in the situation.

"Brian and Joe about freaked when they found the bomb under the car," Heather said.

"Why? Didn't they believe Walt when he told them what she said was under her car?"

"Not exactly. They figured it was a case of some emotional

woman who happened to look under her car and imagined something was there. Us women are often hysterical; we imagine things and are clueless about cars. Crap like that."

"He said that?"

Heather scoffed. "Not in so many words. But it's kind of what he was saying. He's lucky he didn't tell me in person."

"Why?"

"Because I probably would have kicked him. And you know how I'm trying to control my violent impulses. But those idiots could have gotten themselves blown up by underestimating a woman. I still might give him a smack."

"You are talking about your boyfriend," Danielle teased.

"Doesn't mean he can't be an idiot. And I certainly don't want the idiot to blow himself up. I kind of like him. Not sure why, but he's grown on me. So what did Olivia say? Brian said they left her with Walt."

"She has no idea who could have put the bomb on her car and seems sincerely perplexed—and freaked—about all this. By the way, we told her you saw the airport videos and no longer believe she was the woman you saw with Betty. We figured she was so upset about everything that has happened since she arrived in town that she needed some good news. I hope that's okay."

Heather let out a sigh. "I suppose. But honestly, whoever it was, she looked just like Olivia. And perhaps that jacket wasn't the same one, but it sure looked like it to me."

"While it might not have been Olivia, she must be involved someway. After all, someone tried to blow her up."

"True."

"What does Brian say about the bomb? Do they have any leads?"

"No. I guess Brian and Joe were on their way to the library to talk to Josephine Barker. They're trying to find out who was working for the library on the day the letter opener disappeared. One of the janitors, Kenny, don't remember his last name, was there that day, according to Becca. But they haven't been able to track him down. And they also want to find out who checked out books or returned them that day. They assume there would be records on that. But then Walt called about the bomb, and they went to investigate that instead. So not sure when they're going to talk to Josephine."

WALT FOUND Max in the attic office, napping on the desk chair. He walked over to the cat, picked him up and sat back down on the chair, setting the cat on his lap. Max refused to open his eyes immediately and stretched out and made no attempt to jump off Walt's lap.

Walt moved his palm over Max's back, repeatedly stroking the feline while whispering, "Wake up, Max. We need to talk."

POLICE CHIEF MACDONALD sat at his desk, staring blankly at the computer screen. This case made no sense to him. He had just finished looking at the security camera footage available along the alleyway behind Beach Drive. It was the only house along that stretch with a camera aimed at the alley.

A familiar female voice at the open doorway interrupted his concentration. "Hey, Chief."

MacDonald looked up and found Walt and Danielle standing in his doorway. He waved them in, asking them to close the door behind them. After they did, he asked, "Please tell me you've spoken to Betty's ghost?"

"Sorry, Chief, we haven't seen her," Danielle said, taking a seat in one of the chairs facing his desk.

"We haven't seen Betty, but Max told me some things that might be helpful," Walt said as he sat down in a chair next to Danielle.

The chief shrugged. "Hey, I'll take help where I can—from a ghost or a cat. I don't care. What did he have to say?"

"He saw our bomber," Walt began.

The chief abruptly sat up straighter in his chair. "Who was it?"

"Unfortunately, he had never seen him—or her—before," Walt explained.

The chief slumped back in his chair. "He can't tell if it was a man or woman?"

"No. But after a great deal of back-and-forth—you need to remember a cat doesn't describe things the way you might, and it's not like we actually talk words—but he did tell me a few things."

The chief let out a sigh. "Anything that might help us catch this person?"

"Unless I misunderstood Max, the way he described this person, our bomber wore dark pants, a dark hoody, with the hood pulled up over his head, concealing not just his hair. Or her hair. But also much of the bomber's face. And the person wore a dark backpack. I'm fairly certain it was the same color as the jacket and pants. The backpack is where he carried the bomb."

Once again, the chief sat up straight. His hand moved to his computer mouse. "Come look at this. It's footage I received from one of your neighbors on Beach Drive. It's about a half mile from Marlow House."

Walt and Danielle stood up and walked behind the desk and looked over the chief's shoulder at the computer monitor. The chief played a video clip caught that morning from a security camera. They watched. In the video, several cars drove by, and then someone dressed in black, wearing a hoody and backpack, jogged down the street.

Danielle pointed to the monitor. "There they are!"

"That same person—or at least someone the same size and wearing similar clothing—showed up in a video captured by the same camera on the morning they found the letter opener in Davis's trash," the chief explained.

"Whoever planted that letter opener is our bomber?" Danielle asked.

"I suspected it when I first saw this last video. Yet I also figured it could very well just be a jogger, not connected to our case, someone who regularly runs this route. Like Heather does. But now that Max has confirmed that's our bomber, my guess is it is the same person who planted the murder weapon."

"Do Brian and Joe have leads on who might have taken the letter opener?" Danielle asked.

The chief shook his head. "No. They wanted to interview Josephine again, but on their way to the library, Brian got Walt's call."

"Yeah, Heather told me that," Danielle said.

"They finally made it to the library, but Josephine is out of town with a friend of hers, and she won't be back until Thursday," the chief explained. "Brian tried calling her, but the call keeps going to voicemail."

"Surprised she left town right now. I'd think the library would be a little shorthanded with Betty's death, and Olivia hasn't started work yet."

The chief shrugged. "Right now, Brian and Joe are trying to track down Kenny, who used to be the library's janitor. It seems he has disappeared."

Danielle nodded. "Heather mentioned something about that."

"According to what Becca told Brian, Kenny, the library's janitor, and Betty had a disagreement after the letter opener disappeared. He quit a few days later. Right after leaving Becca, Brian called Josephine to find out what she knew about all this, but she wasn't there during the argument, and wasn't sure why he quit. We've been trying to track down this Kenny, but he moved, and his landlord doesn't know where."

"Doesn't he have a cellphone? Everyone has cellphones these days," Danielle asked.

"Yes, Josephine gave Brian the number. But like Josephine's number, it keeps going to voicemail."

WALT AND DANIELLE stopped at Old Salts Bakery after leaving the police station. They both needed their cinnamon roll fix. After making their purchase, they hurried back to Danielle's car, using their rain jackets instead of an umbrella to protect them from the downpour.

Once back in the car and out of the rain, Walt tossed the sack with the purchase in the back seat while Danielle blurted, "I know how we can find Kenny!"

While fastening his seatbelt, Walt frowned at Danielle. "How can we do that?"

"I just figured out who he is! When we stopped at Adam's office on Saturday, we met his new handyman, Kenny. I thought he looked familiar, but I couldn't place him. It just dawned on me. I remembered where I've seen him before. He used to work at the library. I bet he's the janitor the chief was talking about."

"He looked rather familiar to me, too. You want to call the chief and tell him?"

Danielle considered the question for a moment and shook her head. "Let's just stop by Adam's office and find out if I'm right. His office is just down the street. Adam will be able to tell us if Kenny is the same Kenny who worked for the library. And if he is, we'll get his current contact information to the chief. I don't want to send the chief on a wild-goose chase if I'm wrong. He's got enough going on right now."

BY THE TIME they pulled up in front of Adam's office, the rain had stopped.

"Please wait for me to open the door for you," Walt told Danielle as he unbuckled his seatbelt.

"Umm, I appreciate how you are a gentleman, but I can open the door myself."

Walt narrowed his eyes at Danielle. "I understand you are fully capable of opening a car door, but the sidewalk is slippery, and I don't want you to fall. Just wait for me."

Danielle resisted the temptation to roll her eyes and instead unbuckled her seatbelt and patiently waited for Walt to open her car door for her. A few minutes later, they walked arm in arm to Adam's office while Danielle silently wondered what would happen if Walt slipped and fell and then pulled her down with him. Wouldn't it be better if he simply let her walk by herself, and then if she fell, he could use his telekinetic powers to keep her from falling?

She asked herself that question as she and Walt entered the front office of Frederickport Vacation Properties, and she might have whispered the question to Walt, but something distracted her the next moment. She spied a person sitting at Leslie's desk. It was Adam's handyman, Kenny.

TWENTY-TWO

K enny, who sat at Leslie's desk, looked up from the cellphone in his hands and smiled at Walt and Danielle. "Hi. If you're looking for Adam, he left for the post office, and then he has some errands. Not sure when he's going to be back."

"Are you taking over for Leslie?" Danielle asked, only half joking.

Kenny grinned. "I stopped by to drop something off, and Adam asked if I'd hang out here and answer the phones while he's gone. Leslie is still sick. And hey, he offered to pay me. I'm happy to sit in a warm, dry office and surf on my phone while getting paid."

"Gosh, I'm sorry Leslie's still sick," Danielle said, now standing in front of the desk, Walt by her side.

"Adam said she'd be back tomorrow. I guess she's feeling a lot better, but not enough to come in today."

"I have a question," Danielle began.

Kenny smiled at Danielle. "Sure."

"I thought you looked familiar the other day when we stopped in here, and Adam introduced us. And I've been trying to figure out where I'd seen you before. Did you used to work at the library?"

Kenny nodded. "I did. I worked there for three years."

"So I guess you know about Betty Kelty," Danielle said.

Kenny smiled sadly. "I suspect everyone in town knows what happened to Betty."

"I didn't really know her," Danielle said. "But she was killed just a few doors down from our house. It's chilling. A killer is still out there."

"Yes, I knew they found her on Beach Drive. I know you're the ones who own Marlow House. I heard they found her body only a few doors from your place," Kenny said.

"Did you know her well?" Walt asked.

Kenny shrugged. "We both worked for the library. We were friends. But I haven't seen her since I quit. I'm really sorry to hear what happened. I can't imagine why anyone would want to hurt her. My guess, it was some random killer. Maybe a mugger. Hopefully, the police will figure it out, because I agree, it's chilling thinking a killer is still out there. But I suspect whoever did it is long gone."

"It's an open investigation, and if they have any leads, I haven't heard," Danielle lied.

"I imagine if they have any leads, they aren't telling anyone," Kenny said.

"You're probably right." Danielle smiled at Kenny and then asked, "Did you like working at the library? Personally, I love libraries. Something about all those books..."

Kenny chuckled. "Well, I didn't get much of a chance to check out the literature. I spent most of my time cleaning the bathrooms, mopping the floors, and maintaining the building. Actually, it wasn't a bad job."

"You just wanted a change?" Danielle asked.

"Something like that."

"Our new neighbor is the new head librarian."

"Yeah, I heard that," Kenny said. "From what I understand, Betty was supposed to be taking over Josephine's job, and they were hiring this new person to take over Betty's spot. But I guess this new person got an instant promotion, and they're now looking for someone else to replace Betty."

Danielle nodded. "Yes, that's what I heard too."

"I'm surprised Josephine wants to retire. That place was her life," Kenny said.

"I don't really know Josephine. Oh, I know who she is, but I don't really know her," Danielle said.

"I always got along with Josephine. She's the one who hired me. I was sad to hear she was thinking of retiring. I kind of figured Betty might get her job."

"You didn't want to work for Betty?" Danielle asked.

"I didn't say that."

"Kenny," Walt interrupted, "do you just work for Adam? I'm asking because we occasionally hire a handyman to make repairs around Marlow House. We often use Bill Jones, but he's so busy these days, it's hard to get him."

"Sure. I'm always looking to pick up extra work. Heck, here I am answering phones for Adam." Kenny chuckled.

"Great. Can I have your number?" Walt asked.

Kenny grabbed a blank piece of scratch paper from the desk and jotted down his phone number. While he was writing the number, Walt asked, "I assume you live in Frederickport?"

"Yeah. I rent a room over the hardware store. It's more convenient and cheaper than my last place."

"WOW, YOU ARE A SNEAKY ONE," Danielle teased Walt after they left Adam's office and got into her car.

"You're not the only sneaky one in this family," Walt returned.

"You got his phone number and where he lives. Good job!"

Walt put the key into the ignition and turned to Danielle. "It might be the same phone number Edward already has, but now we also know where Kenny lives. You want to call the chief and give him the information?"

After Danielle finished buckling her seatbelt, she pulled her cellphone from her purse and said, "I really wanted to ask Kenny what he and Betty argued about after the letter opener went missing."

145

Walt turned on the ignition. "I'm glad you didn't. Kenny would wonder how you know about that."

"I resisted the temptation," Danielle said before calling the chief.

BRIAN HENDERSON DROVE to Adam's office, hoping to catch Kenny after Danielle had called the police station. When he walked in, he found who he assumed was Kenny sitting at Leslie's desk, looking at a cellphone. When Kenny looked up to see who had just walked into the office, his eyes widened.

"Umm, if you're looking for Adam Nichols, he's out running errands. But I can call him for you," Kenny asked nervously.

"And you are?" Brian asked, certain he already knew the answer.

"I'm Kenny Chandler. I do odd jobs for Adam."

"Actually, you're the man I'm looking for. I heard you worked for Adam."

Kenny frowned at Brian. "Is there a problem?"

Brian handed Kenny one of his business cards and then said, "I'm investigating Betty Kelty's murder. I understand you used to work together."

The next moment, Adam Nichols walked into the office.

"Hey, Brian," Adam greeted him. "What's up?"

"He needs to talk to me about Betty Kelty," Kenny answered for Brian.

KENNY AGREED to meet Brian at the police station to answer questions. Fifteen minutes after leaving Adam's office, the two sat in the interrogation room, with Joe and the chief in the adjacent office, watching through the one-way mirror.

"I'm so sorry about Betty," Kenny began. "But I really don't see how I can help you. I haven't talked to her since I quit the library."

"Why did you quit?" Brian asked.

Kenny shrugged. "I just wanted a change."

"I understand you and Betty had an argument a few days before you quit."

Kenny frowned at Brian. "Did Becca Hammond tell you that?"

"Why do you ask?"

Kenny gave another shrug. "She was the only one in the library at the time."

"So you did have a disagreement?"

"Betty was just upset, and she was venting to me. And I guess I didn't appreciate it, so the exchange got a little heated."

"Venting about what?"

"There's a display case off the lobby used to showcase different displays throughout the year. They change every month or so. They had one on the lost art of letter writing. Something from the display disappeared, and Betty totally flipped out. She blamed me, but I had nothing to do with the display, and it was certainly not my responsibility to watch it. That wasn't my job."

"You're talking about the missing letter opener?"

Kenny frowned at Brian. "You know about that?"

"I understand it was an antique. According to one antique dealer, it is worth around five hundred dollars."

"I don't know about that."

"Does the display case lock?" Brian asked.

"Yes. That's one thing that had Betty so upset. She swore she locked the display, but when she discovered the letter opener missing, she realized the display wasn't locked. And it didn't look like anyone had tampered with it. She found the key where she always kept it, still hanging in the back office on a hook. I know the letter opener belonged to her friend Becca Hammond, because Becca came into the library to see if Betty had located it.

"I got the impression Betty may not have been up front with Becca about it being missing. Becca knew someone had removed it from the display, but I think she believed it had been taken out for some reason, not stolen. Anyway, that day, Betty pulled me aside and started grilling me. Insisting I must have opened the display to dust it or something and had forgotten to lock it. And then she asked me to remember where I set the letter opener. I hadn't touched the thing, but she kept telling me to just try to remember."

"How did the conversation end?"

"I finally said something like, 'I don't know what else I can tell you,' and then I walked away and left for my lunch break."

"And you quit a few days later?"

"Yes, I felt it was time for a change."

"Did you quit because of the missing letter opener?" Brian asked.

Kenny frowned. "Why would I quit over the letter opener?"

"I meant, did you quit because of how Betty reacted?"

Kenny considered the question for a moment and then shrugged. "Not exactly. I had been considering leaving for a while, and I guess that was the final straw."

"You are saying this wasn't your first problem with Betty?"

"Hey, I didn't have a problem with Betty. Certainly not what you're talking about."

"And what am I talking about?" Brian asked.

"You're investigating her murder. And I totally get that. You're looking at people who knew her, who might have had an issue with her. But just because Betty took out her frustration on me over that missing letter opener doesn't mean I had a reason to go homicidal."

TWENTY-THREE

L ily stood at her kitchen counter, dicing celery to add to the
macaroni salad. She intended to bring it to tonight's potluck
dinner at Marlow House, where the friends had agreed to gather to
discuss the recent unsavory events of Beach Drive.

She glanced over to her husband, Ian, who sat at the breakfast
bar, looking down on his cellphone, while Connor napped in his
bedroom. "Who are you texting?"

Ian looked up from his phone. "I'm not texting anyone. You sure
I can't help you?"

"Nah, I got this." Lily resumed her dicing, and Ian turned his
attention back to his phone.

After a moment of silence Lily stopped what she was doing and
looked back to Ian. "I forgot to tell you. With the bomb scare and
everything, it just slipped my mind."

Ian looked up at Lily. "What?"

"Yesterday, when Dani and I were having lunch at Lucy's Diner,
before you guys showed up, your sister stopped at the diner. She had
been at Adam's office picking up some information on new listings.
She said something really funny."

"I suspect you're not talking funny, ha ha."

"Not unless you find humor in your mother's tears."

Ian frowned. "My mother's tears?"

"Yeah. Your sister said she stopped by your folks' house to discuss having the wedding at Pearl Cove."

"She's accepting the offer?"

"I don't know. Anyway, when your sister started talking to your mom about the wedding, your mom broke into tears, started crying. She wouldn't say why she was crying, but she made your sister promise not to tell you about it."

"And of course, Kelly promised not to tell me, yet did not promise not to tell you. And she told you, and now is waiting for you to tell me, so I can, in turn, tell her why Mom was crying, assuming I know."

Lily's eyes widened. "Wow. You know your sister well."

Ian shrugged. "This is pretty typical Kelly reasoning."

"So?"

"So what?" Ian asked.

"Do you know why your mom was crying?"

Ian let out a sigh and set his cellphone on the counter. "I think so."

"Are you going to tell me?"

"I suppose. But I would rather discuss this with Kelly myself, so if she asks you about it, tell her to come to me directly."

"But won't that be breaking her promise to your mother?"

"Not really."

"So why was your mom crying? What did you do?"

"Why do you assume I did anything?" Ian asked.

"It obviously has something to do with you."

Ian let out another sigh. "I'm not positive, but I have to assume Mom may have broken into tears because of a conversation I had with her the other day. It certainly was not my intent to make her cry, but it's the only explanation that makes sense. She must be upset over what I said."

"What kind of conversation?"

"You might say I set down some boundaries with Mom. I told her if she could not respect those boundaries, then we might not attend her Sunday dinners, and we probably would not see them as much in the future."

Lily's eyes widened. "Wow." Instead of asking questions about the boundaries he set, she resumed making her macaroni salad and told herself if Ian had wanted to elaborate, he would have told her about the conversation with his mother before now. Lily would respect that. Plus, she had a good idea what the conversation was about, because like Ian knew his sister well, she knew her husband.

After a moment of silence, Lily looked up from the macaroni salad to Ian, who sat quietly staring off into space, no longer looking at his phone. "Hey, Ian," Lily began in a quiet voice, "I don't know if I have mentioned it today, but I love you. And I hope your mom is going to be okay."

Ian smiled at Lily. "I love you too. And me too, I don't get any pleasure making Mom cry. I love her, but she will get over this, and when she does, all of us will be happier."

I hope you're right, Lily said to herself.

DANIELLE PLACED the food along the buffet in the dining room. She had made fried chicken, Lily brought her macaroni salad, Heather brought sourdough bread and mashed potatoes, Brian brought dessert from Old Salts, and Chris picked up coleslaw and beer at the grocery store.

After filling their plates, they sat around the dining room table, Walt, Danielle, Lily, Ian, Connor, Heather, Brian, and Chris.

"Do you have any leads on this Olivia look-alike?" Lily asked.

About to take a bite of chicken, Brian paused and glanced at Lily. "Unfortunately, no. And nothing adds up."

Danielle looked at Brian. "Did you ever talk to Josephine? I remember you said you were trying to interview her again."

"Yes. She repeated much of what she told us before. She didn't get back to the library until after the letter opener was gone. But she gave me a list of people who checked out books or returned them on the days the letter opener could have been taken, along with which employees worked those days."

"I thought you knew what day the letter opener went missing?" Chris asked.

"According to Becca Hammond, she stopped at the library on Saturday morning to pick up the letter opener, since that was the last day of the exhibit. But when she got there, Betty explained that while Saturday was officially the last day, it wouldn't end until the library closed on Saturday, and they planned to change the display on Monday," Brian explained. "Becca regrets not returning right before the library closed on Saturday and asking for the letter opener back, instead of waiting until Monday. After all, at that point, it wasn't necessary to leave it in the case since they were closed the next day and breaking down the display on Monday."

"Monday was the day Josephine returned from vacation?" Lily asked.

Brian looked to Lily. "Yes. But she didn't come into the library until later that day, after Betty discovered the letter opener missing. According to Becca, when she stopped at the library on Saturday morning, the letter opener was still in the display case. But we really aren't sure when it was taken. It might have been gone when they closed up on Saturday. And the library is closed on Sunday. Betty didn't notice it missing until about an hour after the library opened on Monday, and that was when she went to switch out the display and found the case unlocked."

"It would sure make things a lot easier if they had cameras in the library," Danielle muttered.

"I'm surprised they don't," Chris said.

"But I found out something interesting. It seems our ex-handyman, Kenny, has a record for theft."

Danielle looked up from her plate to Brian. "Really? Are we talking jewel thief or grand theft auto?"

Brian looked at Danielle. "Neither. He was working at a warehouse in Washington and helped himself to some of the merchandise. He spent a little time in prison."

"Wow, did Josephine know that when he applied for the job?"

Danielle asked. "Kenny said that's who hired him. I wonder if Adam knows."

"Not sure about Adam," Brian said. "But Josephine was aware of his record before she hired him. After talking to him, I ran a background check. When I talked to Josephine again, she brought it up before I did. She told me about his record, but insisted he was innocent. From what he had told her, someone had set him up, and he made a plea deal to reduce his sentence. She felt sorry for him."

"Let's say the handyman is the one who took the letter opener," Chris said. "I don't imagine someone like that takes an antique letter opener because he thinks it's pretty."

"Supposedly, it was worth about five hundred dollars," Brian said.

"I'd think he would want to sell it," Chris said.

"It disappeared a little over a month ago," Ian reminded him. "Not sure that's enough time to find a buyer. It's not like he can list it on eBay or Craig's List. If I were the letter opener's rightful owner, that's where I'd be checking."

"While I can understand why he would still have the letter opener after a month, even if he intended to sell it, I can't come up with a scenario where he ends up using that letter opener to kill Betty. Why?" Danielle asked.

"We need a motive or what led up to the murder," Brian admitted. "But if we can find who took that letter opener, we are one step closer to finding the killer."

They debated the topic a few minutes longer when Connor reached toward his mother's plate and said, "Bread!"

Lily relinquished her bread to her son and then stood up, preparing to replace hers from the basket of bread Heather had set on the buffet. Ian, seeing his wife about to get up, told her to sit back down, and he would get her the bread. But then Walt stopped them both and offered to do it. The next moment, the basket of bread floated across the room to the table while all the friends watched.

"Hey, Walt, think you could bring that platter of chicken over here?" Chris asked.

"I suppose I could do that." After the basket of bread landed on the table in front of Lily, Walt turned his attention to the platter of chicken. It lifted from the buffet and floated across the room toward them.

"Please don't drop that," Danielle teased. "I'd hate to see all that fried chicken land on the floor."

Like a flying saucer, the platter made its way to the table, and as it prepared for landing, it hovered above the center of the tablecloth for a few seconds. Yet, instead of making a slow descent, it abruptly dropped the two feet to the table, sending pieces of fried chicken bouncing across the tablecloth.

"Walt!" Danielle started to scold, yet quickly noticed Walt's attention was no longer on the platter of chicken, but on something on the other side of the room. Danielle looked to see what had captured Walt's attention, as did everyone else at the table.

Danielle's first thought: how did she get in here? Their new neighbor, Olivia Davis, stood at the end of the dining room next to the kitchen. Eyes wide, Olivia stared at the table for a moment. By her expression, she had obviously just witnessed the platter of chicken flying across the room. Olivia then looked at the faces now turned in her direction. The next moment, she vanished.

"Holy crap!" Heather blurted.

"Did you guys just see that?" Danielle squeaked.

"You mean Walt dropping the plate of chicken?" Lily asked. "What are you guys staring at?"

The mediums exchanged glances.

"Can someone explain what just happened?" Brian asked. "Aside from Walt trying to be funny."

"He wasn't trying to be funny," Heather said.

Ian stood up and began picking the chicken up off the table and returned it to the platter, which, fortunately, hadn't broken in the fall. "You guys saw something. What was it?"

"Brian, I think we have a problem," Heather announced.

"I don't like the sound of that." Brian groaned.

"I think what Heather is trying to say," Danielle began. "Whoever was trying to murder Olivia, it looks like they have succeeded. Her ghost was just here."

TWENTY-FOUR

B rian stood abruptly. He looked from Danielle to Heather. "Are
you saying Olivia is dead?"

"Nooo, don't say that!" Lily groaned.

Connor pounded on his highchair's food tray and then pointed
across the room. "Lady bye-bye!"

Chris looked at Lily. "Unfortunately, where there's a ghost,
there's a dead body."

"At least until it's cremated or decomposes," Heather quipped.

"Heather!" Lily gasped.

Heather shrugged. "Well, it's true."

"Her ghost was really here?" Ian glanced around the room as if
he could see her if she suddenly reappeared.

Danielle let out a sigh and stood. She walked to where she had
seen Olivia minutes earlier. "Yes. Unfortunately. She was standing
right here when Walt dropped the chicken."

"I wouldn't have dropped the chicken if a woman appearing out
of thin air hadn't distracted me."

"She could have at least stuck around and told us what
happened to her," Heather grumbled.

"She seemed startled at the floating platter of chicken hovering over the table," Chris said. "Unlike Walt, I missed her arrival. At first, I didn't realize she was a ghost. I thought, this is terrific; someone left the kitchen door open, and our new neighbor barged in without knocking. How are we going to explain a floating platter? And then I heard it fall on the table, and the next moment she vanished."

"You thought all that in just the few seconds she was here?" Heather asked.

"What, you couldn't?" Chris countered.

"We can't have another murder on our street!" Lily moaned.

"We really don't know if it's murder," Chris reminded. "There were no visible wounds on her body."

"That means nothing," Danielle said.

Heather looked at Brian. "Now what?"

"I need to go over there, but I have no idea what I might walk into. I can't exactly call for backup. What do I say? A ghost dropped by, so we need to find the body?" Brian asked.

"You think someone might still be there?" Heather asked.

Ian stood. "This is serious. The second murder on our street in less than a week. And we don't seem to be any closer to finding the killer."

"Your mother is going to love this," Lily muttered under her breath.

Walt stood. "I think Brian and I should go over there. I can be his backup, and the rest of you stay here and keep the doors locked."

"Instead of barging over there, can't we go upstairs first and look out the window and see what's going on over at her house?" Danielle suggested.

Brian considered the question for a moment. "Okay. Maybe we'll see something, and that'll justify me calling for backup."

"I'm going to check and make sure all the doors are locked. I'll meet you upstairs," Chris said as he stood and tossed the napkin from his lap onto the tablecloth.

"I have an idea," Walt said before calling, "Max!" A moment later, Max, who had been lying in the hallway with Hunny and

Sadie, came strolling into the dining room, panther like, while Hunny and Sadie, who now stood at the entry, leaning into the room, wanting to come too, but understood they were not allowed into the dining room until Walt gave the okay.

Walt leaned down and stared into Max's eyes. Instead of verbally repeating what message he conveyed to the cat, he remained silent. Max let out a meow and then dashed to the open doorway leading to the kitchen door. A moment later, they could hear the pet door in the kitchen swing back and forth. Max had gone outside.

"What did you tell him?" Danielle asked.

"I sent him on a recognizance mission," Walt said. "He's going to check out next door and let us know what's going on over there."

FIFTEEN MINUTES LATER, the friends stood upstairs, looking toward Olivia's house from the windows of one of the guest bedrooms. They did not turn the bedroom lights on but stood in the darkness. Ian held Connor in his arms. Chris had joined the group after checking all the doors, and Max had not yet returned. Hunny and Sadie had remained downstairs after Walt told the two to patrol the first floor and let him know if they heard anything suspicious.

The sun had set within the last hour, and next door at Olivia's, all her blinds were closed and lights off, save for the bedroom window upstairs. While its blind was closed, the room light was on. Yet they saw no movement or silhouette in the window. They could see the shadow of Olivia's car still parked in her driveway behind the house.

A meow broke their concentration. Walt turned to the open doorway leading to the hallway and spied Max's silhouette, backlit by the hall light.

"What did you find, Max?" Walt asked. Everyone in the room grew silent, waiting for Walt and Max to finish their conversation. Like the last time, whatever additional questions Walt might have had, he did not voice them out loud, but instead remained quiet.

Several minutes later, Walt turned to Brian and said, "According to Max, it's quiet over there. No one was outside. And there are no strange cars parked in the back alley or on the street by the house. There is a stack of empty boxes on the back porch."

"She's been unpacking all day," Heather said. "She was putting empty boxes outside when I was walking over here."

"I suppose we're lucky Max made it back to tell us what he did. He was rather intrigued by those boxes. Wanted to return and further investigate them. I told him no. If there is a crime scene over there, Max doesn't need to compromise it," Walt said.

"Thanks for that," Brian said.

"So now what?" Lily asked. "It doesn't sound like our neighbor's body is outside in her yard."

"I'm more concerned about a killer still lurking in the area," Danielle said.

"It's possible she wasn't murdered. She might have fallen in the house while moving some of those boxes," Chris suggested. "She could have fallen down the stairs, like Pearl."

"Pearl didn't just fall. She was pushed," Heather reminded him.

Chris shrugged. "I'm just saying if she was alone over there, carrying boxes up and down those stairs, it's possible she tripped, fell, and hit her head."

"I hope you're right," Lily said. "While tragic dying from a careless accident, it's much better than being murdered."

"You mean much better for the neighborhood," Chris said.

Lily shrugged.

Brian looked at Walt. "Before we go over there, I should call the chief and tell him what's going on."

Walt nodded. "I thought you would probably do that."

Brian stepped out into the hallway alone and called the chief on his cellphone. He was there for a few minutes. When he returned to the room, Danielle asked, "What did the chief say?"

"He wants us to go over there and look around. He doesn't want us to break in, but if the door is unlocked, he wants us to go inside and check it out."

"And of course, when you find Olivia's body, you'll say the door was open, and you heard something suspicious, which is your reason for going inside in the first place," Heather said.

"Something like that." Brian turned to Danielle and added, "He said since meeting Danielle, he forgot how to play by the rules."

Danielle shrugged. "You aren't much better."

"No argument there," Brian agreed.

"You guys, please be careful," Danielle urged. "I do not want to raise twins with a ghost."

AFTER REACHING THE FIRST-FLOOR LANDING, Walt and Brian headed to the kitchen and then went outside through the side door.

"I have the flashlight on my phone, but I'd rather not use it. If someone is out there, I don't want them to see us. Can you see okay?" Brian whispered.

"Well enough," Walt whispered back.

Holding his gun in one hand, Brian pointed toward the back gate. He wanted to enter Olivia's property from the alleyway so they could check out her car first. Walt gave a nod, and together, the two men walked to the back of the yard. Careful not to make any noise, Walt unlatched the back gate, and the two men left Marlow House's backyard.

When they reached Olivia's driveway, they noticed nothing out of order. Brian walked around her vehicle and found all the doors locked. When they finished checking out the car and driveway, they entered Olivia's backyard, both men looking for anything out of the ordinary.

The night was quiet, the only sound an occasional hooting of an owl in a nearby tree. Because of the darkness, they failed to notice the pile of cardboard boxes Max had told Walt about. Brian tripped over them, and he might have fallen to the ground had Walt not caught him with his telekinetic energy. Yet he didn't catch the boxes now scattered on the ground along the side of the house.

"Thanks," Brian told Walt. "Maybe I should use my flashlight."

While Brian turned on his flashlight app, Walt checked the back door. When Brian joined him a moment later, Walt said, "The door is unlocked."

"It is?"

"Well, it is now," Walt said.

"You unlocked it?"

"How else are we going to get inside?"

"The chief said not to break in."

"The chief also said to go in if the door was unlocked," Walt reminded him. "It's unlocked. Did you see me do anything to the door?"

"You moved the locking mechanism with your energy, didn't you?"

"And if you told Joe what I did, would he believe you? If he looked at this door, I imagine he would say it doesn't look like it was forced, so it must have been left unlocked. Of course, the chief will want us to say it was also open."

Brian shook his head and sighed. "Before those crazy witch wannabes kidnapped us, I wouldn't believe this either."

"Should we go in?" Walt whispered.

Brian handed Walt his phone, its flashlight app on. Gun ready, he moved in front of Walt and turned the doorknob. It opened, and he slowly pushed the door into the dark house. He entered first, followed by Walt, who left the door wide open.

Brian's cellphone in hand, Walt moved the beam of the flashlight app around the room to get familiar with their surroundings so they wouldn't trip over something like Brian had done with the boxes outside. Unlike the last time Walt had been in the house, it now had living room furniture.

They didn't find Olivia's body in the living room, so they headed to the kitchen. She was not there. From the kitchen, they went back out through the living room and made their way toward the staircase.

When they were about five feet from the base of the stairs leading to the second floor, an overhead light turned on, illuminating the staircase and living room. Both men froze.

"Hold it right there!" a female voice shouted.

Walt and Brian looked up and found Olivia standing on the top of the staircase, pointing a rifle at them. Neither man moved an inch.

"Olivia?" Brian stammered, his gun now pointing at her.

"You can see her?" Walt asked.

"Yes, I can see her," Brian snapped.

TWENTY-FIVE

When Walt first spied Olivia on the staircase, he assumed she was a ghost, whose energy had turned on the overhead light. He didn't find the rifle threatening, believing it was nothing more than an illusion. But if Brian could see her, he wasn't so sure she was a ghost, despite seeing her spirit over at Marlow House. Was it possible the spirit who had interrupted their dinner was actually the ghost of the woman Heather had seen with Betty? Had someone murdered Olivia's look-alike?

"I want you to put that gun on the floor," Olivia demanded, her rifle still aimed at the two men.

Brian lowered the gun, yet instead of setting it on the floor, he said, "We're not here to hurt you. I'm a police officer. Please lower your rifle."

"I don't care who you are. You broke into my house, and you pulled a gun on me. I could shoot you now, and I would be justified."

"Walt?" Brian whispered.

"It's okay. I'm watching the rifle," Walt whispered back.

Brian set the gun on the floor, never taking his eyes off Olivia.

"This is a misunderstanding," Walt said.

Olivia arched her brows while shifting the aim of her rifle, pointing it directly at Walt. "Misunderstanding? You breaking into my house was a misunderstanding?"

"We didn't break in. Your back door was unlocked and—" Walt began, only to be cut off by Olivia.

"I locked all my doors tonight. I checked them before I came upstairs. And even if it had been unlocked, which it wasn't, that doesn't mean you can just walk into someone's house."

Walt resisted the temptation to point out that many of the neighbors on Beach Drive had no shyness about walking into Marlow House uninvited. But he didn't think now was the time for levity. While he felt confident he could remove the rifle if Olivia got trigger-happy, he didn't want to take any chances. Danielle was quite serious that she didn't want to raise their children with a ghost. Because if he got himself killed, he'd be a ghost again, and while he would, of course, stick around, it was not the family life Danielle had envisioned.

"We noticed someone lurking around your house," Walt lied. "We were next door, having friends over for dinner. After we took them upstairs to show them the work we were doing on the house, Brian looked outside and noticed someone."

"It's dark out. How could you have seen anything?" Olivia demanded.

"I thought I saw someone going over your fence," Brian lied.

"Considering all that had gone on, Brian wanted to come over and check it out," Walt said.

"Why not just call the police?" Olivia asked.

"I am the police," Brian said.

"Yes, I'm aware of that. But do you always break into people's houses because you thought you saw something?" Olivia now pointed the rifle at Brian.

"We didn't break in. Your door was open," Brian lied.

"No, it wasn't. I said I checked it before I came upstairs."

"Brian called the police before we came over," Walt told her.

Olivia shifted the rifle, again taking aim at Walt. "So when are the police cars going to show up?" she snarked.

"They aren't, because we told them we were going to come over here and check it out and call if there was a problem," Brian said.

"Then I'll call the police station and ask them. But I need you both to sit over there on the floor, and don't try anything." She pointed to where she wanted them to sit.

"What are you going to do?" Brian asked.

"I'm going to call the police station and check out your story."

"I spoke to Police Chief MacDonald. He's at home. You won't reach him at the station this time of night," Brian explained.

"You didn't call anyone, did you?" she snapped.

"Yes, I did. But I called him at home. I tell you what, I can give you his number, and you call him," Brian offered.

"And how do I know it's really the police chief's number?"

"How about this, you call the police station," Walt suggested, noting her rising agitation. "Explain it's an emergency and you need Police Chief MacDonald to call you about Officer Henderson's recent phone call."

Olivia considered the question for a moment. She eventually said, "Fine. But I want both of you over there in the corner, and don't touch that gun."

After Brian and Walt sat in the corner, Olivia started down the stairs, the rifle still pointing at the men.

"Can I ask one favor?" Brian called out.

Olivia stopped walking. "What?"

"While you're coming down those stairs, can you please not point that thing at us? If you trip, you might shoot one of us."

Olivia frowned at Brian but lowered the rifle while coming down the stairs. But once she reached the landing, she again pointed the firearm at them while making her way to the coffee table near the sofa, where she had left her cellphone before going upstairs. It was one reason she hadn't called the police instead of coming downstairs with a rifle when hearing someone breaking into her house.

She sat on the sofa, resting the rifle on the coffee table while reaching for her cellphone. With one eye on the men, she looked up the number for the police station on her cellphone and then placed her call. When she got off the phone, they waited in silence for the chief to return her call.

But instead of her phone ringing, Brian's cellphone rang. Walt, who held Brian's phone, glanced down at it. "It's the chief."

Olivia frowned. "Answer it."

Walt handed Brian his cellphone.

"Hello, Chief," Brian said dully.

"I just got a strange call from the station. They claim Olivia Davis just called and wanted me to call her. Do you have any idea what's going on? Have you gone over there yet?" the chief asked.

"Like I told you earlier, I saw what I thought was someone going over the fence to her house, which is why I called you, considering the recent attempt on her life," Brian began.

"Someone is there? Aren't they?" the chief asked.

"Yes. And we took your advice; we came over to check it out. Everything was dark, the door was wide open, and we thought it best to go in, in case she was being attacked. But when we got inside, there was no one downstairs, and then the lights turned on, and Ms. Davis was there, with a rifle pointing at us."

"And she's not dead?" the chief asked.

"Obviously not," Brian said.

"Crap." The chief immediately caught himself and added, "I don't mean crap, she's alive, I mean—"

"Yeah, I get it," Brian answered. "I feel the same way." He then looked to Olivia and asked, "Do you want to talk to the chief?" Still sitting on the floor with Walt, he reached out his hand, offering his cellphone to her.

She frowned at the cellphone and shook her head. "No. What guarantee do I have that you are talking to the police chief? Anyone could have called you."

Brian turned his phone around for her to see the screen. But she was too far away to make out the caller's identification.

"You tell him to call me. He should have my number; I gave it to the person I spoke to at the police station."

Brian put his cellphone back to his ear. "Chief, she wants you to call her."

Seconds after Brian ended his call with the police chief, Olivia's phone rang. She answered it. Walt and Brian sat quietly while listening to her side of the conversation. When the call ended, she looked at Brian and asked in a shaking voice, "Was the door really open?"

"You can look at it, see it wasn't forced," Brian said.

"But someone got it open," she said, looking nervously around the room. "Does that mean someone might be hiding somewhere in this house?"

"I understand you checked the lock," Walt began. "But I also remember when Pearl had this house, she sometimes had a problem with the lock on that door. The wind could have pushed it open, and it is entirely possible what Brian saw was a cat going over the fence, not a person. But we can check out your house and make sure there's no one here."

Still sitting on the sofa, Olivia nodded. Gingerly, she moved the rifle to the coffee table, no longer pointing it at the men.

"Can we stand up now?" Brian asked.

Olivia nodded again.

As Brian and Walt got to their feet, Brian said, "We're sorry we scared you. But someone tried to kill you the other day, and we were just trying to make sure you were safe. When we found the door open, we were concerned someone was in here with you. We really couldn't call out your name or knock, and risk someone hurting you."

Olivia nodded. "I understand that now. And I am sorry for pointing a rifle at you."

Brian walked over and picked up his gun. He looked at Olivia and said, "I tell you what, Walt can stay here, and if it's okay with you, I'll check out the house and make sure no one's hiding."

"THIS WAS SUCH a mistake to move here," Olivia muttered after Brian left her alone with Walt.

Walt, who sat on a chair facing the sofa, smiled weakly at Olivia.

When first seeing her on the staircase and realizing she was not a ghost, he speculated the spirit they had seen earlier must have been the ghost of the woman Heather confused for Olivia. The double was dead, not Olivia, Walt decided.

Yet now, having the chance to study Olivia, he realized it was more complicated than a mere doppelgänger. The spirit he had seen in the dining room wore the same outfit as Olivia currently wore. Why?

Was it possible she was really a spirit and not a living person? Was she manipulating her energy to show herself to Brian? But then he remembered she had called the police station, and they obviously heard her voice since the chief had returned the call. Could a spirit use a telephone? He certainly couldn't when he had been one.

He could only think of one way to rule out the possibility Olivia was a ghost. Focusing his energy, he studied her. The next moment, she let out a little yelp and grabbed hold of her arm.

"What's wrong?" Walt asked innocently.

After rubbing her arm, she looked down at it and frowned. "It felt like someone just pinched me. Dang, did I get bitten by a spider? Can this week get any worse?"

"THE LIES just roll off our tongues," Brian told Walt after they left Olivia's house and were well out of earshot.

"We didn't have a choice."

"You were certainly quick on your feet, making up crap," Brian quipped.

"Something I learned from my wife. But you didn't do too bad yourself."

"Now we have to figure out who in the hell you saw in the dining room. It obviously wasn't Olivia." Now at the gate, Brian paused. He looked at Walt, who stood in the darkness. "It must have been that woman Heather saw with Betty. She must be dead now."

"I considered that too. But what's odd, the ghost was wearing the same outfit Olivia was wearing tonight."

"Really?"

"Yes."

Brian considered Walt's words for a minute. "Well, the first time Heather saw her, she was wearing the same thing Olivia wore later that day. This must mean something."

"But what?"

Brian opened the gate. "Is it possible Olivia is really a ghost? Maybe I'm a medium now."

The two men walked through the gate into Marlow House's backyard.

"I don't think so," Walt said.

"Why do you say that?"

Walt shrugged. "Because I pinched her."

TWENTY-SIX

The friends of Beach Drive stood in one of Marlow House's upstairs guest bedrooms, looking through the window at where Pearl used to live. They hadn't turned on the bedroom light, so they stood in darkness. Earlier, they'd watched the shadows of Walt and Brian move across the side yard to the back gate and leave the property. Since that time, they had seen very little until the downstairs light of Olivia's house turned on. Prior to that, the only light from next door came from an upstairs bedroom window. Even if it had been daylight, the fence separating Marlow House's property from its southern neighbor obscured the view of the rear side door of said neighbor's house.

"I wish Brian or Walt would at least text us," Heather said. "What's going on over there?"

"I assume they found the body, and they're probably busy calling the police," Ian suggested.

"I wish Marie or Eva were here. It would have been a lot easier if one of them could have gone over there to find out what was going on," Danielle grumbled. "At least then, Walt and Brian would know what they were walking into."

No one asked where the two spirits were this evening, because they had discussed it before dinner. Earlier that day, Danielle had asked Eva and Marie to take a trip to Astoria, where Betty's family lived, hoping to find Betty's ghost. Now, Danielle regretted the suggestion. She would rather have them here, instead of her husband walking into what might be a murder scene.

"Is that them?" Lily asked, leaning closer to the window. The friends looked outside into the darkness and watched as what looked like two shadows moved across the yard to the kitchen door. A moment later they heard Hunny and Sadie barking downstairs. The friends turned from the window and rushed from the dark room, with Ian carrying Connor.

Just as they reached the hallway, Walt and Brian stepped out from the kitchen.

"You're back?" Danielle said.

With tails wagging, Hunny and Sadie were already greeting the two men.

"We've been watching for the police to arrive. What's going on?" Heather asked.

Brian shook his head. "No one's coming."

Danielle frowned. "You didn't find her body?"

"Yes, we found her body," Walt said.

"How did she die?" Heather asked. "Was it murder?"

"Shouldn't the coroner or something show up to get her?" Lily asked.

"The coroner wouldn't want her the way she is right now," Walt said.

With a frown, Heather looked from Walt to Brian. "What's going on?"

"She's alive," Brian announced.

"What do you mean she's alive? We saw her ghost," Danielle said.

Walt pointed to the dining room. "Why don't we go in there, and we'll explain what happened."

After the group moved to the dining room, Ian put Connor back into the highchair, and the others sat down where they had been sitting earlier. Brian and Walt proceeded to tell them what had happened after going next door.

"If that wasn't Olivia's ghost in the dining room earlier, it has to be whoever Heather saw Friday morning. The woman who looks like Olivia. And it seems she's now dead. Or maybe she was already dead when Heather saw her the first time," Chris suggested.

"What's interesting," Walt began. "When we were over there tonight, Olivia was wearing the same outfit as the ghost. Same blouse, same pair of pants. She even had her hair tied back in a red ribbon like the ghost."

"Whoever was with Betty on Friday morning wore the same clothes Olivia had on later that day," Heather reminded him.

Danielle, who was finishing up what she had left on her plate earlier, paused and said, "Perhaps she's a ghost. It's possible she's harnessed her energy so people who aren't mediums can see her. That can happen."

"Brian and I already discussed that possibility. Our neighbor is not a ghost. For one thing, she made that call to the police station. We know she called someone, and they heard her, because the chief called us because of what she told the people on the other end. I've never heard of that happening before," Walt said. "When we hear a spirit, it's not sound waves in the traditional sense. Not something that can travel through a phone."

Danielle shrugged. "It doesn't mean it's not possible. We don't know all the rules. Maybe a spirit can be in one location, and someone in another location can hear them. It might even seem to come from a phone when it isn't."

"Walt also pinched her," Brian said.

Chris frowned. "You pinched her?"

"With my energy, not my fingers; that would rather defeat the purpose. If she had been a spirit, my energy would not have a body to pinch. She could only pretend to feel the pinch if she saw it coming. Which she didn't."

"What did she say?" Lily asked.

"She said something like 'ouch.'" Walt shrugged. "She assumed something bit her."

"This is bizarre," Ian muttered. "I didn't think things could get stranger around here. Boy, was I wrong."

They all sat in silence for the next fifteen minutes, finishing what was on their plates and contemplating the recent events. When they were done, Heather began clearing the table. When Danielle and Lily started to get up to help, Heather told them to sit down, yet flashed the men at the table a look that told them, *are you just going to sit there?*

They all understood what they had to do. Chris and Ian went into the kitchen while Brian held the door open between the two rooms, and Walt, who remained sitting at the table, turned to the buffet. Platters and bowls lifted off the buffet and floated toward the open doorway and into the kitchen.

Lily looked at Danielle and grinned. "I suppose there are some perks to being pregnant."

Danielle giggled. "And having a husband with telekinetic powers." The next moment, they heard something crash in the kitchen. Danielle cringed. "Someone didn't catch a plate."

When Heather returned to the dining room fifteen minutes later, she said, "I'm sorry. We had a minor problem with the control tower." She looked at Walt and said, "You might want to work on that. Chris is cleaning it up."

A few minutes later, everyone returned to the dining room, and Lily had placed Connor on the floor, who now played with Hunny and Sadie.

When Chris sat back in his chair, he said, "You know what I started thinking about in there? This whole thing with our new neighbor rather reminds me of my out-of-body experience." He was referring to his head injury during a kidnapping, which left him temporarily in a coma.

"That crossed my mind too," Lily said. Lily, like Chris, had experienced a similar out-of-body experience.

"Yes, that's an instance where someone who is alive can present as a spirit to mediums. But they also have a comatose body some-where. It sounds like our neighbor was fully conscious and appeared healthy when Brian and Walt were over there," Danielle reminded them.

Snowflakes fell from the ceiling. The mediums looked up.

"Looks like Eva is on her way," Heather mused. "I wonder if Marie is with her."

The next moment, Marie materialized in the space between the buffet and dining room table while Eva floated down from the ceiling in a shower of snowflakes. When Eva's shoes touched the floor, the snowflakes vanished.

"We're back!" Marie announced.

"Did you have any success?" Danielle asked.

Marie let out a sigh. "Unfortunately, no." The next moment, Marie reached down and picked up Connor, who had put his arms out to greet her. To the non-mediums, it looked like the small boy had taken flight. Meanwhile, Eva took a seat in an imaginary chair.

"Poor family, parents are utterly devastated. They're having her body cremated. They said the coroner is releasing the body for cremation tomorrow," Eva explained.

"We also stopped at the morgue just in case Betty had finally showed up. But she wasn't there or in Astoria with her family. I have a feeling the girl has moved on," Marie said.

"That's the feeling I get, too," Eva said.

"Are they having a funeral?" Danielle asked. "We all know spirits often show up at their funeral."

"That's typically when a spirit follows their body," Eva said. "Although that's not always the case."

"They're having a memorial service on Saturday," Marie said. "In Astoria."

"I guess it would be strange if one of us attended her memorial, especially since it's in Astoria. It's not like any of us really knew her," Heather said.

"I hate these one-sided conversations," Lily whispered to Ian. He nodded in agreement.

"Walt knew her a little," Danielle said. "She helped him with research at the library."

"I have no clue what you guys are talking about," Brian interrupted. "But don't you think you should tell Marie and Eva what happened tonight? Maybe they can figure out what's going on."

"What happened?" Marie asked.

Walt told Marie and Eva about the evening's strange events. When he was done, Eva said, "That is most curious."

"Do you have any idea what might be going on?" Heather asked.

"No. But it is most interesting, especially considering whatever you saw not only looked like your neighbor, but dressed the same," Eva said.

"What does this mean?" Marie asked.

"It means one of us needs to stay with this new neighbor and catch the spirit when she shows up next door again," Eva said. "I'll happily volunteer for this mission. I'd like to find out what mischief is underfoot."

"Why do you assume this mystery spirit would show up next door?" Danielle asked.

"If your neighbor is alive and there is a ghost that looks like her hanging around the neighborhood, and this ghost dresses like her, I would have to assume this ghost is spending some time with the neighbor. Otherwise, how else would she know what she wore each day?" Eva asked.

"Are you suggesting there is a ghost impersonating our neighbor?" Danielle asked.

"Damn, I wish I could hear what they're saying," Lily grumbled.

"Me too," Brian and Ian said at the same time.

"We have a ghost, and we have a living neighbor. If the ghost looks like the neighbor, I assume that ghost is probably some deceased relative of the neighbor. One who bears a striking resemblance to her. The clothes tell me this spirit is hanging around the neighbor. If I decided one day to dress like Heather, I would need to first visit her and find out what she was wearing. How else would I know what outfit to imagine?" Eva explained.

"Why in the hell would you want to dress like Heather?" Chris snarked.

Heather glared at Chris. "Shut up."

"Okay, you guys! Enough! What are you talking about?" Lily blurted.

Danielle repeated for the non-mediums what had been said. After the telling, both Marie and Eva went next door. They had a spirit to catch.

TWENTY-SEVEN

Marie and Eva arrived at Olivia's house Tuesday evening and found her sitting at her kitchen table, eating a bowl of cold cereal while looking at her cellphone. The phone sat on the table next to her bowl. Olivia wore a long green flannel robe over her pajamas and her hair pulled back in a red ribbon.

Marie and Eva hadn't changed their clothing—at least the illusion of clothing—since leaving Marlow House minutes earlier. Had Olivia been a medium, she would have found an elderly woman, wearing a yellow gingham fabric dress and straw hat, standing in her kitchen with a much younger, stylishly dressed woman who looked as if she had come from the early 1900s, wearing a blue-gray dress, with its hemline falling to the floor.

Like Eva and Marie's last visit, Olivia did not flinch when the two ghosts suddenly appeared. She simply kept eating her cereal while surfing on her cellphone.

"I will never understand why they're always looking at their phones," Eva said. "And to be honest, I'm not really sure why they call that thing a phone. It certainly looks nothing like the telephones from my day."

"Nor from mine. At least, not when I was a younger woman."

Eva frowned down at the bowl of cereal. "Is that what she's having for dinner?"

"It could be a late-night snack. I used to eat cereal at night when I ran out of ice cream. I rather miss ice cream." Marie let out a wistful sigh.

Eva glanced around. "It looks like her furniture may have arrived. I don't remember a kitchen table the last time we were here."

Marie walked to the wall in the kitchen where someone had stacked a row of open cardboard boxes. She peeked inside. Most were over half full, filled with items wrapped in brown paper. She glanced up at the overhead cabinets and back to Olivia, whose back was to her. Looking again at the cabinets, she willed their doors to open and quickly close. Unfortunately, too quickly, they made a loud slamming noise. Olivia jerked around and stared at the cabinets. Slowly, she stood and walked to them for a closer look.

"Careful, she's going to think the house is haunted." Eva smirked.

Olivia reached up and grabbed hold of one cabinet door. She opened it and pushed it close. It made a sound similar to what she had heard a moment earlier. Frowning, she repeated the action several times. Finally, she shook her head and returned to the table while glancing back at the cabinets several times.

Eva chuckled.

"I'm just surprised she hasn't put more of her kitchen things away. That's what I'd unpack first," Marie said. "She's put hardly anything away. Those cabinets are practically empty."

"Why? You said you didn't like to cook when you were alive," Eva asked.

Marie shrugged. "Well, I did like to eat." Marie walked through the wall leading to the living room and disappeared. A moment later, she reappeared. "Her living room is put together nicely. But I suppose the movers did that."

The cellphone Olivia had been looking at rang. She picked it up and said, "Hello?... I'm okay... It wasn't just finding the men in my living room... Yes. I should be grateful I have neighbors looking out for me. But what kind of people are these, really? I told you what I saw… I was not imagining things… No. I don't care what you say, I was not dreaming… Okay, I'll do that… I can't make that promise… And remember, what the other neighbor said. Explain that!"

There was a long silence from Olivia's side of the call as she listened to whatever the person on the other end said. Finally, she let out a sigh and said, "Okay. I'll try, but no promises… Love you, too. Bye."

Olivia tossed her cellphone back on the table and finished her cereal. She picked up the bowl and drank what milk remained. Standing, she took her now empty bowl and spoon to the sink, rinsed them both, and put them in her dishwasher. After she finished, she picked up her cellphone from the table.

Marie and Eva followed Olivia out of the kitchen, through the hallway, and up the stairs, while she turned the lights off as she left each room. She continued up the staircase and to the master bedroom. She stayed in the bedroom long enough to toss her cellphone on the bed before turning and leaving the room and going into the bathroom. Marie and Eva stayed in the bedroom instead of following Olivia into the bathroom.

"Oh my, this room looks so much different from when Pearl lived here." Marie glanced around the bedroom. A mission-style queen bed with drawers under the mattress was against the wall facing the window, with a matching dresser under said window. The bed had one side table, on the right, with a lamp. Along the wall next to the door stood a five-foot-wide bookcase filled with books.

"This looks more like a library than a bedroom," Eva noted.

Marie stepped closer to the bookshelf. "Goodness, apparently this is the first time she has ever moved."

"Why do you say that?" Eva asked.

"Who puts books away before the kitchen?"

Eva shrugged. "Olivia Davis, obviously. I guess she likes to read."

Marie frowned as she glanced over the titles in Olivia's bookshelf. She read them aloud, more for herself than for Eva. "*Adventures Beyond the Body, Ultimate Journey, The Out-of-Body Experience, Astral*

Dynamics, Mastering Astral Projection... Goodness, what an odd collection of books." Marie surveyed the rest of the books in the case. "I don't see a single novel or dictionary."

Eva shrugged. "Some people enjoy nonfiction."

"Not sure I would call these nonfiction, more science fiction."

Eva stepped closer to the bookshelves and looked through the titles. "They sound quite interesting."

From the adjacent room came the sound of a toilet flushing. A moment later, Eva and Marie heard a door open and shut, followed by Olivia entering the bedroom. Had either of them wondered if Olivia could really see them, that notion would have been dispelled when Olivia walked through Eva en route to her bed.

"Oh, I hate when they do that!" Eva said with a shiver.

The two spirits turned and watched while Olivia removed her robe, folded it, and placed it neatly along the end of the mattress. She wore flannel pajama bottoms and a matching long-sleeved shirt. Without pulling back the bedspread, Olivia climbed onto the mattress and assumed the yoga lotus position.

"What is she doing?" Eva asked.

Marie shrugged. "It looks like she's doing yoga, but she shouldn't be doing it on a bed mattress. Too much give."

The two spirits each took a seat in imaginary chairs in the far corner, facing the bed. Olivia continued to sit in the lotus position, her eyes now closed.

After about ten minutes of watching Olivia, Marie said, "If we're going to sit here and wait for our mystery ghost to show up, why don't we do something to pass the time? After all, she might not even show up tonight."

"What do you suggest?"

"I wouldn't mind playing a game of gin rummy," Marie suggested. "Have you ever played?"

"Yes. But I'm afraid you need cards to do that. And even if we found a deck of cards in this house, I can't levitate them like you can, and even if I could, I imagine if she opened her eyes and witnessed playing cards floating around the room, she wouldn't accept it as calmly as she did the slamming kitchen cabinets."

"Ahh, but she won't see these!" Marie waved her hands, and a deck of cards appeared.

Eva sat up straighter, her gaze fixed on the cards in Marie's hands. "How did you do that?"

Marie shrugged. "I wondered, if you can conjure up snowflakes and glitter, why couldn't I imagine playing cards?"

"Yes, but I have no energy left to do all that you do," Eva reminded her.

"Perhaps you aren't doing it right. After all, Walt conjured up cigars, and he still moved objects. Shall we try?"

Eva smiled. "Might as well!"

The next moment, a tabletop appeared between the two spirits —not an invisible one like the chairs they sat on, but one they could see. It floated in midair between them. Eva watched as Marie laid out the playing cards on the table.

Marie looked up at Eva. "Try to pick one up."

Eva reached for a card and attempted to pick it up, but her hand moved through it.

"Oh dear, I was afraid that might happen," Marie grumbled.

"If you can do it, I'm sure I can figure it out," Eva insisted. "That was only my first try."

"You've never levitated anything before."

"Yes, but we are talking about illusions. Remember, I've mastered glitter and snowflakes."

Both spirits focused their attention on the cards while Eva reached for one. Before she picked it up, a voice from the bed shouted, "How did you get in here?"

The two spirits immediately turned their attention toward the bed. When they did, they found two Olivias, one sitting on the bed, still in the lotus position, her eyes closed, and another standing by the bed, staring at the two spirits.

"It looks like our mystery spirit has arrived," Marie said, waving her hand over the table. Both the tabletop and cards vanished.

The eyes of the mystery spirit widened, staring dumbly at where the cards and tabletop had been moments before. She looked back at Eva and Marie. "Who are you? How did you get in here?"

"I believe the real question is, who are you? And what are you to Olivia Davis?" Marie asked.

"What kind of question is that? I am Olivia Davis! And you are in my house!"

"If you are who you say you are, who is that?" Marie pointed to the woman on the bed, still with her eyes closed, in the lotus position.

The mystery spirit turned to where Marie pointed and frowned. The next moment, she vanished. After she did, the woman on her bed opened her eyes. She looked around the room in a panic, as if expecting to see something, yet it wasn't there.

"What happened?" Marie asked.

Eva shook her head. "I have no idea."

Olivia scrambled off the bed. When she did, she rushed out of the room and into the dark hallway. After turning on the upstairs hall lights, she looked over the railing to the downstairs, the lights there still off. She turned and returned to the bedroom, closing and locking the door behind her.

Oblivious to the two spirits watching her, Olivia reached for her cellphone, which she had tossed onto the mattress when first coming into the bedroom that evening. Eva and Marie watched as Olivia sat on the edge of the mattress, cellphone in hand. She looked down at the phone and pressed the screen, making a call. She then put the cellphone by her right ear.

The next moment Olivia said into the phone, "Hi. The craziest thing happened. If you think what I told you before was nuts, this is even crazier... I was doing it again, opened my eyes, and there were two women in my bedroom... no, they aren't here now... I didn't see them leave. But they were here."

"Is she talking about us?" Marie asked as she and Eva frowned at Olivia.

"I am serious. It was an old lady. She was wearing a straw hat and a yellow gingham dress... she was playing cards with the Gibson Girl. Yes, you heard me right. The Gibson Girl. At least it looked just like her! No, I was not dreaming. They were here!"

TWENTY-EIGHT

Cellphone in hand, scrolling for interesting news stories, Danielle sat at Marlow House's kitchen table on Wednesday morning. She had set the table for breakfast and now sipped a glass of orange juice while Walt stood at the nearby stove, cooking french toast and bacon for breakfast. Danielle had offered to help, but he insisted on making the morning meal.

Danielle's cellphone rang. She answered it and talked a few minutes before ending the call.

"Was that Heather?" Walt asked, now placing the french toast on the plate with the cooked bacon.

Danielle glanced at her husband. "Yes. She wanted to know if we've heard from Marie or Eva yet. I told her I'd call her if I see them before she does."

Walt carried the plate with french toast and bacon to the table. Danielle looked at the food as Walt set the plate down. She smiled. "This was sweet of you."

"I am a very sweet guy," Walt said with a chuckle as he sat down next to Danielle.

"Yes, you are." She leaned over and gave him a quick kiss on the lips and then divided the french toast and bacon between two plates. She handed Walt a plate, while she kept one for herself.

"So you didn't see anything?" Danielle asked. Before starting breakfast, Walt had gone outside to look over at Olivia's house, curious to see if he might glimpse Eva or Marie through a window.

"Not with all the blinds closed. Although I admit, I was tempted to try opening the blinds a little so I could peek inside."

Danielle chuckled. "Great, the telekinetic Peeping Tom."

A knock came at the door, and before they had time to answer it, the door opened, and in walked Lily. She wasn't alone. Ian was with her.

"Why don't you have that door locked?" Lily asked. "Have you forgotten we have a killer in our neighborhood?"

Ian followed Lily into the house and gave Walt a hello nod before closing the door behind them.

Still sitting at the table, Danielle looked at Lily and said, "Walt was out there a few minutes ago to look over at Pearl's house. I guess he forgot to lock the door. He wanted to see if Eva and Marie are still over there."

"Are they?" Lily asked, walking to the table.

"All the curtains are still closed, and I can't see through walls," Walt said. "But I assume they are, since they haven't been back since they left last night."

"That's why we're here," Ian said. "Curious if you found out anything yet."

Now standing at the table, Lily eyed the bacon and french toast on Danielle's plate. "Oh, yummy, my favorite breakfast." Lily reached for the bacon, not intending to really grab it.

Danielle quickly placed her hand over her plate of food and glared at Lily. "Don't you dare touch my bacon."

Lily stuck her lower lip out in a faux pout. "Dang, you are mean when you're pregnant."

"If it were a cinnamon roll, you would've lost your hand," Walt teased. "I'd offer to make you some french toast, but I used up all the bread."

"Looks like sourdough," Lily said, still eying the french toast.

"It's from last night's leftover bread," Walt explained, referring to the sourdough bread Heather had brought over for dinner.

"That makes great french toast. But I was teasing. We already had breakfast." Lily turned to Danielle, and before sticking her tongue out, she said, "Walt is the nice one."

No longer guarding her plate, Danielle giggled and said, "No argument there."

Lily flashed Danielle a smile, and she and Ian joined them at the table.

"I'm surprised they haven't been back," Ian said.

"By the time they went over, it was late," Danielle said. "And if this mystery ghost showed up sometime last night, they probably figured we were already asleep."

"Yeah, and knowing Marie, no way is she going to wake Dani up," Lily said. "Marie is big on letting us pregnant gals get our sleep."

"What are you guys up to today?" Walt asked as he poured syrup on his french toast.

"Where's Connor?" Danielle asked before they could answer Walt's question.

"Kelly's watching him," Lily said.

Danielle arched her brows. "This early?"

"She needed to borrow some of my books for a blog post she's working on," Ian explained. "She was going through my bookshelf when I told her we were coming over here for a minute. We were going to bring Connor, but she told us to leave him."

"Has she decided about the wedding?" Danielle asked.

"Yes. She's going to have the wedding over at Pearl Cove. When we go back home and she finishes getting the books she needs, we're going to talk about it. They need to set a date. I guess she talked to Laura already to find out what dates work for her. Laura's going to be Kelly's maid of honor," Lily explained.

"Ahh, you'll get to see your sister," Danielle cooed.

Lily rolled her eyes. "Honestly, the entire thing is a little weird. Sure, they bonded, or whatever, but it's not like they've actually spent a lot of time together."

"Unfortunately, Kelly hasn't made many close girlfriends here. And she says she feels funny choosing one of her sisters-in-law, worrying it may cause hurt feelings," Ian said.

"I don't have a problem with Kelly asking Joe's sister to be her matron of honor," Lily insisted.

Walt cocked a brow at Lily. "But you have a problem with your sister being her maid of honor?"

Lily frowned at Walt. "Oh, shut up. I was wrong. You aren't the nice one."

Ian chuckled and reached over and patted Lily's hand. "I think in some way Lily feels Kelly stole her sister."

"That's not true." Lily did not sound convincing.

"But I keep telling her she has Danielle, and I think both Kelly and Laura are a little jealous of that friendship," Ian said.

Danielle frowned at Ian. "Really?"

Ian shrugged in response, and Lily said, "Well, they shouldn't be. Dani won't even share her bacon with me."

Danielle picked up a piece of bacon from her plate and offered it to Lily.

Lily looked at it and wrinkled her nose. "Nah, you don't have to give me your bacon. I'm just being hormonal."

"Here, take it as a sign of our friendship." Danielle grinned.

"Gee, thanks, Dani." Lily accepted the bacon and brought it to her face, giving it a sniff before taking a bite. But instead of eating the bacon, she dropped it on the table, jumped from the chair, and raced from the room, out into the hall.

"What was that about?" Walt asked, looking toward the doorway where Lily had disappeared through.

With a groan, Ian stood. "I'll go check on her."

"What just happened?" Walt asked after Ian left the room in search of his wife.

"My guess, morning sickness hit," Danielle said.

"I thought she said she was feeling good?" Walt said.

Danielle shrugged. "The way she turned green after smelling the bacon, that's my guess." Danielle reached out and picked up the abandoned piece of bacon, setting it back on her plate.

Danielle and Walt were just finishing breakfast when Lily and Ian finally returned to the kitchen.

"Are you okay?" Danielle asked as she removed plates from the table.

"Yeah. Just don't offer me any more bacon," Lily groaned. "I thought I was going to whiz through this second pregnancy without morning sickness. That breakfast I had earlier, it's gone now." Lily sat down at the table, intentionally looking away from the plates being cleared.

"I cleaned up the bathroom," Ian told them while helping himself to a glass from the overhead cabinet. He filled it with cold water and set it on the table in front of Lily.

Returning to the table, Danielle looked sympathetically at Lily. "You didn't make it?"

Lily shook her head. "Nope. I guess it serves me right. Karma for calling you mean."

Now sitting at the table, Danielle reached over and patted Lily's hand. "I'm sorry."

Lily shrugged and gave Danielle a weak smile.

Walt stood at the sink, rinsing the dishes Danielle had just cleared, when Marie suddenly appeared in the kitchen.

"Marie's here," Danielle announced as Ian rejoined them at the table.

"Hi, Marie, wherever you are," Lily said in a dull voice.

"Is Eva here too?" Ian asked.

"Eva stayed back with Olivia," Marie explained, knowing Lily and Ian could not hear her. "Some strange things happened last night."

Walt returned to the table, and Marie, who took a seat in an imaginary chair, told them what had happened at Olivia's house. When she finished the telling, Danielle repeated the tale for Ian and Lily.

"I'm confused. Marie said this mystery ghost, the one who looks like Olivia's twin, claimed to be Olivia?" Lily asked.

Marie nodded. "Exactly."

"That's what Marie said," Danielle confirmed.

"And when she was talking on the phone, she described seeing two people who looked like Marie and Eva standing in her bedroom?" Ian asked.

"Yes. But I didn't appreciate her calling me an old lady," Marie grumbled. "But she did describe my dress, and we all know Eva looks like the Gibson Girl."

Once again, Danielle repeated Marie's words for the non-mediums.

"How does she even know who the Gibson Girl is?" Lily asked. "Seriously. It's not exactly current pop culture."

Danielle looked to Lily. "She's a librarian, so she's obviously a reader."

"She is a reader, but the books she reads are odd, if you ask me," Marie said.

"Odd how?" Walt asked.

"She has a bookshelf in her bedroom, filled with books. Odd girl. She unpacked all her books, but her kitchen was practically still in boxes. She doesn't know how to properly move into a new home," Marie said.

"What kind of odd books?" Walt asked.

Marie listed off the book titles she could remember.

"What is this about odd books?" Ian asked.

Danielle repeated all that they had missed, including the list of titles Marie had rattled off.

"I'm familiar with a few of those titles," Ian said. "Most of those are about astral projection."

Lily frowned at Ian. "You mean like an out-of-body experience?"

"Not like you and Chris experienced. More like Shirley MacLaine's book *Out on a Limb*," Ian explained.

They all grew silent for a few moments, digesting what Ian had just told them while considering what Marie had described happening next door.

Danielle looked at Walt. "Is it possible? Is this ghost we have been seeing not a ghost at all, but the detached spirit of our next-door neighbor, who somehow can step out of her body and go—well, wherever she wants?"

"That's pretty freaky," Lily muttered.

"If true, it would mean her spirit left her body when she was in that plane, thousands of feet in the air, to visit her new home," Walt said.

"Kinda risky too. I've learned, not a good idea to leave your body unattended." Lily cringed at the idea.

TWENTY-NINE

After Ian and Lily returned home and Marie headed back to Olivia's house, Walt and Danielle retired to the parlor, where Danielle called Heather to tell her what Marie and Eva had experienced at their new neighbor's the night before. When she got off the phone, Walt said, "So we're going to Lucy's Diner for lunch?" He had heard her mention it while talking to Heather.

"Yeah. Heather agreed we need to get together to discuss this. But Chris has Zoom meetings all morning, but she's certain he'll be done by one. We'll meet them both over there."

"I take it, only the four of us?" Walt asked.

Danielle nodded. "After what happened to Lily here this morning, I don't imagine she's up to Lucy's. I'm afraid that grilled-burger smell will do her in. And Brian is working, so he won't be joining us."

"Is Heather going to tell Brian what Marie told us?" Walt asked.

"I'm not sure."

Walt stood. "We have a few hours before we meet them. I'll go upstairs and do a little research on astral projection."

"You think that's what might really be happening?" Danielle asked.

"There was a time I would have found the idea ludicrous. But considering everything that's happened since my former brother-in-law murdered me, I realize this world we live in is far more complicated than I ever imagined."

"That's an understatement." Danielle sat down at the desk.

Walt walked over to her and kissed her forehead. "I'm going upstairs."

"I'll stay down here and do my own research." She glanced at the laptop sitting on the desk.

ACROSS THE STREET AT THE BARTLEYS', Ian sat with his sister, Kelly, in the living room. She had just finished going through the books she needed. Connor played on the floor nearby while Sadie napped at Ian's feet.

"I hope Lily's okay," Kelly said. After Ian and Lily had returned from Marlow House, Lily had excused herself and gone to their bedroom.

"I'm afraid a wave of morning sickness hit her when we were across the street," Ian said. "She's going to try taking a nap. Hopefully it will pass," Ian explained.

"That sucks."

"But now that we're alone, we need to talk about Mom."

Kelly frowned. "Mom?"

"Lily told me about Mom crying, and how she said not to say anything to me about it."

Kelly cringed. "Umm, remember, I never told you."

Ian smiled. "Yeah, I get it."

"But what is the deal? What happened between you two?"

"Honestly, I didn't expect quite this reaction from her. Assuming that's why she's crying."

"What did you do?"

"I had a little talk with our mother about boundaries." Ian then told Kelly about his conversation with their mother, without going into too much detail.

When Ian finished the telling, Kelly let out a sigh and said, "I wish I were more like you. I'd like to have my own boundary talk with Mom. But I doubt that would work out. She's always treated you differently. It's like she accepts the fact you're an adult. And I never will be one. Not in her eyes. Oh, and after I told her I was going to accept your wedding gift, she demanded I bring over the catering menu from Pearl Cove so she could decide on the menu for the wedding. I told her I was doing that with Lily, but she told me not to be ridiculous; as the mother of the bride, that's her job."

"I suspect Lily won't be as eager to help you decide on the menu options now. You and Mom might need to handle this."

"Umm, because of the morning sickness?"

Ian nodded in response.

————

WHEN WALT and Danielle showed up at Lucy's Diner Wednesday afternoon, Heather and Chris hadn't yet arrived. Taking a seat at a booth, Walt and Danielle sat side by side, leaving the bench across from them empty for Chris and Heather.

They had just started looking at their menus when a voice said, "Hello, Walt and Danielle." Both looked up to find the art teacher, Elizabeth Sparks, standing by their table.

"Elizabeth, hi," Danielle greeted her. She glanced around, wondering if anyone was with Elizabeth. "You meeting someone here?"

"I was. They just left. We already had lunch," Elizabeth explained. "I suggest today's special. It was really good."

"Hmmm, I'll look at that. We're waiting for Chris and Heather. They're joining us for lunch," Danielle explained.

Elizabeth glanced around and looked back at Danielle. "Do you mind if I sit down for a minute before they get here? I kinda wanted to ask you something."

"Certainly." Walt motioned to the empty bench across from them.

Elizabeth sat down. "I heard about what happened to Betty

Kelty. I understand they found her body on your street. Have they made any progress on the case?"

"Not really. Did you know her well?" Danielle asked.

"Yes. We worked together on the library's art displays. She always supported the local art community, especially any programs for Frederickport's children. I haven't met the one replacing her. I understand she's your new neighbor."

Danielle nodded.

"Do you have any idea who had a problem with Betty?" Walt asked.

Elizabeth shook her head. "No, not really. She always seemed to get along with everyone. Sometimes, her persistence could be a little annoying. But in retrospect, that was probably a good trait."

"She never had any problems at the library?" Walt asked. "Anything you can think of?"

Elizabeth considered the question for a moment before answering. "The only problem she ever discussed with me was about how things at the library would disappear."

"Are you talking about theft?" Walt asked.

Elizabeth nodded in response.

"What kinds of things?" Danielle asked, yet she already knew about the stolen letter opener that had been used to kill Betty.

"We're not talking about anything that they would bother calling the police about. For example, she bought an expensive ink pen, cost her like forty bucks, claimed it disappeared from her desk."

"Ink pens are notorious for vanishing," Danielle said.

"True," Elizabeth agreed.

"What else went missing?" Walt asked.

"Random stuff, like sunglasses, coffee cups, staplers. Some of the stuff belonged to library employees, but sometimes a visitor to the library would complain that they set something down and someone took it. I know she talked to Josephine about it, but Josephine told her you expect that sort of thing when you have people constantly coming and going out of the library, especially kids," Elizabeth explained. "But she was really upset when a letter opener from one display disappeared. Now, that's something she should have made a police report on. It was an antique."

"Do you think she ever suspected any of the employees?" Danielle asked.

"We talked about it a few times. At first, she wondered if it was the janitor, because he was usually around when something disappeared. But after she got to know him better, she didn't think it could be him. For one thing, she couldn't see him taking the stuff that went missing. And it didn't sound like anything he could sell. She figured Josephine was probably right. Chances are it was kids or someone with sticky fingers. Probably no one person."

The server came to the table. Walt told her they were waiting for Chris and Heather, but he ordered something to drink for him and Danielle, while offering Elizabeth to order something for her. Elizabeth declined the offer, chatted a few more minutes after the server left the table, and then said her goodbyes. She had been gone for about five minutes when Heather and Chris finally showed up.

"Sorry we're so late," Heather said after sitting down where Elizabeth Sparks had been five minutes earlier. She scooted down the bench, making room for Chris. After he sat down, they chatted a few minutes before the server returned to the table with the beverages. She took their food orders, along with beverage orders for Heather and Chris.

After the server left the table, Heather said, "Chris and I were talking on the way over, about the possibility this was some out-of-body experience. Could that really have been Olivia I saw Friday morning? Was that who was in the dining room at Marlow House? Is this actually possible?"

"You're asking me if something as outrageous as an out-of-body experience is possible?" Walt laughed.

"We all know out-of-body experiences are possible," Chris said. "But I never imagined them being something a person could voluntarily do while not in a coma."

"Both Danielle and I researched the topic before we came here. And while it seems fanciful—I'm not sure what else it could be," Walt said.

"Now what?" Chris asked. "How do we find out?"

"If it is true, I'm not thrilled knowing our neighbor can barge into our homes whenever she wants," Heather grumbled.

"I know what you mean," Walt said with a snicker.

Danielle silently elbowed Walt and then said, "I say we confront her."

"What do you mean, confront her?" Heather said.

"After what I read today, and after what Marie and Eva witnessed, including the spirit claiming to be Olivia, and the fact after she reconnected to her body, she told someone on the phone she just saw two women in her bedroom. Two women who look like Eva and Marie. It is the only answer. We have to confront her. For one thing, she was with Betty before she was killed. She must have seen something. But she probably feels she can't say anything. After all, she was mid-flight during the murder."

"How do we confront her?" Chris asked.

"I should invite her to Marlow House this evening. On some pretense. I don't know what yet. But we can come up with something. And the four of us meet with her. Tell her what we know about her."

"Yeah, right," Heather snarked. "Like that will work out."

"Why not?" Danielle asked.

"This whole thing is crazy," Heather muttered. "And if you will remember, I told her I saw her on Friday. I was adamant. But she kept swearing she was not there."

"How was she going to admit being there?" Walt asked. "This is not something she is likely to admit to strangers."

"Then why bother confronting her?" Heather asked. "We're practically strangers to her."

"We are going to have to tell her our secret so she feels comfortable discussing her secret with us," Danielle said.

Heather frowned at Danielle. "You're going to tell her about Walt?"

"That might be a little much for her to digest right now," Walt said.

"But we could tell her we are mediums. And I could tell her about my out-of-body experience," Chris suggested.

Heather looked at Chris. "You think this is a good idea?"

Chris shrugged. "It's the only thing we can do at this point."

"And you don't think it's some look-alike spirit just trying to mess with us?" Heather asked.

"If Marie and Eva hadn't overheard the phone call, where she admitted seeing two women in her bedroom, then I would question it. I could see the possibility of some spirit messing with us," Danielle said.

Heather considered all that had just been said. "I guess you're right. And this isn't something we can ignore. After all, I really don't want her popping into my house uninvited."

Danielle looked at Walt and said under her breath, "Don't say it."

THIRTY

They had finished lunch and still hadn't come up with a plan to get Olivia to come over to Marlow House.

"No matter how we phrase the invitation, there is no guarantee Olivia will accept," Danielle said after the server removed the plates from the table and left them alone.

"It was your idea," Heather reminded.

"I know. But the more I think about it, I have this gut feeling she'll find some excuse not to come. And then what do we do?"

"Maybe we shouldn't expect her to come to Marlow House. Perhaps we should show up on her doorstep," Chris suggested.

Heather looked at Chris. "How would that work?"

Chris considered the question for a moment and smiled. "We go over there like the welcoming committee. I'll stop at Old Salts and have them make us a basket of goodies. Who can resist Old Salts' cinnamon rolls?"

"Hmm, sort of like a housewarming gift?" Danielle said.

"And we get pushy and get her to let us into the house," Chris said.

Heather eyed Chris for a moment and then gave a little shrug. "It could work. She hasn't seen you yet. And when she does, I imagine she'll invite you in without us having to ask. The trick will be to get the rest of us in with you."

Chris frowned at Heather. "Oh, shut up."

Heather grinned. "Come on, I've seen how the girls go all weak-kneed the first time they see your pretty face."

"She has a point, Chris," Danielle agreed.

"She already saw Chris," Walt said. "When she visited Marlow House during her out-of-body experience."

"Did she see him? I think what she saw was you levitating a plate, which is probably the reason for her hasty exit," Heather said.

"And it might be a reason why she'd turn down my invitation," Danielle added. "After seeing flying dinnerware taking a crash landing in our dining room, she might be reluctant to come over for a visit."

The server brought their dessert. After she left the table, they discussed how to approach Olivia that evening, and what they would say once they got in.

EVA AND MARIE sat at Olivia's kitchen table, playing cards, while Olivia unpacked the boxes for her kitchen and filled her cabinets. That morning, Eva had finally figured out how to manipulate the cards Marie had imagined, yet now she was having doubts about the playing cards, considering she had lost ten games in a row.

"Marie, there is definitely something wrong with these cards," Eva insisted.

"What do you mean?" Marie asked. "They seem to work fine. Aren't you having fun?"

"I've lost every game," Eva said.

Marie frowned. "I'm sorry. I suppose it's no fun to always lose. But you'll get better when you get the hang of this game."

"I used to play this all the time when I was alive."

"But dear, that was a century ago. You're just rusty. I could let you win, but that wouldn't be any fun for you. When I played cards with Adam and his brother, I never let them win, even when they were little. That way, when they finally won, it was something they could be proud of. You'll see."

Eva let out a sigh. "Marie, darling, I suspect these cards don't work quite like regular playing cards."

Marie frowned. "What are you suggesting?"

"When you imagined them—as I imagine snowflakes or Walt his cigar—we have ultimate control. We determine when they vanish, or the shapes of the snowflakes, or the color of glitter. In Walt's case the fragrance of the cigar, and in playing cards, what number and suit shows up on each card."

"Are you suggesting I'm cheating?"

Eva smiled. "Not intentionally. But you were so excited to create the illusion of playing cards, you didn't consider the unconscious way you've been manipulating each card. Think about it. When playing a hand, before you draw a new card, aren't you imagining what card you need to draw in order to win the hand?"

Marie's eyes widened as she considered Eva's suggestion. She looked from Eva to the cards in hand. After a moment of reflection, she gasped, "Oh my! You're right!" The next moment, all the playing cards vanished.

"I'm sorry, you didn't need to unimagine them. We could have finished the hand, at least."

Marie shrugged. "What is the point?"

The front doorbell rang. The spirits stopped talking and turned to Olivia, who had set whatever she was unpacking on the kitchen counter so she could answer the door. They followed her out of the kitchen.

WALT, Danielle, Chris, and Heather stood on the front porch of Olivia's house. The sun was still up, yet it would set within the hour. Heather held the large gift basket Chris had purchased at Old Salts Bakery. On their way back to the office after lunch, Chris and Heather had stopped at the bakery to order the gift basket, which they picked up twenty minutes earlier.

Several minutes after ringing the doorbell, the front door opened. Standing in the open doorway stood Olivia, with Marie and Eva standing behind her. Marie flashed a smile at her friends and gave a wave, while Eva simply smiled, followed by a brief snowfall, all of which Olivia failed to see.

"We come bearing gifts," Danielle announced.

"To officially welcome you to the neighborhood," Walt said.

"And to ask your forgiveness for making you uncomfortable," Heather added.

"And to meet you, I'm Chris. I live down the street." Chris turned his legendary smile on Olivia.

Heather hadn't been wrong. The instant Olivia's gaze set on Chris, she momentarily froze, staring at the ridiculously handsome man and his charming smile. Heather and Danielle exchanged glances, both speculating on what the woman might be thinking. Walt, who often found amusement at the feminine reaction to Chris, seized the opportunity. He snatched the basket from Heather and said, "Here, let me bring this in for you. It's rather heavy."

Before Olivia knew what had happened, Walt was already in her house, with the others close behind him. He didn't ask, but he headed straight for the living room coffee table, where he deposited the basket.

Flustered, Olivia shut the front door and joined her uninvited guests in the living room, while the two lingering spirits each took a seat in an imaginary chair to watch the events unfold.

"Umm, what do we have here?" Olivia asked awkwardly as she looked down at the basket now sitting on the table.

Not waiting to be asked, Both Danielle and Heather sat on the sofa while Danielle said, "A little welcome gift. It's from Old Salts Bakery here in town. They make the most amazing cinnamon rolls."

Danielle thought her neighbor's smile was forced when she looked at her and Heather, who sat on the sofa as if they didn't intend to leave any time soon. She felt a little sorry for the woman, especially when Walt and Chris joined them on the sofa, leaving Olivia standing in the living room by the coffee table.

"Umm, this is really nice of you all. Maybe we can visit later, but I really need to finish unpacking the kitchen."

"Oh, do you have food sitting out?" Heather asked. "Something that might spoil?"

"Umm, no, but…"

"Why don't you sit down?" Walt pointed to the chair facing the sofa. "We promise we won't stay long, but we have something we need to talk to you about."

Olivia glanced from Walt to the others and then to the empty nearby chair. Reluctantly, she sat down, now facing her uninvited neighbors, who made no attempt to leave.

"What did you want to talk to me about?" Olivia asked.

When Walt had sat down a moment earlier, he noticed a book on the coffee table next to the basket. Its title was one he had looked up when researching astral projection earlier that day. Seeing it as a perfect opportunity to open the conversation, he picked up the book, looked at it, and then turned the cover to Olivia.

"This looks like a very interesting book," Walt said.

"Umm, yes, it is." Without thought, Olivia jumped up from the chair, snatched the book from Walt, and sat back down, hugging the book to her chest. "I like to read."

"So do I," Walt said. "The next time you come to Marlow House, you'll have to visit our library."

"Umm… thank you, but I really must—"

"Do you believe in astral projection?" Walt asked, cutting off what Olivia was about to say.

Olivia glanced briefly at the book in her arms and then back to Walt. She shrugged. "I suppose I believe anything is possible. It's an interesting topic."

"A long time ago I read *Out on a Limb* by Shirley MacLaine," Danielle said. "Have you read it?"

Olivia nodded. "Yes."

"You know what I find fascinating about astral projection?" Walt asked.

Olivia shrugged and clutched the book tighter.

"You know what a medium is, right?" Walt began.

Olivia furrowed her brow and continued to hug the book. "Someone who claims they can communicate with people after they die."

"I wonder where they're going with this conversation," Marie asked Eva.

"I think I know," Eva whispered.

"There are different types of mediums," Danielle said. "Some mediums can actually see the spirits of dead people, not only communicate with them. The spirit can look like the person looked when alive. Sometimes the vision is transparent, and other times a medium might actually mistake a spirit for a living person."

Olivia looked at Danielle. "You believe in mediums?"

Danielle smiled. "I do."

"In astral projection, the spirit leaves the body of a living person," Walt said. "And then it returns to the body."

"I've read the book," Olivia said.

"And you know what can happen when that type of spirit encounters a medium?" Chris asked.

Olivia looked at Chris and shook her head. "No."

"The medium can see the spirit, just as a medium can see the spirit of a dead person," Chris explained.

"I don't remember ever reading that," Olivia said.

"It's true," Heather said.

Olivia looked at Heather. "How do you know?"

Heather smiled. "Because I am a medium. And so are Chris, Danielle, and Walt. I saw you—or your spirit—Friday morning, when you were up in that airplane. Well, your body was in the airplane, but your spirit decided to check out your new house."

Olivia jumped to her feet, still clutching her book. "You should all go."

"You know it's true," Danielle said. "We saw you the other night. When you barged into Marlow House while we were all having dinner. That's why Brian and Walt came over here. We were afraid whoever had tried to blow up your car had finally succeeded and killed you. They expected to find your body over here and hoped your spirit was still around so they could find out who killed you. They were surprised when it was your living body they found."

"No, this can't be true." Olivia shook her head in denial.

"You witnessed something at Marlow House that scared you," Walt said. "But it's really not much different from astral projection. While you have mastered the ability to disconnect from your body, I have mastered telekinetic powers and can use my energy to move items like that plate you saw flying across our dining room. Or that basket." Walt looked at the basket from Old Salts. It rose off the table.

Olivia fainted.

THIRTY-ONE

O livia opened her eyes and found her four neighbors standing by the sofa, anxiously looking down at her. Blinking, she tried to remember what had just happened. She glanced over to the nearby coffee table, where Walt Marlow had set the basket of pastries, and it all came back to her. Walt, Danielle, Chris, and Heather had been sitting on the sofa, talking about mediums, astral projection, and telekinesis when the basket took flight. Then everything went black. But now she was the one on the sofa, as if she had been napping, and by their looks, they had been waiting for her to wake up.

"You should see a doctor," Danielle said.

Olivia frowned and sat up while rubbing her head. The others moved back a few steps, giving her more room. "I don't feel like I hit anything."

"No, because Walt intervened again," Danielle said. "I'm serious about the doctor. We only met you five days ago, and you've fainted twice. That's not normal."

Now sitting on the sofa, Olivia shook her head. "No. I'm okay. With the move and all, I haven't been eating well this last week. And

I need to drink more water. Plus, it's kind of freaky when baskets fly around the room."

"Sorry about that," Walt said. They all sat back down, with Heather and Danielle sitting on the sofa with Olivia, and Chris and Walt each taking a seat on nearby chairs. "I was proving a point."

"I'm kinda surprised you didn't faint when you saw that bomb under your car. I know that would freak me out more than Walt's trick," Heather said.

"How can this be true?" Olivia muttered, now leaning forward, her elbows resting on her knees as she buried her face in her palms.

"Let me get you some water." Heather stood and dashed from the room. A few minutes later, she returned with a glass of water and found Olivia still with her face in her palms as the others looked on silently.

Shoving the glass of water at Olivia, Heather said, "Drink this." After Olivia reluctantly took the glass, Heather snatched a cinnamon roll from the basket and handed it to Olivia. "Maybe you need something to eat, too."

They all sat quietly while Olivia sipped the water, set the glass on the coffee table, and took a bite of the cinnamon roll. After a few moments, her expression changed from confusion to wonder. She looked down at the cinnamon roll. "Wow, this is amazing."

"Yeah, they are pretty darn good," Danielle agreed.

Olivia looked around the room at all the faces quietly watching her. Hesitantly, she asked, "Umm, you want some?" She motioned to the basket with the cinnamon roll in her hand.

"No, thank you," Walt said as the others shook their heads. "Are you ready to talk about this? About your adventures in astral projection?"

Olivia took another bite of the cinnamon roll, leaned forward, and set it in the basket. Sitting back on the sofa, she licked the sweet residue off her fingers before saying, "I'm not sure about all this. Too far-fetched."

"You are the one doing the astral projection," Heather reminded her. "Are you suggesting you didn't do it?"

Olivia shook her head. "About the medium stuff. You guys are seriously saying you can communicate with ghosts?"

"There are two of them in the room with us right now," Heather said.

Olivia frowned at Heather. "Are you suggesting Pearl Huckabee's ghost is haunting this house?"

"Nah, Pearl's ghost hung around for a little while after she died," Heather said. "Actually, she made a better neighbor as a ghost than when she was alive. But after she did what she needed to do here, she moved on."

"Last night, you made a phone call to someone. You told them there were two women in your bedroom. One was an older woman, wearing a yellow gingham dress and straw hat. The other was a younger woman, who you said looked like the Gibson Girl," Danielle said.

Olivia narrowed her eyes at Danielle. "Is my house bugged?"

"No. At least, not in the way you suggest." Danielle pulled her cellphone out of her jacket's pocket. She opened her photo app and showed a picture to Olivia. "Is this one of the women in your house last night?"

Olivia stared dumbly at the image. After a moment, she looked at Danielle. "Who is she?"

"She was a dear friend of ours who passed. Her name is Marie Nichols. Her spirit decided to stick around. She is here now with us. And she witnessed your spirit leave your body last night. And she listened to you make that phone call."

Danielle took back her phone. She flipped to another photo, this one of the portrait of Eva in the museum. She handed the phone back to Olivia.

"The Gibson Girl," Olivia muttered, staring at the image.

"Her name was Eva Thorndike. When you get around to visiting the local museum, you'll find this portrait there. She bears a remarkable resemblance to Dana Gibson's drawing. Eva was a silent screen star, and she died about a hundred years ago. She, like Marie, has decided not to move on. They are both here with us now."

Olivia shook her head and handed the cellphone back to Danielle. "This is insane."

"As insane as you leaving your body?" Heather asked.

Olivia slumped back on the sofa. She looked from Heather to the rest of them. "You are all mediums?"

"We are," Danielle said, "but please keep this between us. While a few people are aware of our gifts, many of our friends aren't."

"And you all live on this street?" Olivia asked.

"Yep. We are the mediums of Beach Drive," Heather chirped.

"But I'm not a medium, so how could I see a ghost?" Olivia asked.

"When your spirit leaves your body," Chris explained, "you can communicate with spirits of those who've died yet haven't moved on. Even if your physical body has not died."

"What makes you think this is true?" Olivia asked.

"Over three years ago, I suffered a head injury," Chris began. "I was in a coma for a few days, and during that time, my spirit moved from where my body was in Arizona back to Frederickport. I wasn't dead, but Danielle could recognize and communicate with my spirit when it disconnected from my body."

Olivia considered Chris's words for a moment. Finally, she said, "Maybe it explains how a medium like Danielle could communicate with your detached spirit, and you also claim to be a medium. But I'm not. So I don't understand why you believe a non-medium's spirit would suddenly become a medium."

"We have another friend who was in a coma. She is not a medium, yet while out of her body, not only could I see her, she could see spirits," Danielle explained.

Once again Olivia grew quiet while digesting the information. Finally, she said, "The waitress at Pier Café told me about my neighbors. And from what she said, you all moved here at different times."

"Carla," the mediums chorused.

"Yes, I believe that was her name. Were you all friends before you moved here? The way she explained it, you met here."

"True, we met each other after we moved to Frederickport," Danielle said.

"Then, I don't understand. I guess I can believe in mediums. After all, astral projection is real. But how is it four mediums are living on the same street?" Olivia asked.

With a smile, Danielle glanced at Eva and then back to Olivia. "Sometimes the Universe has a reason for bringing certain people— certain spirits—together. I believe we were all destined to meet each other, to be part of each other's lives. And I suspect the Universe has a reason for bringing you here."

"If so, I wonder what the reason could be. To make me more miserable? Ever since I got here, things keep going wrong," Olivia grumbled.

"Why don't we focus on your visit here on Friday morning, when you were with Betty," Chris suggested.

Olivia looked at Heather. "When I picked up my keys at Marlow House, it freaked me out the way you looked at me. When I saw you earlier that morning and looked you right in the eyes, I never imagined you could actually see me. I never considered that was possible. But then later, you came to my house and confronted me. I wasn't sure what to think."

"But you thought it might be possible," Heather said. "Because you told me you wouldn't expect an apology from me after the police received the video from the airport. Why else would you say that?"

"True. I wondered if maybe you had seen me. I don't understand how all this works," Olivia said.

"Tell us about that day," Walt asked.

With a sigh, Olivia leaned back on the sofa. "I was on that flight, eager to get here. I'm not a big fan of flying and wondered if I could leave the plane without my body. So I gave it a try, and then suddenly I was standing in my new house. But right after I arrived, a woman ran by the kitchen window. I learned later it was Betty Kelty. At the time, I was just wondering who was going through my yard, so I followed her."

"Did you witness her murder?" Chris asked.

"Goodness no! In fact, I had no idea she had been murdered until the police questioned me. And when I found out who she was, I was shocked to learn she was going to be my boss. None of it made sense."

"What happened after you walked down the street with her?" Heather asked.

"I followed her. She stopped at someone's house and knocked on the door. She waited a while, and when they didn't answer, she turned around and started back down the street. I wondered if she was going back to my house, so I kept following her. But then a car pulled up beside her. Right through me. That freaked me out. Having a car drive through me. The next moment, I was back on the airplane."

"You say the car pulled up next to Betty? Do you know if it stopped?" Walt asked.

Olivia nodded. "Yes. Like I said, I was walking next to her. Of course, she thought she was alone. And then this car, it just plows through me and stops. Like I said, it freaked me out."

"Did you see who was in the car?" Walt asked.

Olivia shook her head. "No, not really. I mean, sort of. Kinda the back of their head. But they were wearing something like a hoody or something covering their head. Like I said, it happened so fast. I'm pretty sure there was just one person in the car."

"Can you describe the car?" Chris said.

"No. Not really." Olivia closed her eyes, trying to visualize that point in time. After a moment she said, "There was a bear hanging on the rearview mirror."

Walt frowned. "A bear?"

Olivia flashed Walt a smile. "A little pink stuffed bear. Like one of those Beanie Babies."

"That could be our killer," Heather said.

Danielle looked to Walt. "We need to tell the chief."

"The chief?" Olivia asked.

"Police Chief MacDonald," Danielle explained.

"Isn't he going to wonder where you got this information?" Olivia asked.

Danielle chuckled. "Yes. And I can already hear him groaning after I tell him."

Olivia frowned. "And he will believe you?"

"Like I said, a few of our friends know about our abilities. The chief is one of them," Danielle explained.

"There is one thing that just makes little sense to me," Walt said.

"You think any of this makes sense?" Olivia muttered.

Danielle looked at Walt. "What's that?"

"Someone put a bomb in Olivia's car. They tried to kill her. We all assumed it was because she was involved with Betty's murder. But if all Olivia tells us is true, then why did someone try to kill her?"

Heather groaned. "It was probably my fault."

They all looked at Heather. "What do you mean?" Danielle asked.

"I kept insisting I saw Olivia that morning with Betty, right before her murder. The killer must know I told the police I saw her, and they think she really was there that morning and might be a witness. I could have gotten Olivia killed!"

THIRTY-TWO

"I don't blame you," Olivia told Heather. "And I have an apology I need to make to Walt and Danielle."

They all looked at Olivia.

"For what?" Danielle asked.

"When you saw me in your dining room last night, it wasn't the first time I came into Marlow House that way."

"You did it on Saturday, didn't you?" Walt asked.

Olivia turned to Walt. "How did you know?"

"Max saw you," Walt said.

Olivia frowned. "Max? Your cat?"

"Yes. Some animals can see spirits. Not sure if it's all animals, but dogs and cats can," Danielle explained.

Olivia scrunched up her nose. "Really? That's interesting."

"Did you look in our window once? The bedroom window upstairs?" Danielle asked.

Olivia grimaced. "I'm sorry. When I realized it was your bedroom, I left. But I was just so curious about Marlow House. When I was a kid and visited Frederickport with my mom and sister after we moved, we'd go by Marlow House, and back then no one lived there. It seemed spooky, and we always thought it was haunted.

I just wanted to see inside. I figured since no one could see me, it really wasn't wrong. But I realize now it was wrong on both counts."

"I can understand that," Heather said. "Come on, who wouldn't be tempted to explore? Especially if you believed there's no way someone could catch you?"

"Please keep those books on astral projection away from Heather," Chris groaned.

Heather rolled her eyes at Chris. "That's not something you need to worry about. I don't like the idea of leaving my body unsupervised."

Olivia turned to Heather. "When you came over here and claimed you saw me with Betty Friday morning, I didn't think it was possible, but you were so insistent, sounded so sincere, and I knew I had been with her that morning. Heavens, if I were you, I would have been terrified to confront someone who I believed was a killer. In fact, well, you took an enormous risk doing that. What if I had been the killer? I could have hurt you."

Heather shrugged. "I wasn't all that reckless. I had backup."

Olivia frowned. "You did?"

"Marie was with me," Heather explained.

"Marie? Isn't that the name of one of the ghosts you say is here?"

"Yes. And like Walt, Marie has telekinetic powers," Heather explained.

"I think we need to call the chief," Danielle interrupted. "He needs to know about the car that ran over Olivia."

EDWARD MACDONALD LOUNGED on a recliner in his living room, watching television while his sons sat in the kitchen, finishing their homework. From the side table, his cellphone rang. He picked it up and looked at it. Danielle was calling. He set the phone back down, picked up the remote, muted the television, and then picked up the cellphone again.

"Evening, Danielle."

"That woman Heather saw with Betty before she died, let's just say it was a ghost. She had nothing to do with the murder."

"Who was she?"

"It's a long and, well, unbelievable but true story."

"Isn't it always with you?"

"I suppose. I'll explain it all later. But for now, I wanted to tell you what this woman saw."

"You mean what this ghost saw?"

"Whatever. She didn't witness the murder, but not long after she left Pearl's house following Betty, a car drove up next to Betty and stopped. The car drove right through her, which freaked her out."

"Betty wasn't hit by a car."

"No. I'm talking about the woman with Betty."

"You mean the ghost with Betty?"

"Oh crap. I thought this would be easier if I just gave you the abbreviated version for now, but I see this is not going to work."

"What are you talking about?"

"Please just listen."

"I'm listening."

"Do you remember that book by Shirley MacLaine, *Out on a Limb*, and how she experienced out-of-body experiences, like the ones Chris and Lily had when they were in a coma, but in MacLaine's case, she wasn't in a coma?"

"I never read the book, but I heard about it. So?"

"Olivia Davis can do that. Heather saw her on Friday. But that was Olivia's spirit experiencing an out-of-body experience while her body was still on the plane."

"Danielle, you're not supposed to drink when you're pregnant."

"I'm not drinking! Focus, Chief!"

"WHAT DID HE SAY?" Heather asked Danielle when she got off the phone with the chief.

"Not much. I think he's trying to process what I just told him."

"It is a lot to process," Chris said.

Heather looked at Olivia. "I'm curious about something."

"What?"

"How did you get into this astral projection thing?" Heather asked.

"I'm rather curious about that myself," Walt said.

Olivia shrugged. "Umm… well, it's kind of a long story."

"We have the time," Chris said.

Olivia glanced around the room, noting the anxious way they all looked at her. She took a deep breath, exhaled, and then said, "I married my high school sweetheart. His family was very religious; mine wasn't. In fact, his father is a pastor. Before we got married, I joined his church."

"Interesting way to solicit new church members," Heather muttered under her breath.

Danielle silently listened with the others. She wondered how all of this led up to Olivia playing with out-of-body experiences.

"Let's just say my marriage didn't quite work out like I thought it would. After our youngest graduated from high school, I left my husband. It was, well, not what you would call an amicable divorce. My sons were furious with me. And, well, my church family sided with my husband. To make matters worse, I never had a job before, and I didn't have any money."

"What did your husband do for a living?" Heather asked.

"He owned… owns… a construction company in my hometown. Both of our sons work for him."

Heather frowned. "If you guys owned a construction company, isn't it half yours?"

Olivia smiled at Heather. "The company was in my husband's name. I never had my own bank account. I would get a monthly allowance from my husband to pay the household expenses, like groceries."

"But you're a librarian?" Heather said.

"I am now. We were living in Texas when I met my husband. My parents moved not long after I got married. Dad got a job in California, so I only saw them once or twice a year. When I decided to leave my husband, like I said, I had nothing. They sent me a plane ticket. I moved in with them. I ended up going to college, with their help, and I became a librarian."

"And how did this get you to experiment with astral projection?" Chris asked.

"I had spent almost two decades being the obedient wife. Being a wife and mother was my entire identity. And then I wasn't anymore. I started reevaluating my beliefs. My faith, the church. What they had taught me. I also spent more time reading the New Testament and realized that what my father-in-law preached from the pulpit didn't align with the teaching of Jesus. Jesus taught love and forgiveness, but my father-in-law preached hate and control."

"I suspect you started reading more than the Bible at this point," Walt said.

Olivia smiled at Walt. "Yes. I read about different religions, philosophy, new age. When I started reading about astral projection, I found it so fascinating. I ended up reading everything I could find on it. And one day, well, I did it."

"When did you have your first out-of-body experience?" Heather asked.

"About six months ago," Olivia said.

"As I mentioned, I had a similar experience when I had a head injury. And one thing I learned: it is frightening to be separated from your body. Because when you do that, you no longer have control over what happens to your body. Personally, I wouldn't willingly want to do that again," Chris said.

Olivia looked at Chris. "I understand what you're saying. But there is power in having full control over one's spirit. Because we never have total control over our body. Never. Especially if you are a woman. But if we can remove our mind from that body, then we never need to feel pain ever again. No matter what someone does to me, if they beat me or torture me, no matter what hell they inflict, I can simply remove myself from this body and be free. Free from pain. Free from physical abuse."

THIRTY-THREE

On Thursday morning Danielle stared unimpressed at her bowl of oatmeal. Instead of sugar, she had added frozen blueberries, and instead of cream, she used milk. With the tip of her spoon, she repeatedly stabbed the clump of icy blueberries that had formed after adding milk. She jabbed them several times, pushing the clump under the milk, trying to separate the blueberries.

"I should go next door and ask Olivia for one of the cinnamon rolls she offered us last night." Danielle looked across the table to Walt, who sat quietly reading the morning newspaper while drinking his coffee. "Why don't we have any cinnamon rolls?"

About to take a sip, Walt paused and looked across the table at Danielle. He smiled. "Because you ate all that we bought."

"Why didn't we buy more?"

"Because you decided to cut down on sugar and not buy as many as we normally do. Remember?"

Danielle wrinkled her nose. "I'm too old to start listening to Cheryl."

"Why, because she's dead?"

Danielle shrugged. "I miss my cinnamon rolls."

Walt took a sip of his coffee.

"I miss coffee too," she grumbled, and then turned her attention back to her breakfast.

After returning from Olivia's house the previous evening, they had stayed up late, rehashing all that they had learned. Worried that Olivia might still be a target if the killer believed she had seen something, Marie had agreed to stay next door and monitor things with Eva, on the condition Olivia loan them a deck of playing cards. Danielle could only imagine what Olivia thought of it all, especially after she was left alone with the two spirits and witnessed cards floating. She wondered if Olivia might decide to have an out-of-body experience and join the card game. Danielle smiled at the thought and at the absurdity of her life.

A knock came at the door, followed by, "It's Heather!"

Without standing, Walt focused his energy on the doorknob. The next moment, the door swung open.

Heather walked into the house, followed by Brian. With a cup of hot tea in hand, Heather said, "Good morning. I'm all out of coffee, and Brian stopped over before going to work, and he's not really a tea guy."

Walt motioned to the coffeepot with his mug. "Help yourself."

"Morning, Brian," Danielle greeted. "Heather."

Heather took her mug of tea and sat at the table with Walt and Danielle while Brian said a quick hello and walked to the coffeepot. He grabbed a mug from an overhead cupboard and began pouring himself some coffee. "Sounds like Olivia might have been in an abusive relationship."

"Yeah, Walt and I were talking about that last night," Danielle said. "I thought it telling how she said she needed control of her spirit to avoid physical pain. Yet it didn't surprise me considering what Marie had told us."

Brian walked to the table with his coffee and sat down. "After Heather told me about last night, I asked myself, is anything ever going to surprise me again?"

Danielle chuckled. "You just accepted the fact our new neighbor can travel without her body?"

Brian shrugged. "Considering Marie's ghost doesn't have a problem giving me a slap when she finds me annoying, why not?"

"Marie is more a pincher than a slapper," Heather reminded him.

"She also likes those earlobes," Danielle added.

"I also knew about Chris's and Lily's out-of-body experiences. And I remember when MacLaine's book first came out, and all the talk of her claiming to have this experience. Of course, at the time, I thought she was just another Hollywood crackpot. But if it's possible for it to happen to someone while in a coma, why not someone who isn't in a coma?"

"I like the way you are so open-minded and willing to accept these things," Heather said.

Brian looked at Heather and chuckled. "After you see Walt chatting with a mountain lion, it tends to get easier to accept other insane ideas."

Walt smiled and then said, "I heard you worked late last night."

"Yes. I was going to come over to Heather's afterwards, but she said she wasn't afraid to stay home now that she didn't see Olivia as a threat."

"Brian told me he knows whose car it was that ran over Olivia," Heather interjected. Both Walt and Danielle turned to Brian.

"We're fairly certain it was Betty's car," Brian said.

Danielle frowned. "Betty's?"

"Last night after the chief called me about the stuffed animal on the rearview mirror, I remembered seeing that somewhere. Drove me nuts. And then I went to where we have the car stored, and sure enough, there is a stuffed bear hanging from the mirror."

"You impounded the car?" Danielle asked.

"It's evidence in a crime. And for now, we have it locked up. Which is a good thing. Had we turned the car over to her family, they might have removed the bear or contaminated the car. They're going through it again. If what she says is true, and the driver killed Betty, then they may have left some DNA evidence in the car."

"I thought they already went through it," Danielle asked.

"Yes, but the chief wants them to go through it again. The only prints they came up with the last time were Betty's and Josephine's, both of whose we would expect. Josephine admitted driving the car that morning, and it is Betty's car," Brian explained.

"Now what?" Walt asked.

"After I leave here, I'm going down to the station. I spoke to Darren Newsome, who agreed to meet me down there at ten thirty. He's the only library employee we haven't interviewed yet," Brian said.

"That's the new janitor, the one who replaced that Kenny guy," Heather explained.

"We haven't been able to talk to him," Brian said. "He left Friday morning for Bend. Josephine told me he was supposed to be back today and gave me his phone number."

"Possible suspect?" Walt asked.

Brian shook his head. "No. He's only been at the library for a couple of weeks. Was hired to replace Kenny. So he wasn't even working at the library when the letter opener went missing. But maybe he saw something."

———

AFTER BRIAN ARRIVED at the police station on Thursday morning, he headed for the chief's office while checking the messages on his cellphone. Not paying close attention to his surroundings, focusing more on the cellphone in his hand than where he was walking, he pushed open the door and stepped into the chief's office, but stopped abruptly when he looked up and spied the chief standing with Joe at his desk. By the serious expressions of both men, and the way the chief rested one hand on Joe's right shoulder, Brian knew he had just blundered into a private conversation.

Both men looked up, and Brian immediately apologized for walking in without knocking and started to back out when Joe said, "That's okay, Brian."

The chief dropped his hand from Joe's shoulder, and Joe said, "I was just leaving." He started to walk away when Brian asked, "Did you get to talk to Josephine Barker again?"

Joe paused and looked back at Brian. "No, I tried calling her, but she's in interviews all day for the new position at the library." He looked at the chief and said, "Thanks." After leaving the office, Joe closed the door behind him.

"Is Joe okay?" Brian asked.

The chief motioned to one of the empty chairs and took a seat behind his desk while saying, "Charlie Cramer called him this morning." Charlie Cramer had been one of Joe's best friends from high school. He had recently been arrested for the murder of two of Joe's other high school friends and for the attempted murder of Heather. He was currently being held without bail, pending trial.

"What did he want?"

"He wants Joe to visit him."

"Joe's not going to, is he?" Brian asked.

The chief shook his head. "I don't think so, but I'm not sure."

The desk phone rang. MacDonald answered it, and then after he hung up, he looked at Brian and said, "Darren Newsome is here."

"DO you have any idea who did this?" Darren asked after Brian joined him in the interrogation room and sat down at the table across from him.

"It's still early in the investigation," Brian said. "I understand you've been with the library for two weeks?"

Darren nodded. "That's right. I still can't believe someone murdered Betty. I can't imagine why anyone would hurt her. She was a nice lady."

"When was the last time you saw Betty?" Brian asked.

"Thursday. I worked that day and was planning to leave on Friday morning. My parents live in Bend. I was going to visit them."

"And you saw Betty that day?"

"Yes. That was the last time I saw her."

"How did she seem? Did she act like anything was wrong? Anything bothering her?"

Darren considered the question for a moment and then shook his head. "No. Not at all. I think she was excited about her promotion. She told me she was going over to Josephine's the next morning to inventory files the library has stored over there. They wanted to do that before Josephine's last day. She talked a little about the new librarian who was coming in this week. I think she's starting tomorrow. Josephine told me the new woman is going to be the head librarian now. I guess Josephine's going to stick around a little longer to get someone hired for Betty's old job. As for Betty, she didn't seem upset about anything. Just the opposite."

"You don't remember her having a problem with anyone?" Brian asked.

Darren shook his head. "No. But I really didn't know her that long. I just moved from Bend right before I started the job. It's not like she ever confided in me about her personal life."

"Did you ever notice anyone Betty was especially close with?"

Darren shook his head.

"Anyone that might have acted strange toward Betty. Or perhaps Betty acted strange toward them?"

"Not that I noticed." He paused a moment and then said, "Well, the only thing that I can think of, there is this one woman who I've seen a few times at the library. Josephine told me she works at the museum. The first time I saw her, I was emptying some trash cans, and she asked me if I was the new janitor. I introduced myself. Then she asked me if I was married. I said no. And then she said if I liked my job, it would be a good idea not to get too friendly with Betty, because that's why the last janitor left."

"What did she mean by that?" Brian asked.

Darren shrugged. "I sorta took it to mean they got romantically involved. But I could be wrong. I didn't ask her what she meant, and I didn't ask Betty. I just asked Josephine who the woman was."

"Who was it?" Brian asked.

"Sorry, I don't remember what she said the name was. It was an older woman. I just know Josephine said she worked at the museum."

"Is there anything else?"

Darren shook his head. "No."

"Josephine tells me she ran into you at the library early Friday morning before you left for Bend."

"That's right. I had left my jacket in the back room, so I stopped to pick it up before heading off to Bend. It was around six, I think. She was picking up a box of files she wanted to add to the inventory and told me Betty had loaned her the car. I wasn't surprised. Betty had already told me she was going to Josephine's early that morning. I just can't believe after she left Josephine's, someone killed her."

THIRTY-FOUR

Walt walked into the parlor at Marlow House on Thursday afternoon and found Danielle sitting at the desk, talking on the phone, with Max curled by her feet, sleeping. Walt took a seat on the sofa, quietly waiting for her to get off the phone.

"That was Heather," Danielle said after ending the call a few minutes later. She turned to face Walt, careful not to disturb the sleeping cat. "She talked to Brian after he interviewed the library's janitor." Danielle then told Walt what the janitor had told Brian about the remarks a woman from the museum had made about a possible relationship between Betty and Kenny.

"Who was this woman?"

Danielle shrugged. "He doesn't know. For some reason, he can't talk to Josephine until tomorrow. But I'm sure curious. This Kenny guy works for Adam. And he could be the killer."

"Even if he had a personal relationship with Betty, it doesn't mean he was responsible for her death."

"Statistically, women are more likely to be murdered by an intimate partner than a stranger. And Kenny never mentioned his personal involvement with Betty," Danielle reminded him.

"It doesn't sound like the museum gossip actually knew if there was a personal involvement or not."

Danielle arched her brows. "Museum gossip?"

"What else should I call her? We don't know her name."

"There are a lot of docents at the museum—many of whom are older women—but my gut feeling, he was talking about Millie Samson."

"Then I guess Brian will be talking to Millie."

"I think we should go to the museum."

Walt arched his brows. "Why?"

"Until Brian talks to Josephine, he won't know for sure if it's Millie or someone else. And it sounds like he can't talk to her until tomorrow. I think we should go down to the museum and see if Millie is working today."

Walt shook his head. "I don't think we need to butt into the police's investigation."

"I'm not going to butt in. But if it is Millie, and Brian interviews her about it, chances are she won't be as open as she might be if she was just—as you say—gossiping with a friend. She might not want to say anything, knowing it's a murder investigation. Especially if it's just a feeling she had after watching some interaction between the two."

Walt shook his head. "I don't think it's a good idea."

"I hate sitting here and doing nothing while a killer is running free. Someone who murdered a woman just a few doors down from our house. I want to do something to help."

"But—"

"How about if I run it by the chief first?"

"I SHOULD HAVE KNOWN you'd talk Edward into this," Walt said when he pulled the Packard up to the museum.

A few minutes later, Walt and Danielle walked into the museum. To Danielle's delight, they found Millie Samson working in the museum gift store.

"Walt, Danielle, so nice to see you both!" Millie greeted them from where she stood behind the counter. She then turned her full attention to Danielle and asked, "How are you feeling? I heard a rumor. Is it true?"

Danielle smiled at Millie. "If that rumor involves twins, yes."

Millie grinned. "Oh my! You are going to have your hands full! Congratulations!"

"Thank you," Danielle said as Walt draped his arm around her shoulder.

"What can I do for you today?" Millie asked.

"Oh, Walt and I were just driving down the street, and I mentioned we haven't been by the museum lately. Wondered if there were any new exhibits."

"Nothing since the last time you were here. You know how it is, slow this time of year. In fact, I'm the only one here. You two are our first visitors today!"

Danielle smiled in response.

"Oh, I heard about poor Betty Kelty," Millie whispered. "And on your street!"

"Yes. It's horrible," Danielle said.

Millie shook her head. "And from what I hear, they haven't arrested anyone yet."

"No, no, they haven't. Did you know Betty very well?" Danielle asked.

"Yes. The museum and library frequently work together. I can't believe we've lost Betty, and in a few weeks, Josephine will be retiring. Although, I hear she's now staying on a little longer until they hire someone to take Betty's old job."

"Yes, we heard that too," Danielle said.

Walt removed his arm from around Danielle. "Go ahead and visit with Millie. I'm curious to check something about one of the exhibits." Walt smiled at Millie and added, "It's for the book I'm working on." Walt really didn't need to check on any exhibit, but on the way over to the museum, he and Danielle had agreed Millie might be more prone to unfiltered gossip if speaking one on one with Danielle.

After Walt left the two women alone, Danielle said, "I didn't know Betty very well. Walt said she was always helpful at the library. But we don't know anything about her personal life. I don't even know if she had a boyfriend."

"I don't think she was currently dating anyone. But she got involved with someone who worked at the library a while back. It didn't work out; those things never do."

Danielle frowned. "What things?"

"A man dating someone who is basically his supervisor. Someone who is more educated. Although, I suppose just because he was a janitor doesn't mean he isn't college educated."

"Betty dated the janitor from the library?"

"Not the janitor there now. The one who worked there before."

"That's interesting. I never heard anyone mention those two once dated."

"It wasn't public knowledge. Josephine certainly wasn't aware of it when I mentioned it to her."

Danielle arched her brows. "How did you know?"

"I was visiting with friends in Seaside, and I saw Betty and her janitor at a table, holding hands. Before I had a chance to go say hello, they left. I don't think they saw me. About a month later, someone told me he was no longer working at the library. Those relationships never work. To be honest, that poor girl didn't have the best judgment in men."

"What do you mean?"

Millie lowered her voice to a whisper, which wasn't necessary since she and Danielle were the only ones in the museum gift shop. "I wouldn't want this to get out. After all, the poor girl is dead, and no reason to talk ill of her. But after the janitor quit the museum, she and Dave Hammond got a little too close. Not exactly an appropriate relationship for a single woman and married man."

"Are you talking about Dave Hammond who lives up the street from me? His wife is Becca?"

"It's no secret that Becca and Betty had a falling-out. Everyone knew. Goodness, they had a screaming match in front of Betty's house. Eden Langdon told me herself."

"I understood Becca and Betty's falling-out was over a missing letter opener."

Millie shook her head. "That's what they told people. I doubt either of them wanted the truth to get out. Would you?"

"How do you know this?" Danielle asked.

"It's just something someone close to them confided in me the other day."

"Have you mentioned this to the police?"

Millie frowned. "Why would I do that?"

"Someone murdered Betty. The police need to question any suspects."

"If I thought for a moment Becca or Dave were involved, I would call Chief MacDonald. But I know for a fact that Becca and Dave were on their way to Salem when someone murdered poor Betty."

"How do you know?" Danielle asked.

"I will confess, when I first heard about the murder and the fact they found Betty just down the street from the Hammond house, my first suspect was Dave."

"Why Dave? Why not Becca?"

"While Becca might end her friendship with Betty, she wouldn't kill her over it. After all, this wasn't Dave's first time."

Danielle arched her brows. "It wasn't?"

Millie shook her head. "No. Before you moved to town, Dave and Becca separated for a while. He had an affair. Becca kicked him out. They got back together after the other woman left town; but I heard Becca swore if he ever cheated on her again, she wouldn't just divorce him, she would take everything. That house they live in belonged to her grandfather. He left it to Becca. The house belongs to her. Not to Dave."

"Why are you convinced of Dave's innocence?" Danielle asked.

"I ran into Becca on Monday, and we talked about the murder. I was curious about where Dave was when all this happened. Of course, I didn't tell Becca that I wondered if her husband had killed Betty. But I asked her if she noticed anything on Friday morning, since they found the body on her street. She told me she and Dave were on their way to Salem for a wedding when the murder happened."

"I'm curious; who was it that told you Betty and Dave were having an affair?"

"She didn't say affair, actually. It was more an innuendo when I asked her if it was true about things going missing at the library. I knew about the falling-out between Becca and Betty. I'd been told it was about some missing letter opener, but when I asked her about it, she said it wasn't a letter opener Betty almost walked away with." Millie flashed Danielle a knowing smirk and arched her brows up and down a few times.

"Who is she?" Danielle prodded.

"Someone who knows what is really going on at the library. But according to her, whatever was going on between Betty and Dave, it ended before her death. That's why I said she wasn't seeing anyone."

"AND SHE NEVER NAMED HER SOURCE?" Walt asked as they drove away from the museum.

Danielle looked out the side window and let out a sigh before saying, "No. But my guess it was Josephine. Who else would it be?"

"You want to stop at the police station and tell the chief what you found out?" Walt asked.

"I'll just call him. I was hoping we could stop at Adam's office before we go home." Danielle reached down and pulled her cellphone from her purse.

"Sure. Any specific reason?"

"I'm going to tell Adam it's about the wedding."

"But it won't be," Walt said.

"Exactly. I'm curious how well he knows Kenny, his handyman." Danielle then called the chief and told him about her conversation with Millie.

THIRTY-FIVE

W hen Walt and Danielle arrived at Frederickport Vacation Properties, they found Leslie alone in the front office at her desk.

"Good to see you're back. How are you feeling?" Danielle asked.

Leslie smiled up at Danielle. "Much better, thanks. You here to see Adam?"

Together, Walt and Danielle stood by Leslie's desk. "Yes. Is he here?" Danielle asked.

"He's in his office. You can go on back."

THE DOOR to Adam's office was open, but instead of stepping inside, Danielle and Walt stood in the open doorway while Danielle knocked loudly on the doorjamb and called out a hello. Adam looked up from his desk, where he had been sorting papers.

"Hey, come on in!" Adam stood, waved them in, and watched Walt and Danielle enter the office. He motioned to the two empty chairs facing his desk. Before sitting down, Walt shook Adam's hand while saying hi.

"So, what do I owe this visit? You decided to buy some investment property?" Adam sat down behind the desk, facing the couple.

Danielle grinned. "Maybe some other time. We were just in the neighborhood and figured we'd stop and say hi. And I wondered if Mel said anything to you about the email I sent her about the wedding."

Adam returned Danielle's grin. "She did. In fact, she emailed me a copy. Looks like you might have a career as a wedding planner." Danielle had sent Melony an itemized list of all the things that needed to be done for the wedding, including suggestions along with a breakdown of what Danielle could do for Melony.

"Lily helped me," Danielle said.

"With Lily doing Joe and Kelly's wedding, maybe you two need to go into business together," Adam teased.

Danielle flashed Adam a grin. "I'll consider it. By the way, Kenny gave us his business card when we were in here, in case we need a handyman, and Bill seems super busy lately. I'm assuming he's good, since he works for you?"

"Kenny knows his stuff. I've been happy with him."

"Have you known him for a long time?" Walt asked.

"A couple of years." Adam shrugged.

"Do you know anything about what he did before he worked for the library?" Danielle asked.

Adam let out a sigh. "You heard something about Kenny's past, didn't you? One thing about Frederickport, can't keep secrets in this town."

"I don't agree. Frederickport is good at keeping secrets," Danielle argued.

Adam arched his brows. "How do you figure?"

"Let's see, for years Daisy Morton assumed her sister's identity while hiding her sister's body next door to Marlow House. Then there is that secret tunnel under Beach Drive—"

"True," Adam interrupted. "But they didn't stay secrets, did they?"

"They did for decades. What's Kenny's secret?" Danielle asked.

Adam studied Danielle. "So you didn't hear anything?"

"Someone might have said something about him spending time behind bars," Danielle said.

Adam leaned back in his desk chair. "He told me when he applied for the job, so it wasn't really a secret from me. And I checked out his story. After all, I have to trust someone before I send them into a renter's house to make repairs."

"The story isn't true?" Danielle asked.

"Yeah, it's true, the part about his time behind bars, anyway. He worked at a warehouse and got involved with some sketchy co-workers. He let these friends store some boxes in his garage, but what he didn't know, it was stuff they ripped off from the warehouse where they all worked. Someone tipped the cops off that they'd find stolen merchandise on the property. He didn't have the best public defender; the guy talked him into making a plea deal, which included testifying against the guys who put the hot merchandise in his garage and serving some time."

"If he didn't realize the stuff was hot, and he cooperated with the police, why did he get sent to prison?" Danielle asked.

"Like I said, he didn't have the best public defender. After he told me his version of the story, I asked if Mel could talk to his attorney. He agreed. After she did, Mel said the public defender was a freaking idiot. Anyway, Kenny's a good guy. Frankly, Bill and I did some pretty stupid crap when we were younger that could have gotten us locked up."

"Did he ever find out who tipped off the cops?" Walt asked.

"He's pretty sure it was the ex-girlfriend of one of the guys who had ripped the stuff off. She knew what her boyfriend was doing, and after she caught him cheating, I guess she figured she'd burn him. Of course, it didn't just burn her ex."

"Do you know if Kenny had any kind of personal relationship with Betty Kelty?" Danielle asked.

Adam frowned. "Whoa, that's quite a leap from storing hot merchandise to murder suspect. That is where you're going. Right?"

"No," Danielle lied. "Someone said they dated for a short time."

"Who told you that?" Adam asked.

Danielle shrugged. "I don't remember."

"Well, that's a new one on me."

―――――

INSTEAD OF GOING HOME, Walt and Danielle stopped at the police station and found the chief in his office with Brian. Danielle told them what Adam had said about Kenny and rehashed the conversation she'd had with Millie.

Brian glanced at his watch and then looked at the chief. "Kenny should be here any minute." He looked at Walt and Danielle and said, "I spoke to him on the phone earlier, and he agreed to come in and talk to me again."

"I'm assuming you're going to talk to Becca and her husband again?" Danielle said.

"Yes. I called them already," the chief said. "They're coming in tomorrow morning."

"Where's Joe?" Danielle asked. "Isn't he here?"

"Joe left for home early," the chief said.

"Everything okay?" Danielle asked.

Brian and the chief exchanged quick glances before looking back at Danielle. "This morning Charlie Cramer called Joe; he wants Joe to go see him," the chief explained.

Danielle looked at the chief. "Is he going to?"

"That's what I asked," Brian said.

"And then this afternoon, Kelly called. She was rather upset because she received a letter in the mail today―from Charlie."

"Why would Charlie be writing to Kelly?" Danielle asked. "Was he trying to persuade Kelly to talk Joe into seeing him?"

"The letter was written before Charlie called this morning," the chief explained. "And it wasn't about Joe going to visit him. It was about how Charlie was looking forward to their wedding."

Danielle frowned. She looked from the chief to Brian and back to the chief. "Why would Charlie be looking forward to the wedding? It's not like he's going to attend."

"I didn't read the letter," Brian said. "But from what Joe told us before he left, it sounded like Charlie assumed he would be out on

231

bail when they were getting married, and he was looking forward to being there."

"Well, that would be kind of awkward. Since Heather is going to be there and he was planning to burn down her house with her in it," Danielle said.

The desk phone rang. The chief answered the call. After he hung up, he said, "Kenny's here."

BRIAN SAT across the interview table from Kenny, whose folded hands fiddled nervously on the tabletop.

"It surprised me you wanted me to come in again," Kenny said. "Not sure what else I can tell you. I haven't seen Betty since I quit a month ago."

"The last time we spoke, you implied your relationship with Betty was strictly a work relationship."

Kenny shrugged. "It was."

"Are you saying Betty and you never had a more—personal relationship?"

Kenny visibly swallowed and glanced around the room. He shifted in his chair and then said, "Umm, what are you getting at?"

"Someone has come forward with information that says your relationship was more intimate than what you suggested. It would be a good idea if you weigh your words before you explain the nature of your relationship with our murder victim."

"Do I need a lawyer?"

"It's your right to have one."

Kenny let out a snort and slumped back in the chair. "Yeah, right. The last time I got a lawyer, I ended up spending almost a year behind bars for something I didn't do. But yeah, Betty and I had a relationship, one that ended before I quit the library. And I didn't mention it before because I had nothing to do with her death. And if you're wondering if I killed her because she broke my heart, I broke up with her. She didn't break up with me."

"Why did you break up with her?"

"Because she didn't want anyone to find out about our relationship. Which at first, I didn't mind, because I figured Josephine would frown on her protégé seeing the ex-con janitor. I was good enough to clean the toilets and do some repairs, but as nice as Josephine was to me, I wasn't stupid, and I cared enough about Betty that I didn't want to jeopardize her career. And I confess, there was something a little hot about a secret forbidden relationship. But then I realized Betty didn't want to tell her family either, not because she worried about losing her job, but it embarrassed her to be dating me. But it sounds like she told someone. Who was it?"

"That doesn't matter. When did you break up with her?" Brian asked.

"It was a couple of weeks before I quit. After I broke up, she got all bitchy." He paused a moment and said, "Not bitchy enough that I wanted her dead. Listen, I really don't want to get railroaded a second time for something I didn't do. Hell, I cared about her. I wouldn't have hurt her."

"Were you in love with her?" Brian asked.

Kenny considered the question for a moment. Finally, he shook his head. "No. It wasn't love. Like I said, I cared about her. We had some fun. And while I didn't mind the sneaking around, keeping it from Josephine, I'll admit that when I realized she was ashamed of me, well, it kind of threw ice water on the relationship, if you get what I mean. I don't know about you, but if a woman I care about starts looking at me like I'm crap, well, I start feeling like crap. And frankly, I don't need that in my life. So I broke it off with her, but I sure as hell didn't kill her."

"And you have no idea who might have wanted to hurt her?" Brian asked.

Kenny shook his head. "No."

"And no idea who might have taken the letter opener?"

"No. To be honest, I didn't even realize the damn thing existed before Betty said it was missing. I don't even know what it looks like."

"You didn't see it when it was in the display case?"

"If I did, I don't remember. I never paid much attention to the displays. For one thing, it's not like I was ever involved with setting them up; Betty did that herself. And she kept the case locked. Yeah, I had access to the key, but I never had a reason to open the case. I wasn't responsible for dusting it or anything. Betty always made it clear no one was to touch the displays because they might break something or screw up how she had them arranged. She was sort of obsessive about it. You can ask Josephine."

"What do you know about her relationship with Dave Hammond?" Brian asked.

Kenny frowned. "Becca's husband?"

"Yes. Were they friends?"

Kenny shrugged. "He was married to one of her close friends, but from what Betty said, she wasn't a fan. She once told me it creeped her out how he looked at her sometimes."

"Looked at her how?" Brian asked.

"I asked her that too," Kenny said.

"And what did she say?"

"She said he looked at her like a predator."

THIRTY-SIX

Olivia doubted she would tell her sister, Shanice, how she had spent the previous evening. While Shanice had accepted Olivia's stories about her adventures in astral projection, she suspected Shanice might wonder if her younger sister was actually experiencing a mental breakdown. She wouldn't blame Shanice, because even she was finding it difficult to believe two ghosts had babysat her Thursday evening while playing cards. Witnessing those cards floating around hadn't helped her accept what she had just learned. Instead, it made her question her own sanity.

Eva had left before sunrise, and only Marie remained by Olivia's side and was now with her as she walked to her car, preparing to head off to the library for her first day on the new job. When she reached the car, she peeked under the vehicle, checking to see if the bomber had returned. Convinced nothing suspicious had been attached to the underside of her vehicle, she stood by the engine, wondering if the bomber might have put the mechanism under the hood. If so, how could she check? Just opening the hood might trigger the bomb—if there was one.

MARIE STOOD BY HER SIDE, watching. When Olivia initially looked under the car, Marie assumed she was looking for Max. After all, he had been under the car before. But when Olivia began staring at the engine and absently chewing on her lower lip as if in deep contemplation, Marie had an aha moment.

"You are looking for another bomb, aren't you?" Marie asked, knowing the woman couldn't hear her. "I can understand why you're reluctant to open the hood. Let's see if I can help." The next moment, Marie stuck her head through the hood and was annoyed to find it was too dark to see anything.

Marie pulled her head out of the engine and looked over at Olivia. She did the only responsible thing she could do before opening the hood to check for a bomb. She sent Olivia flying over the fence to Marlow House, depositing her in the middle of the yard. After placing Olivia at what she believed a safe distance away, the engine hood popped open.

———

DAZED, Olivia found herself sitting in the middle of Marlow House's side yard. "What just happened?" she muttered, getting to her feet. The next moment, an invisible force picked her up and sent her flying over the fence, back into her own yard, and this time set her on her feet in front of her car, its hood open.

"What are you doing, Marie?" Olivia heard Heather call from the other side of the driveway. She looked up to see Heather walking over from next door.

Still confused, Olivia looked at Heather. "Did you see what happened?"

"Yes, I did. Marie sent you flying next door and back again." Heather turned her attention to the other side of the car and started talking as if someone was standing there. "Well, you're lucky she didn't faint again… You sure?… I suppose I can understand." Heather stepped closer to the car and looked at the engine. After inspecting it, she reached up, grabbed hold of the engine hood, and slammed it shut.

"What is going on?" Olivia demanded.

Heather turned to her. "Marie said you were worried about another bomb, and she just wanted to help. Good news. There is no bomb."

OLIVIA WASN'T sure how she felt knowing a ghost sat in her passenger seat, going to work with her, to keep her safe until they felt the bomber had no reason to try again. At least, that was how Heather explained it all. Had Heather not been getting ready to go to work herself and witnessed her flight over the Marlow fence and back, Olivia doubted she would be on her way to work right now. Instead, she might be checking into a mental institution.

When she arrived at the library, Josephine greeted her with a part-time employee who was filling in for Betty until they hired someone. Josephine took Olivia into her office to discuss the head librarian's job in private.

"Are you okay, dear?" Josephine asked after noticing Olivia seemed distracted and kept glancing around the office as if looking for someone.

Olivia smiled weakly at Josephine. "I'm just a little out of sorts. This week has been stressful."

"I'm so sorry your first week in Frederickport has been, well, I imagine something of a nightmare. Is it true someone put a bomb under your car?"

Olivia nodded. "Yes. Fortunately, it didn't go off."

"Do you have any idea why someone would want to hurt you?"

"You mean kill me?"

Josephine cringed. "I didn't want to say it that way."

"That's what would have happened had the bomb gone off. But I suspect whoever killed Betty placed the bomb on the car, and that's what the police think, too."

Josephine frowned. "Why would they do that?"

"Someone told the police a woman who looked like me was with Betty right before she died. Right in front of my house. This person is probably convinced it was me, and I think the police did too, at first."

"And they don't now?"

Olivia shook her head. "No. They have video footage from the airline showing me getting on my flight, proving I was thousands of feet in the air when Betty was killed. But the killer, whoever he is, thinks I was with Betty right before her death, and is obviously worried I might have seen something I shouldn't have. Someone from the police station must have mentioned I was seen with Betty before they saw that video. And whoever they told must have said something to the killer."

"Oh dear." Josephine gasped. "That might have been me!"

"Excuse me?"

"I was told someone who looked like you was seen with Betty right in front of your house. I might have said something to someone, and it got to the killer. Oh dear, I could have gotten you killed! I am so sorry!"

Josephine's phone rang. Flashing Olivia an apologetic grimace, she answered the call. When she hung up a moment later, she said, "I'm afraid I'm going to have to leave you alone in a little while. That was Police Chief MacDonald. They have more questions for me."

BRIAN SAT with Josephine in the interrogation room, silently cursing the chief for telling him, right before Josephine's arrival, how much she looked like Blanche Devereaux from *The Golden Girls*. He hadn't noticed it before, and now he couldn't stop seeing Blanche, and waited for the prim Josephine to say something sexually provocative. He shook his head at the absurd notion and focused on the interview at hand.

"Have there been any breaks in the case?" Josephine asked before Brian asked his first question.

"No, but it's still early in the process. And I have a few more questions I need to ask you. First, the last time we spoke, I asked if you knew of anyone Betty was seeing? A romantic involvement?"

"I know for a fact she wasn't seeing anyone. That morning, when she was doing the inventory at my house, I made us some coffee, and we chatted a bit. I said something in jest about how her new promotion might cut into her love life, and she laughed, said that wasn't a problem; she didn't have a love life."

"What about any recent love interests?" Brian asked.

Josephine shrugged. "We didn't discuss those kinds of things. Aside from my joke, I didn't pry into her personal life."

"But you knew she once dated Kenny?"

Josephine arched her brow. "Kenny our old janitor?"

"Yes."

"Who told you that?" She then smiled and said, "I bet it was Millie Samson."

"It wasn't true?"

Josephine gave another shrug. "Like I said, I didn't pry into her personal life. But Millie did say something to me about seeing Betty and Kenny having lunch in Seaside. Even claimed they were holding hands. But no, I don't believe there was anything going on between the two. You should talk to Kenny."

"I have."

Josephine started to say something but stopped. She studied Brian through narrowed eyes and asked, "He told you they had a relationship, didn't he?"

Brian shook his head. "I really can't say."

"Oh! Millie was right!" Josephine slumped back in her chair.

"The last time we spoke, you didn't mention Kenny had a record."

"I honestly didn't think to mention it. I assumed you probably already knew, and if you had questions about it, you would have asked me. Maybe I was wrong. Wrong about everything."

"What do you mean?"

"I was with Olivia Davis this morning at the library. It's her first day at work. We talked about someone putting a bomb on her car, and she told me the bomber was probably Betty's killer, and that whoever the killer is, they believe Olivia was with Betty right before the murder, and they're afraid she might have seen someone. But of course, Olivia wasn't there that morning. She told me how the airline video proved she was on the flight at the time of the murder, so she couldn't have seen anything. I knew someone who looked like Olivia was seen with Betty that morning. I was questioned about it. And I foolishly told some people. It's possible one of those people told the killer."

"And who exactly did you tell?" Brian asked.

"Kenny, for one."

"When was that?"

Josephine shrugged. "I don't remember what day exactly. Since the murder, I haven't been able to keep things straight. But I ran into him at the grocery store, and we talked a moment about Betty, and I said something about the person seen with Betty before the murder and how much she looked like our new employee."

"Do you remember his response?"

"He didn't really have one. Not really."

"Did you mention where Olivia Davis lived?"

"I suppose."

Brian frowned. "You suppose?"

"In a roundabout way. Because the woman seen with Betty was standing at the gate of Olivia's new house, on the same street where they found Betty's body."

"Did you tell anyone else?"

"That same day, I ran into Becca and Dave Hammond. Umm, I might have said something to them."

"About Dave Hammond, do you know what his relationship was with Betty?"

"I know he was flirty with her, but then, Dave Hammond tends to be a flirt, which got him into trouble before."

"Do you think they had any sort of relationship?"

"Oh, goodness no! Betty and Becca were friends. I can't see Betty doing that to her friend; plus, I always got the feeling Dave's attention made Betty uncomfortable. Of course, it's not like I saw them around each other very much. It's just the impression I got the few times I saw them together."

WHEN BRIAN FINISHED the interview with Josephine, he walked her to the front office and was surprised to find Danielle chatting with Joe in the waiting area. After Josephine said her goodbyes and headed for the exit, Brian joined Danielle and Joe.

"What are you doing here?" Brian asked Danielle.

"Walt's writing, and Joanne is on a cleaning frenzy, so I thought I'd do a little shopping, and while out, stop by and see if there are any breaks in the case. It's nerve-racking knowing the killer is still on the loose." She paused a moment, glanced at Joe, and then looked back at Brian and said, "And Joe was telling me about Charlie's weird letter."

Brian nodded. "Yes, he let me read it this morning."

Danielle glanced at the door where Josephine had just walked through and then looked back at Brian. "I see Josephine was here. Did you get anything new from her? Something that might help solve this?"

Brian shrugged. "Not really. But that person Millie was talking about who she insinuated worked at the library. It wasn't Josephine. Josephine felt Dave's attention made Betty uncomfortable. She wasn't encouraging it."

THIRTY-SEVEN

Danielle was about to head home when her cellphone rang. Sitting in her car, preparing to insert the key in the ignition, she instead answered the phone. "Hey, Walt."

"Where are you?" came Walt's voice.

She looked over at the store she had just left. "At the moment, I'm sitting in the parking lot at the grocery store, getting ready to come home. Do you need me to pick up something?"

"How do you feel about Chinese food?"

"Why, you want me to pick some up for dinner?"

"No. Chris called, and we started talking, and if you're up to visitors, he's offered to bring dinner."

"Is Joanne finished?" Danielle asked.

"Yes. She left about fifteen minutes ago. We have a sparkling clean house."

"And now our friends can come over and mess it up?" she teased.

Walt laughed and then asked, "So what do you think?"

"Sounds good. Who's all coming?"

"Just the Beach Drive group. Along with Brian, but he's working, so he'll be a little later."

ONE THING DANIELLE hated about late November and early December in Oregon were the shorter days. She didn't mind the rain as much as she did a four-thirty sunset. But it was now the second week of January, and sunset was being pushed back to almost five. But not quite. She wouldn't see a five o'clock sunset until next week.

Home from running errands, she had already put away the groceries and now sat in the kitchen with Walt, chatting about her afternoon outing and drinking a fruit smoothy she had picked up on her way home. If she couldn't enjoy a glass of wine on a Friday night, she would have a smoothy.

While Danielle recounted her visit to the police station, the sound of the pet door swinging back and forth caught her attention. She and Walt glanced at the door and watched as Max strolled into the room. Once inside, the cat looked at Walt and let out a meow.

"Heather's on her way over. She came in the back gate," Walt announced.

"See, we don't need that doorbell camera Adam told us to get. We have a watch cat."

Walt focused his attention on the back door. It unlocked, and the next moment the door swung open just as Heather stepped onto the back porch.

"Wow, that's service," Heather said as she walked into the house.

"Hi, Heather. Is Chris with you?" Danielle asked.

"No, he wanted to go home and change before picking up the food." Heather kept walking through the kitchen, heading toward the door leading to the hallway. "I have to use your bathroom."

When Heather returned to the kitchen five minutes later, she said, "I can tell Joanne was here today. Everything looks so clean." She took a seat at the table with Walt and Danielle. "I wish I had a Joanne."

"She is great," Danielle agreed. Danielle glanced upwards and said, "Thanks, Aunt Brianna, for originally hiring Joanne."

"Wasn't that Renton who actually hired her?" Walt reminded her.

"Yeah, I suppose." Danielle glanced upwards again and said, "But I am not thanking you, Renton. You were a jerk."

"You may be looking in the wrong direction if you're trying to talk to Renton." Heather pointed downward.

Danielle giggled. "You have a point."

"Before you arrived, Danielle told me about her visit to the police station this afternoon. Brian said the Hammonds were coming in for another interview today. Did you talk to Brian after he spoke to them?" Walt asked.

"Yeah, I did. He told me what Millie had told Danielle, about something going on between Dave and Betty, and that Josephine claimed that story didn't come from her," Heather began.

"What did they say?" Danielle asked.

"Becca claimed it wasn't true. And Dave admitted he found Betty attractive, but that if he was going to screw around on his wife, it certainly would not be with one of his wife's best friends. Not unless he wanted to be caught."

"They're both denying it," Walt said. "I assume Brian is going to interview Millie and find out who told her there was something going on between Betty and Dave?"

Danielle groaned. "I hate that. Millie is going to know I left her and marched right over to the police station."

"Hey, Millie was the gossip here. What does she expect?" Heather asked. "But you don't have to worry about it."

"Why?" Danielle asked.

"They both have alibis. Not just were they together, they have a gas receipt showing where they were at a specific time that morning. And the chief already obtained video footage proving they were at the gas station at the time they claim they were. So they couldn't have been the ones who killed Betty."

"What about the phone call?" Danielle asked.

"The time of that call corresponds to when they were at a gas station. And Becca claims she was getting in her purse then, to get her credit card. So it is entirely possible she made a butt call to Betty. It happens," Heather explained.

The next moment, Marie appeared in the middle of the kitchen.

"Hi, Marie," the three chorused.

"Olivia is right behind me. She's on her way over here," Marie explained.

"Is she with anyone?" Walt asked.

Marie frowned. "No, why?"

Walt looked to the door and focused his energy. The next moment, the door unlocked and then opened. A few moments later Olivia stood at the back porch, looking into the kitchen while the three people sitting at the kitchen table stared back at her. She could not see Marie.

"Hi, Olivia," Danielle greeted her. "Come on in."

Olivia marched into the kitchen, glanced around, and then asked, "Is anyone else here?"

"Just Marie," Danielle said.

Her back to the open door, Olivia stood up a little straighter, licked her lips nervously, and was about to say something when the door behind her closed abruptly and locked, making her jump. She looked to the now closed door.

"Sorry, I didn't mean to startle you," Walt said.

Turning back to Walt, Olivia said, "I know you're all trying to help me, but please, tell your Marie ghost I really don't need her. Thank her. But tell her she does not need to babysit me. In fact, I implore her don't go back to my house with me!"

They all looked at Marie. "What did you do?" Danielle asked.

Marie scowled. "I didn't do anything."

"You made her fly across the yard this morning," Heather reminded her.

"It wasn't just that," Olivia argued while Marie grumbled, "I was just trying to help."

Walt and Danielle looked at each other while they both mouthed, *Flying?*

"I'm sorry. But this is just nerve-racking. Can't you all understand how creepy it is to know a ghost is following you everywhere?"

Marie frowned. "Is she calling me creepy?"

"I can't even go to the bathroom!"

"I didn't follow you into the bathroom," Marie said with a pout.

"You haven't gone to the bathroom all day?" Heather asked.

"I don't want to talk about it," Olivia mumbled.

Heather shrugged. "You brought it up."

"Tell her I didn't follow her into the bathroom. And it wasn't just because she asked me not to the first time. Frankly, it was insulting that she found it necessary to ask me every single time she used the bathroom. I heard her the first time—which wasn't even necessary for her to say. I may be dead, but I'm not a voyeur."

Danielle leaned over and pulled out a chair. She looked up to Olivia. "Come. Sit down."

Hesitantly, Olivia glanced around the room. She took a step toward the table, then paused. "Where is she now?"

"If the she you are talking about is Marie, she is right there." Danielle pointed to the corner where Marie stood.

"Oh goodness. This is silly. I'm going to go say hi to Connor." Marie vanished.

"Marie just left," Heather told her.

Olivia took a deep breath, exhaled, and walked to the table and sat down. "I'm sorry, but this has been all too much."

"I guess having a ghost hanging around that you can't see might be a little... umm..." Danielle didn't finish the sentence, but instead thought about how quickly Lily had adapted when first learning an invisible Walt shared Marlow House with them. But then she remembered Lily had already met Walt in a dream hop. Perhaps she should try arranging a dream hop with Marie and Olivia.

Heather broke Danielle's train of thought when she asked Olivia, "Aside from your haunting, how was your first day at work?"

Olivia shrugged. "It was okay. I didn't do much. One of the volunteers gave me a tour of the library. Josephine gave me my own set of keys, so I guess I'm official. Next week I'm supposed to help her complete the inventory she started with Betty. But aside from that, she was gone most of the afternoon. We're closing the library tomorrow, in respect of Betty, and to let the library employees and volunteers attend her memorial service if they want."

"You have the weekend off?" Walt asked.

"Yes. It will give me time to finish unpacking."

"If you don't feel it's necessary for Marie to hang out with you, that's okay. She was only trying to help," Danielle said.

Olivia smiled at Danielle. "And I appreciate it. But I hope you understand."

THEY HAD INVITED her to join them for dinner, but she respectfully declined, telling them she really wasn't hungry and wanted to get back to her house to go through some boxes. But when she returned home, she was too tired to unpack. Instead, she removed a carton of Ben and Jerry's from her freezer, peeled off its lid, grabbed a spoon from a drawer, and headed out to the living room to eat a dinner of ice cream in front of the television.

But instead of turning on the television, she sat alone in her living room, eating ice cream out of the carton and thinking about Betty and her funeral tomorrow in Astoria. She remembered what her medium neighbors had told her, that she would be able to see ghosts when on an astral projection journey. Later that night, she fell asleep with that thought in her head.

OLIVIA SLEPT in the next morning. When she woke up, it was almost ten thirty. She sat up in bed, wearing just her white linen night shift, and combed her fingers through her hair. Glancing at the clock on her nightstand, she remembered Betty's memorial service was starting in about an hour.

"I wish I could talk to Betty. She could tell me who killed her," Olivia said aloud. It was in that moment a thought came to her. What if Betty's spirit had not moved on, like the mediums claimed?

What if she showed up at her funeral to watch? *That's what I'd do,* Olivia thought.

"If it's actually possible for me to see a spirit while in an out-of-body state—possible for me to communicate with the spirit—then if I go to Betty's funeral, and she is there, I could find out who killed her. Whoever it is would no longer be a threat to me or anyone else."

Olivia did not consider discussing her idea with her medium neighbors. Instead, she grabbed the smartphone from the nightstand and began surfing for maps of Oregon, along with an obituary on Betty Kelty. After she had what she needed, she positioned herself on the center of her bed, closed her eyes, and prepared to astral project.

THIRTY-EIGHT

Heart racing at the idea of what she intended to do, Olivia took a deep cleansing breath and told herself she must calm down if she wanted this to work. She remained quiet on her bed for another thirty minutes before she maintained the necessary relaxed focus required for an out-of-body experience.

When she had done this while flying, it had been the first time she had ever attempted to do it with people in close proximity. The plane hadn't been full on her flight to Portland, and she had the row to herself, so there was no one sitting next to her on either side. During that projection, she had focused on where she wanted to go, visualizing the place on the map, along with what she had seen during her last visits to the property. While it was the first time she had astral projected while surrounded by people, it was not the first time she had visited her new house by this method.

Her real estate agent believed she had purchased the Frederick-port property sight unseen, aside from photographs sent to her by the agent, online listing photos, and a home tour via video chat. However, she had visited the property prior to making the offer via astral projection.

During her last visit to the house, via astral projection from the airplane, she had initially kept her eyes closed. But when she finally opened them, she found herself standing in the middle of her new living room in Frederickport. She had intended to walk through the entire house, looking to see if she needed to hire a cleaning company before her furniture arrived. Yet before she had a chance to go upstairs, someone had run by her window. Curious to see the trespasser on her property, Olivia had followed the woman—something she now regretted. Had she not followed Betty from her front yard down Beach Drive, Heather Donovan would never have seen her, and whoever tried to kill her would have no motive to try silencing her. But there was nothing she could do about that now. Now, she needed to help the police find the killer.

Sitting on her bed, her eyes closed, Olivia imagined the road to Astoria from Frederickport, visualizing how she would drive if going by car. From her brief research on her smartphone, she had found the location of the church hosting Betty's service.

"OLIVIA DAVIS, what are you doing here?" a female voice called out.

Olivia opened her eyes and found herself looking at two women who stood about six feet away, each staring in her direction. They looked familiar. She glanced around and noticed the rows of pews and, beyond the pews, what looked like an open casket. A few people sat in the pews, some stood by the casket, and others were entering the building through a door to her left. She heard faint organ music. *I made it*, Olivia told herself.

She looked back at the two women, who continued to stare at her. It was then she realized where she had seen them before—standing in her bedroom the other night.

"What are you doing here?" the eldest of the two women asked again.

"Marie?" Olivia asked hesitantly.

"Of course," Marie snapped. "What in the world are you doing here? And goodness, couldn't you have worn something more appropriate for a funeral?"

Olivia looked down at her body. She still wore the linen night dress she had slept in the previous night, its fabric wrinkled. Looking down at her feet, she saw they were bare. She wiggled her toes, noting the peeling nail polish remaining from her last pedicure.

"And you didn't even comb your hair," Marie scolded.

No longer looking at her feet, Olivia looked up to the two women and absently attempted to comb her fingers through her hair, yet there seemed to be nothing tangible to comb. But she knew Marie was right. Olivia hadn't combed her hair that morning.

The attractive woman standing with Marie chuckled and said, "I'm Eva Thorndike. I know you've heard about me. It's nice to meet you. But as Marie asked, why are you here?"

Now self-conscious about her appearance, Olivia glanced around the church again and was relieved when no one seemed to look her way. When a little boy almost walked through her the next moment and then moved through Eva and Marie as if they weren't there, Olivia found comfort knowing the living could not see her. As it was, she felt as if she had just woken up living one of her worst nightmares, the one where she was suddenly at high school without a stitch of clothing. Fortunately, she didn't sleep nude, because standing in the middle of a church in a wrinkled nightdress, barefoot and with uncombed hair was bad enough.

"Why are you here?" Marie asked again.

Olivia looked back at Marie and blinked several times. Finally, she said, "I'm sorry. I am just a little overwhelmed right now."

"Yes, we can see that. But please answer Marie's question," Eva said.

Olivia regained her composure and looked at the two spirits. "I'm hoping to see Betty. If it were me, I'd want to go to my funeral before I moved on. And the mediums told me that when I'm in this state, I can communicate with spirits." She paused a moment and looked the two ghosts up and down. With a shrug, she said, "Like I'm doing now. But why are you here?"

"We're here for the same reason," Marie said.

"You are?" Olivia frowned. "No one told me you were coming."

"I imagine you would have found out had you accepted Danielle's dinner invitation," Marie said. "Both Eva and I stopped over at Marlow House last night, and we discussed the funeral. While Betty's spirit wasn't with her family when we were here earlier, we thought it possible that she might show up at her service."

"Oh." Olivia glanced around and then looked back at the spirits.

"Danielle usually likes to come to these things," Marie explained. "Gives her a chance to talk to the departing spirit. But she barely knew the girl, and while Walt knew her slightly better, it would seem odd for them to travel all the way to Astoria to attend the funeral of a girl they barely knew. Plus, if they ran into Betty's spirit, it would be difficult to have much of a talk with her in these close quarters."

"And it's raining outside," Eva added.

"Marie Nichols, is that you?" a female voice called out.

Marie, Eva, and Olivia turned to the voice and found themselves looking at Betty Kelty. She wore a dress, and had they peeked in the casket earlier, they would have seen it was the same dress her body wore.

"Betty, we were hoping to see you," Marie called out.

Betty stepped closer and looked at the woman by Marie's side. Her eyes widened. "Don't tell me, Eva Thorndike!"

Eva smiled. "You recognized me."

Betty grinned. "Oh yes! Your portrait at the museum is my favorite exhibit over there. I can't believe I'm meeting you!"

"You seem in good spirits—no pun intended. Considering someone killed you," Marie said.

Betty let out a sigh, and her smile faded. "Yes, that. I…" It was in that moment she noticed Olivia standing off to the side. She stopped talking and then looked Olivia up and down. Finally, she asked, "Who are you?"

"I'm Olivia Davis."

Betty's eyes widened. "That's the name of the woman they hired to take my old job."

"Yes, that is me."

"Oh no!" Betty gasped. "You were murdered, too! I am so sorry!"

Olivia shook her head. "No. I'm not dead."

Betty frowned. "Are you a medium or something?" She looked her up and down again. "I thought for sure you were dead like the others I've been able to talk to. Especially since you're wearing that." Betty glanced around the church. No one seemed to look their way. She looked back at Olivia and said, "You might want to go put something on."

"Don't worry, dear," Marie said. "No one can see her. It is a long story; I will explain it later. But first, we need to find out what happened to you."

"I'll be curious to hear the story. But frankly, nothing surprises me anymore. Not since I was murdered. It has been a crazy week."

"Where have you been?" Eva asked.

"Lots of places. After the attack, I suppose the best way to describe it, I was stunned. I couldn't believe what had just happened. I had no idea I had been killed. At first, I didn't realize I had been stabbed. Yes, I felt a sharp pain at first, and then I was pushed down in the bushes. Shoved back. But I wasn't hurting, at least not after that initial sharp pain."

"I suspect when you were stabbed, it killed you instantly," Eva said. "Which explains the brief pain."

"What happened then?" Marie asked.

"I didn't know what to do. I needed to talk to someone, so I just started walking."

"When did you realize you were dead?" Eva asked.

"It wasn't until a Doberman told me."

Marie arched her brows. "A Doberman?"

Betty nodded. "Yes. A very nice Doberman. I don't think he was supposed to be out alone, but I found him running along the beach. I think I had been walking for at least a day when I met him."

"How do you know? Time can be tricky for spirits," Eva said. "Especially for those recently departed."

"I assume it was the next day. It got dark; then the sun came up again. I wondered why I wasn't afraid, being out on the beach alone all night. But then I met the Doberman; he was running along the beach. We talked. He helped me understand."

Still listening to Betty, Olivia glanced from the three ghosts and realized the church was now full, and someone had closed the doors. People filled the pews, and in front of the church, a minister stood at the pulpit, preparing to start the service.

Olivia wanted Betty to simply tell them who had killed her, but she could not bring herself to interrupt the conversation, and a part of her feared that if she raised her voice to get their attention, people would see her—standing in a church wearing just a thin and wrinkled nightdress, or that she might find herself suddenly back in Frederickport, alone in her bed.

The service was about to begin. Marie suggested they all go to the front of the church and stand by the casket so Betty could get a better view.

Olivia disagreed, reminding them why they were there, only to be shushed by Eva, who explained, "All in good time. This is Betty's service. She is the star of the show—the spiritual guest of honor. After the service, she can tell us what we need to know."

Reluctantly, Olivia followed the others to the front of the church. Self-conscious in her nightgown and bare feet, Olivia felt like the emperor in the old fable, and imagined that at any moment the people in the pews would abruptly stand, point in her direction and shout, "She isn't wearing clothes!"

The moment they reached the front of the church and turned around to face the mourners, someone shouted and pointed. It was not the mourners in the pews; it was Betty, who stood by her casket, pointing to one row of pews. "That's my killer! That's who killed me!"

THIRTY-NINE

Olivia bolted upright in bed. She glanced around her bedroom and wondered if Eva or Marie had returned with her. Was it possible Betty had returned to Frederickport?

"Am I alone?" Olivia said out loud. All remained silent. While she knew she couldn't hear them even if they shouted, she figured if Marie was there, she would make herself known. "If you are here, Marie, knock on the wall or something." Nothing.

Convinced she had returned alone, Olivia scurried from the bed to the closet, looking for something to wear. Thirty minutes later, she was dressed and heading downstairs to find help. Before stepping out the side door, she debated where she should go, to Heather's house or to Marlow House? She decided on Marlow House.

A few minutes later, she hurried up the sidewalk to Marlow House. Instead of entering through the side gate, she continued to the front door. Hastily making her way up the front walk and about to step on the porch, she froze when the front door opened, and found Walt Marlow standing at the open doorway, smiling down at her. He wore gray slacks, a long-sleeved blue shirt, and a knit vest. Glancing down briefly, she spied the tips of his freshly polished dark leather shoes sticking out from the hems of his slacks.

Walt opened the door wider. "We've been waiting for you." He stepped back, making room for her to enter.

Olivia walked into the entry hall. "I know who killed Betty!"

"Yes, I do, too," Walt said calmly as he shut the front door behind them. "They're all in the living room, waiting for you."

"They?" Confused, Olivia followed Walt down the hall. When she walked into the living room, she found Brian and Heather sitting on the sofa with Danielle. Across from them sat Chris and Police Chief MacDonald, each sitting in a chair facing the sofa. Since she hadn't noticed the vehicles parked behind Marlow House, she didn't know the Marlows had company.

"Go ahead and sit down," Walt said, motioning to an empty chair. "Now that you're here, we can figure out how to expose the killer."

Instead of sitting down, Olivia turned to Walt. "You said you know who the killer is. How do you know?"

"Because Betty just finished explaining it all," Walt said.

"How could she have done that? I just left the funeral less than thirty minutes ago. Betty's there with Eva and Marie."

"No, they got here right after you left the funeral," Heather said from the sofa. "Marie came to my house, where Brian was. He called the chief. We all agreed to meet here, and Betty explained everything before you arrived."

"You might tell Olivia it's been more than thirty minutes since she returned," Marie said while glancing at the clock. "She left the church almost an hour ago."

Still confused after Heather conveyed Marie's message, Olivia took a seat and silently listened.

"Our killer is the last person I'd expect," the chief said. "And I'm not sure how we're going to prove the killer's guilt."

"You could find the list," Betty said from the corner, where she stood with Eva and Marie. "The letter opener is on that list. And when you compare the items in the box—all of which are on the list —then it will be obvious who had the letter opener last."

Danielle repeated Betty's words for the non-mediums.

"We could get a search warrant for the library and possibly for

the storage room. But that will take a little time. And even if we find
the list and box, it's circumstantial at best," the chief said.

"If you get that evidence legally, it might be enough to get
another warrant to search the computers our bomber had access
to," Danielle said. "How else does someone like that learn bomb
making?"

"How long will a search warrant take?" Heather asked.

"There's no reason to wait for a search warrant. I could get
them for you now!" Olivia blurted.

"How could you do that?" Brian asked.

"I'll bring you the list. Betty told us where she put it. I'm
supposed to clean out Betty's desk. And Josephine already gave me a
key to the storage room."

"Wouldn't you need Josephine's permission to get into the
storage room?" Heather asked.

"I'll be there next week, anyway. We're finishing the inventory." Olivia paused and then cringed. "But then we'd have to
wait."

"If that box hasn't already been moved, I doubt it will be there
next week," Chris said.

"We'll be right back," Marie said. The three ghosts vanished.

"Where did they go?" Heather asked.

Brian glanced around. "Who?"

"Marie, Eva, and Betty just took off," Danielle explained.

They discussed their options, and a few minutes later, the ghosts
returned.

"It's still there," Marie announced. "We visited the storage
room, and Betty showed me where to find it. I opened the box, and
it was all there. All but the letter opener, of course."

"Marie and the others are back," Danielle told the non-mediums. "And the box is still there."

"I have a key to the library. Let me get the list. And then I can
go to storage before Josephine gets back from the funeral. They
were going to the wake at Betty's parents' house after the service. So
we have some time."

"The only problem with that, we don't have a search warrant," the chief reminded them. "I understand you can bring us the list without one, but the box is another matter."

"You don't need one. When Josephine explained the storage room, she said as head librarian, I'm the one who has complete access to the room, and the one who can grant other library employees or volunteers permission to retrieve any of the boxes. So I don't need a warrant to get the box. And I have the key to get in."

OLIVIA CONVINCED the others she didn't need anyone coming with her to the library or to the storage room. After all, the only person to fear was out of town, attending Betty's wake. Plus, it made Olivia uncomfortable having a ghost—one she could neither hear nor see—following her around. And she certainly didn't need three ghosts trailing behind her. Knowing they were there but she could neither see nor hear them gave her the heebie-jeebies.

When Olivia pulled up to the library on Saturday afternoon, there were no cars in the parking lot. She pulled around to the back of the library and parked. From her purse, she pulled the keychain Josephine had given her and used one key on the ring to unlock the back door.

Once inside, she turned on the lights and locked the door behind her. She had to admit, there was something a little creepy about being in the library all alone. Olivia dropped the keychain back in her purse and made her way to Betty's desk. Yesterday, Josephine had told her the not-yet-hired librarian taking over Betty's old job would be assigned to Betty's desk, and it would be Olivia's job to go through it before the new employee started work. Olivia did not know if the killer had riffled through Betty's desk, but considering where Betty hid the list, she didn't think the killer would have found it even if they had gone through her files.

Now sitting at Betty's desk, Olivia put her right hand into a file drawer, reaching to the rear of the drawer. Blindly feeling around, Olivia nibbled on her lower lip as she continued to grope along the inside of the drawer.

"Yes!" she squealed when her hand landed on what felt like an envelope. The next moment, she pulled an envelope from the drawer, taking with it some of the tape Betty had used to secure said envelope on the inside of the drawer.

She gingerly opened the envelope and pulled out a piece of paper. After unfolding the paper, she read what Betty had written. It listed a number of items. Betty had written a different date by each item. Olivia smiled and muttered, "Mission accomplished."

"What are you doing here?" a male voice interrupted the silence.

Upon hearing the voice, Olivia slammed the piece of paper on the desktop, blank side up, and looked up to find Darren Newsome standing in the doorway, looking at her.

"What are you doing here?" Olivia blurted. The last time she had seen him, he had been sitting in a pew at Betty's service.

Darren walked into the room and shrugged. "Just came back from Betty's memorial service, but I didn't go to her parents' house with everyone else. I don't know anyone. I drove by, saw a car parked by the back of the library, and wondered who it was." He stepped to the desk and looked down at the envelope and paper sitting on the desk, Olivia's hand resting on the piece of paper. "What are you doing here?"

She snatched up the paper and protectively clutched it to her chest. "I, uh, thought I would come in and get some work done while no one's here. Josephine wants me to get this desk ready for the new librarian."

"That was Betty's desk."

"Yes. I know." Still clutching the paper to her chest, she picked up her purse. "I need to get going." She rushed from the library, leaving Darren standing by Betty's desk.

———

TEN MINUTES LATER, Olivia pulled up Josephine's street and began looking at the addresses, trying to find where Josephine lived.

When she found it, she parked down the street, not wanting any of Josephine's neighbors to see her parked in the driveway.

Olivia tucked her purse under the passenger seat, got out of the car, locked it, and hastily made her way to Josephine's garage door, keychain in hand. The garage had two doors. One a roll-up door, used for vehicles, and a second door, an exterior hinged door, commonly used to access the storage room from outside. One key on Olivia's library keychain fit that door's deadbolt and doorknob lock. After unlocking both locks, she entered the garage, turned on the overhead light, and closed the door behind her.

From what Marie had told the mediums, which Danielle had conveyed to her, Marie found the box on a worktable along the back wall. It took Olivia only a minute to locate the box. She removed its lid and looked over the items. Confident this is what she had come for, she was about to pick up the lid and return it to the box when she noticed a bucket shoved into the far corner of the worktable. Curious, she pulled the bucket to her and looked inside. It contained wire, random small tools, and a folded piece of paper. She picked up the paper and unfolded it.

After reading what someone had written, she muttered, "This is another list. A list for making a bomb."

"What are you doing here?" a woman's voice demanded.

Olivia dropped the paper she had been reading and abruptly turned to face Josephine, who had just stepped into the garage from an interior door, one connected directly to the house.

Eyes wide and speechless, Olivia stared at Josephine.

"What are you doing here?" Josephine repeated.

"I... I thought you were at the funeral?" Olivia stammered.

"That doesn't answer my question." Josephine moved closer to Olivia while keeping her right hand concealed at her side. But when she saw what Olivia had been looking at, noticing both the bucket and the box with its lid removed, she brought her hand up from her side, revealing the revolver she held, now pointing at Olivia.

Olivia stared at the gun. She swallowed nervously, licked her now parched lips and asked, "Umm, why are you pointing a gun at me?"

Josephine let out a sigh. "I obviously can't let you leave. Not after you found everything."

"I... I didn't find anything. I'm just checking out the storage room. You said I could."

Josephine shook her head. "I'm not stupid. I see what you're looking at. There was always something that didn't feel right about you." Purposely raising the gun slightly, Josephine looked as if she was about to pull the trigger.

"Please don't do this! People know I'm here!"

Josephine smiled at Olivia. Just as Josephine was about to pull the trigger, the pistol flew from her grasp, landing on a top shelf. Josephine screamed, and Olivia fainted.

FORTY

M arie and Eva stood in the garage, looking down at Olivia now sprawled unconscious on the concrete floor.

"Danielle's right. That girl is always fainting." Marie sighed. She looked over at Josephine, who was no longer screaming but now looking frantically for her pistol before Olivia regained consciousness.

The next moment, Josephine spied her gun sitting on a top shelf. It was too high for her to reach. She abandoned her gun and grabbed a hammer from the worktable and headed for Olivia still unconscious on the floor. Just as she was about to strike the helpless woman, the hammer jerked from her hand, as the gun had done moments earlier, and it joined the firearm on the top shelf.

Marie focused her energy on Josephine, and the next moment, the crazed librarian rose into the air, flailing and screaming.

"I'll have Walt send the police over." Eva disappeared.

"I hope they get here soon. Not sure how Olivia is going to react when she comes to," Marie muttered to herself while focusing her energy on Josephine, who hovered above her, wiggling about like a fish on an invisible line.

EVA FOUND WALT, who then called the chief. Ten minutes later, Walt met Brian at Josephine's house, all agreeing they would wait until Brian had Josephine in custody before calling for backup or letting Joe know what was happening.

Olivia had locked the door behind her when entering the storage garage. But it took Walt less than a minute to spring the lock. When they stepped into the garage, they found Olivia huddled in a corner, looking up at Josephine, who hovered overhead, her arms flailing as she cried pitifully. Marie stood next to Olivia, but only Walt could see her.

Standing under the librarian, Brian looked up at her and shook his head, his hands resting on his hips. Walt walked to Olivia and offered her a hand, helping her to her feet while calling out to Marie, "You can let her down now."

Olivia stumbled to her feet and let Walt place a comforting arm around her while the two stood side by side and watched Josephine slowly lowering to the floor, still sobbing. If they expected Josephine to take off running the moment her feet touched the concrete floor, they would have been wrong. The moment she was on her feet, she ran to Brian Henderson, throwing her arms around him.

"I'm being punished," Josephine sobbed as she held onto Brian, burying her face in his chest. "I didn't mean to kill Betty. But she wouldn't listen to me. I tried to explain. I'm so sorry. So sorry."

STRETCHED out on the living room sofa, a menu from Pearl Cove in hand, Lily reviewed the appetizer options. She looked over to Ian, who sat on the floor with Conner playing with toddler-sized Legos.

"You know, Ian, I can't do this." She tossed the menu on the coffee table.

Ian looked up from the floor to Lily. "You don't want to help with Kelly's wedding?"

"I still want to do that. But whatever she wants to order for food,

I don't want to know about it. I'm sorry, just reading the menu is making me nauseous."

"I suspected that might happen."

"Yeah, well, food doesn't sound as good to me as it did before."

The doorbell rang, and Sadie barked. Ian stood up and followed Sadie to the front door. He returned a few minutes later with Walt and Danielle.

"Hey, guys, what's going on?" Lily asked, sitting up on the sofa to make room for her guests.

"Has Kelly called you?" Danielle asked as she passed Connor, ruffled his curls, and then sat on the sofa next to Lily.

Lily frowned. "No, why?"

Walt sat on the recliner while Sadie stuck close to his side, her tail wagging, and Ian sat back on the floor with Connor.

"I wondered if Joe told her, and she told you," Danielle said.

"Told us what?" Ian asked.

"They've caught Betty's killer," Walt announced.

"They have? Who?" Lily asked. "Do we know the person?"

"Josephine Barker."

"Josephine?" Ian frowned. "You can't be serious."

"Unfortunately," Danielle said.

"Why would she kill Betty?" Lily asked.

Danielle looked at Walt. "You tell them. I'm sort of worn out from all this."

Walt looked to Lily and then to Ian. "It seems Miss Josephine is a kleptomaniac. She's been picking up little treasures for some time now. One treasure she snagged was the letter opener."

"Wasn't she on vacation when it was taken?" Lily asked.

"Josephine returned the night before they discovered the letter opener missing. She had rented a car for her vacation and planned to return it the next day. When she got back into Frederickport, she stopped at the grocery store. On her way home from there, she dropped by the library to check on things. It was at night; no one was there. And she saw the letter opener and couldn't resist. So the next morning, when they discovered it missing, no one suspected her. After all, she was on vacation, and she didn't come in until later that afternoon. Plus, who would suspect the head librarian?"

"But why did she kill Betty?" Lily asked.

"Betty started keeping a list of all the missing items, with the dates they disappeared. She was looking for a pattern so she could figure out who was taking things—assuming it was one person. Betty had talked to some docents over at the museum, and they claimed they never had a problem with things just walking off. If visitors to the museum weren't stealing things, she wondered why it was happening at the library," Walt explained.

"And the museum has a lot of interesting things that aren't locked in cases," Danielle added.

"She suspected it was someone who worked at the library, an employee or volunteer, but she didn't know who. And then, when she was over at Josephine's on Friday morning, inventorying the boxes from the library, she came across something that she wasn't supposed to see," Walt said.

"It was all the things that had gone missing," Danielle interjected.

"Why would Josephine keep them there, where Betty could find them?" Lily asked.

"They were on one of the shelves where Josephine stored her personal belongings, and she didn't intend for Betty to get into those boxes. But then she went to the library. She never considered Betty would start looking through the boxes on those shelves. After all, she planned to be right back," Walt explained.

"And she found the letter opener?" Ian asked.

Walt nodded. "She wasn't sure how to handle it, so before Josephine returned with her car, she took the letter opener and started walking to Becca's house to discuss it with her. After all, it was her letter opener."

"Why didn't she just call her?" Lily asked.

"She had left her cellphone in her car," Danielle said. "And Josephine had her car."

"When Josephine returned, found Betty gone, and the box

holding her treasures sitting on the workbench, she panicked. She must have suspected Betty was on her way to Becca's," Walt said.

"And that's who was driving the car when it ran over Olivia," Ian said.

"Yes. I doubt Josephine meant to kill Betty," Walt said. "At least that's what Betty told us."

"Betty's spirit showed up?" Lily asked.

"Yes, but that's another story. Betty said Josephine pulled up beside her and got out of the car when she realized she had already gone to Becca's house, but she wasn't home. Josephine tried to convince Betty not to tell anyone; they argued. Josephine grabbed for the letter opener. They struggled, Josephine stumbled, and in the scuffle, she stabbed Betty. Panicked after realizing what she had done, she pushed Betty down between the bushes and drove off. She took the car back to Betty's and parked it there," Danielle said.

Lily leaned back on the sofa. "Wow."

Walt looked at Danielle and smiled. "I thought you wanted me to tell the story?"

Ignoring Walt, Danielle said, "And that phone call from Becca, Josephine admitted answering Betty's cellphone. She could see the call was from Becca, but all she could hear was background noise, so she assumed it was a butt call."

"Why would she answer the phone?" Lily asked.

"She didn't mean to," Danielle said. "Betty had left her phone on the passenger seat. It started ringing right after Josephine left Betty in the bushes. Josephine picked up the phone to see who was calling Betty but accidentally answered the call. In a panic she dropped the phone while trying to hang up, and it fell between the seat and console."

"I'm surprised she didn't try to retrieve the phone. Wouldn't her prints have been all over it?" Lily asked.

"I asked the same thing. Betty said Josephine was wearing gloves when she grabbed the letter opener. I assume she was wearing them when she picked up the cellphone," Danielle said.

"My gloves don't work on a touch screen. How did she answer the phone?" Lily asked.

"They make gloves that work on touch screens," Ian said.

Lily frowned at her husband. "Really?"

Ian nodded.

"I want a pair of those," Lily muttered.

"I am assuming they've arrested her. What does she say?" Ian asked.

"I'm afraid she wasn't doing well when Brian and I showed up to arrest her," Walt said. He then explained all that had happened, from Olivia going to the funeral, to Marie rescuing Olivia. He then said, "Being suspended in midair in her garage did little for Josephine's mental health. The moment Brian and I arrived at the garage and Marie lowered her to the floor, Josephine threw herself into Brian's arms and told him everything."

"And poor Olivia was sitting huddled in the corner when they arrived," Danielle added. "She was just sitting there, watching Josephine overhead, flailing around like a wounded bird."

"While Olivia didn't like the idea of a ghost companion, I think she appreciates the fact that Marie kept an eye on her just in case she needed help. Apparently, Josephine got home a few minutes before Olivia arrived. She ended up not going to the wake, because the person she rode to Astoria with needed to get back to Frederickport," Walt explained.

"Was Josephine the one responsible for the bomb on Olivia's car?" Lily asked.

"Yes, and for putting the murder weapon in her trash bin," Walt said.

Danielle looked at Lily. "It's one reason I believe she didn't intend to kill Olivia."

Lily arched her brow at Danielle. "She put a bomb on her car. Are you saying she didn't intend for it to go off?"

"Oh no." Danielle shook her head. "Josephine definitely tried to kill her that time. I just meant in the beginning. I don't think she intended to stab her, and even Betty said it all happened so fast and they both slipped right before it happened. After that, I think Josephine went into panic mode."

"When she thought Olivia had arrived early and had been with

Betty, she had no idea what Betty had told her or what she had seen," Walt said.

"Which is one reason she stashed the murder weapon in Olivia's trash. If Olivia started pointing a finger at her, she would point it back and try to make it look like Olivia was the killer," Danielle said.

"But Olivia didn't even know Betty," Lily argued.

"Like I said, Josephine was in panic mode and not thinking straight," Danielle said.

"When Olivia denied being in Frederickport during that time, Josephine believed she was lying for some reason and wondered if she had seen something. Maybe something she didn't realize was connected to the murder, so she decided she needed to get rid of Olivia. Fortunately, Josephine proved better at researching bomb making than making a bomb," Walt explained.

"I don't believe Josephine ever intended to kill Betty to conceal her struggles with kleptomania. But she intended to kill Olivia to cover up manslaughter," Danielle said.

"I'm just glad she's been arrested, and we can stop worrying about a killer on the loose," Lily said.

"Totally agree. In fact, I'd like to invite you over for Sunday brunch tomorrow so we can celebrate," Danielle announced. "I also thought it would be nice to introduce Olivia to some people. She's had a rough first week in Frederickport."

WALT RESISTED the temptation to tell Danielle she might be overdoing it, considering she'd expanded her brunch guest list to include not just their friends on Beach Drive, but also to Kelly, Joe, Adam, Melony, Edward, and his sons. He reminded himself she loved to entertain, so instead of saying anything, he offered to make a run to Old Salts before helping Danielle prepare for their guests.

Danielle arranged the food on the buffet, allowing everyone to prepare their own plate before going to the table. They had been sitting at the dining room table for about fifteen minutes when

Olivia turned to Danielle and said, "I really want to thank you for inviting me. This has been lovely. Both the company and the food."

Danielle flashed Olivia a smile. "You are most welcome."

They all started talking about what a crazy week it had been when Kelly said, "There is just one thing I would like to know."

Joe looked at Kelly. "What's that?"

"Who was that woman Heather saw with Betty? It obviously wasn't Olivia, but according to Heather's description, she looked just like her."

The chief cleared his throat and said, "I can answer that."

Everyone at the table turned to the chief while Chris muttered under his breath, "I'd like to hear this one."

"I got a call this morning," the chief lied. "It was a woman who said she'd read about the murder and, after seeing Betty's photo in the paper, realized she was one of the last people to see her alive."

"Really?" Kelly turned to Joe and said, "You didn't tell me."

Joe shrugged. "First I've heard of it." Joe and the rest of the table kept their eyes on the chief.

"I haven't had a chance to tell anyone about it," the chief said.

"I'd love to hear about it," Danielle said sweetly.

"Me too," Heather said.

"Just some woman who'd driven through town on her way to Canada," the chief said.

Chris arched his brow. "Canada?"

"Yeah, Canada. Anyway, she wanted to take a walk on the pier, and when she drove down Beach Drive, she noticed the for-sale sign and was curious. She walked around the house, and when she was in the side yard, she ran into Betty. At first, she thought it was Betty's house, but Betty told her she had cut through the yard from the alley on the way to her friend's house. When she walked back onto Beach Drive, she noticed the neighbor, and by her description, it was obviously Heather."

"And this woman is Olivia's twin?" Kelly asked.

"I'm not sure if I would call her a twin. But I asked what color hair she had, and it's the same as Olivia's." The chief flashed Kelly a smile.

"Do you have her picture?" Kelly asked.

The chief let out a sigh. "I'm afraid I don't. And it doesn't really matter. She told me she walked as far as Marlow House with Betty, where she got in her car and drove off. And from what Josephine already told us, it's obvious she showed up on Beach Drive after this woman left."

"I'd love to see her picture," Kelly grumbled.

Joe looked at Heather. "See, it's just what I told you. I bet if we had her photo, she might not look as much like Olivia as you thought."

Heather smiled at Joe and, before taking a bite of her cinnamon roll, said, "Yes. You were right all along. It was my mind playing tricks on me, making me think this woman looked like Olivia, just because of her hair color and a similar jacket."

Olivia, who had been silently listening, quickly took a sip of water to suppress a giggle.

Walt jumped in and changed the subject. Ten minutes later, while the group discussed a more cheerful topic—the upcoming nuptials of two couples at the table—the chief's cellphone rang. He picked up his cellphone, looked at it, preparing to send the call to voicemail, when he furrowed his brow, staring at the phone for a moment before letting out a sigh and standing up.

"Excuse me, I have to take this." The chief left the dining room with his cellphone.

When he returned to the dining room five minutes later, he stood by his chair, but did not sit down. With a solemn expression, he looked at Joe. One by one, those at the table stopped talking and looked at the chief, wondering what was wrong.

Clearing his throat, the chief said hesitantly, "I'm sorry to bring down this mood, but there is something you need to know."

"What's wrong?" Kelly asked, noticing how the chief kept looking at her and Joe.

"It's about Charlie Cramer."

"What about him?" Joe asked.

"There has been a jail break. Of the three men who escaped,

two were captured immediately. But one is still on the loose. It's Cramer."

"THE CHIEF SURE knows how to ruin a party," Danielle told Walt Sunday evening as she snuggled with him under the quilts on their king-size bed. Flames flickering in the nearby fireplace provided the only light. Danielle felt the weight of Max as he dozed on the end of the bed—and on her feet.

"Perhaps Cramer is in Canada with Edward's imaginary Olivia look-alike," Walt suggested.

"Or maybe he really is planning to attend Joe and Kelly's wedding."

"Unless Joe told him they changed the wedding date, he's going to miss it."

"I just hope you're right, and he took off for Canada."

"Why? You want him to get away?" Walt asked.

"No. But if Cramer is the vindictive type, I don't want him to show up in Frederickport and exact revenge on the person responsible for his arrest."

"You mean Brian?" Walt asked.

"And Heather. I keep thinking about that letter he sent Kelly, saying he was looking forward to her wedding. And he might also be pissed at Joe for not seeing him."

Walt let out a sigh and drew Danielle closer. "Let's not worry about all that now. They caught the two men who escaped with Cramer, and when we wake up in the morning, I bet we'll hear Cramer is back in custody."

"I hope you're right."

"Instead of worrying about Cramer, let's talk about something more positive, like what we're going to name our babies."

With a chuckle Danielle said, "Silly me, I refused to consider baby names until our ultrasound. I wanted to know if we were having a boy or girl before picking out a name. But now—"

"Now we need two names. One for a boy and one for a girl."

THE GHOST AND THE WEDDING CRASHER

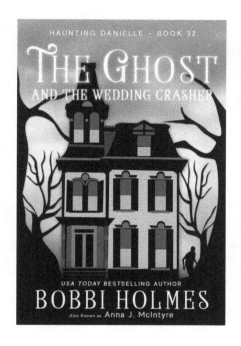

RETURN TO MARLOW HOUSE

THE GHOST AND THE WEDDING CRASHER

HAUNTING DANIELLE, BOOK 32

With two weddings on Beach Drive, Danielle's plan to temporarily close Marlow House Bed and Breakfast is put on hold.

Not everyone showing up on Marlow House's doorstep is a welcome wedding guest.

Nor is everyone from the living world.

BOOKS BY ANNA J. MCINTYRE

COULSON FAMILY SAGA

Coulson's Wife

Coulson's Crucible

Coulson's Lessons

Coulson's Secret

Coulson's Reckoning

Now available in Audiobook Format

UNLOCKED ❤ HEARTS

Sundered Hearts

After Sundown

While Snowbound

Sugar Rush

NON-FICTION BY
BOBBI ANN JOHNSON HOLMES

Havasu Palms, A Hostile Takeover
Where the Road Ends, Recipes & Remembrances
Motherhood, a book of poetry
The Story of the Christmas Village